Indiscretion

By

Tonya Lampley

5 PRINCE PUBLISHING AND BOOKS, LLC
PO Box 16507
Denver, CO 80216
http://www.5PrinceBooks.com

ISBN 13:978-1-939217-79-0 ISBN 10: 1-939217-79-2

Indiscretion
Tonya Lampley
Copyright © 2013 Tonya Lampley
Published by 5 Prince Publishing

Front Cover: Viola Estrella

First Edition/Second Printing January 2014 Printed U.S.A.

Acknowledgements

When traveling the road of life, we never walk alone. Thanks to all who travel with me.

My sister who has read every word, my mother who's encouraging words are like nectar and come when I need them most, my friends for their love and support. And so many others. Thanks also, to Connie Kline, my editor and 5 Prince Publishing for all their efforts to bring this story to readers

Dedications

For my husband

Thanks for walking with me through it all.

Indiscretion

Chapter 1

Damon sat in a red-velvet bishop's chair in one of the back rooms of St. Augustine's Cathedral in downtown Chicago. The 100 year-old church's renowned stained glass window, featuring the Messiah in an array of colors, hung high above him and gently filtered the October sunlight. His eyes rested on the tiny dust particles floating in the air, a useless attempt to distract him from his thoughts.

Three rapid taps on the heavy mahogany door broke through the silence and jarred him from contemplation.

"You ready?" a deep voice asked. Damon recognized the voice of Kurt, who would be his brother-in-law in a matter of minutes. A pretty stand-up guy, in Damon's opinion. Looked nothing like his sisters, and wasn't all that close to them, but he had stepped in per Carmen's request, to fill the role of best man when Damon argued with the original one—his life-long friend Craig. Tempers flared when Craig told Damon he was making the biggest mistake of his life. The conversation ended with Craig refusing to be a part of the wedding. They had since made up, but Craig stood by his original protest. Kurt being in the wedding made Carmen happier, anyway, Damon mused.

Someone knocked again.

"I'll be there in a minute." Damon responded. He walked over to the full-length mirror to give himself a once over. The black tuxedo that Carmen picked out hugged the contours of his svelte body. The white shirt gleamed against his smooth ebony skin. He noticed his white bow tie was crooked and slowly straightened it. His palms were moist as he ran them down the silk stripe of his pants trying to remove the uncomfortable feeling.

He rubbed his freshly cut hair, checked his nose and the corners of his mouth. In a few moments, he would enter the sanctuary. He brought Carmen's image to mind. Good. Sweet. Settled. She possessed an aura of comfort—like baked bread or warm milk. The kind of woman that could hopefully bring him the peace he had been searching for.

Kurt pummeled the door this time. "Everyone is waiting. Carmen's starting to get nervous. You were supposed to be out here a half hour ago."

Damon looked down at his shoes, patent leather, polished to a spit shine. Was he doing the right thing? He cared deeply for Carmen, but was it love?

What he wanted was to feel normal, to be satisfied with his life. The ghost of his past emerged again, as it often did, and reminded him that he had made a mess of things—two children by two different women, and a short stint in jail. The reminder rode in on a tide of regret.

He heard someone trying to turn the worn iron doorknob, but he had locked it. It wiggled back and forth desperately and he could hear mumbling on the other side. The rhythm of his breath sped up and a wave of warmth rose up from his feet. He thought of Rachel, the mother of his youngest son, and the words that spewed from her perfect mouth three years ago when she broke up with him—*I can't be with someone who's content to do nothing with their life.* And when she met Evan Kilgore, M.D. at the hospital where she was taken the night she broke her foot playing softball, she banished Damon to the "friend zone." He accepted his punishment; anything to still be a part of her life. He never thought she would marry him. He never forgave himself for losing her and wasn't about to make the same bet and lose twice. He had to marry Carmen. If he didn't, he might lose her too.

"Go get the key." He heard Kurt say to someone on the other side of the door, along with another knock.

It was time. Damon stood silent in the room. He expanded his chest and forced air deep into his lungs, but it still felt like he was suffocating. His hands registered a slight tremor and as he straightened his tie a second time, he felt a bead of sweat trickle down his temple. He pulled the teal handkerchief out of his pocket and blotted it. His legs felt heavy, like someone cemented them to the floor. Why did doing the right thing feel so uncertain? He closed his eyes and tried to steady his breathing. In a few minutes, it would be over. He willed his legs to start moving. Kurt, and Carmen's sister, Cathy, lunged forward into the room as he opened the door.

The church's pot-bellied groundskeeper walked up behind them carrying a large metal ring, holding several antique keys. He rubbed his shiny dark beard. "Ev-ry-thin'okay?" he asked with his bushy eyebrows raised.

"We got it, sir. Thanks." Kurt said to the man who looked around the room, then shrugged before walking away. Kurt turned his attention to Damon. "The wedding planner is going nuts! We thought something had happened to you."

Cathy huffed, "No *we* didn't." She squinted at Damon. "Why don't you just admit it and save us all a lot of trouble."

He looked right through Cathy. "I'm good, man. I just needed a minute, that's all." Damon brushed past Cathy, dressed in a silly Cinderella-looking, teal, taffeta dress, and lightly grazed her gloved arm. She gritted her teeth as she placed her hand into the center of his back and shoved him forward. He stumbled three un-willful steps at the forceful blow before he managed to get control of his feet. He closed his eyes and drew in a slow deep breath, taking a moment to gather himself—to deny himself the delightful thought of shoving her back—his mother had raised him better than that. He stretched out his arms and adjusted his shirtsleeves, checking his cuff links. Unfortunately, she was part of the deal.

He continued down the hall and opened the double doors to the sanctuary, where 200 guests sat in pews adorned with teal bows, and music from the harp player greeted him. Damon and Carmen argued for two days over the harp player—a total waste of money in his opinion, as was all of it—the courthouse would have suited him just fine. He walked past the harp player strumming like a fool, down the red aisle runner and took his place at the altar in front of the robed Reverend Mallory and the barrage of burning candles.

"Are you ready, Son?" Reverend Mallory was a large man, his voice even louder. The question he asked reverberated through the church and came to rest in Damon's ears.

Damon gave a nod. Reverend Mallory opened his Bible and the wedding planner raised her bony arm toward the back of the church, cuing her assistant to start the music. Time seemed to suspend as the remaining eight members of the bridal party entered the sanctuary, waltzing to Carmen's careful selection of Luther Vandross's *Here and Now*, and took their places at the front of the church. Damon was avoiding Cathy's glare when the collective sound of 200 people standing captured his attention. When he looked up, Carmen stood in the doorway, engulfed in a sea of white. Tulle cascaded all around her. She made eye contact with Damon almost immediately and smiled. He wasn't sure what he was feeling, but he knew her well enough to read the look on her face—that grin and the beam in her eye spoke of her happiness. And when he saw how happy she was, despite everything, he was happy for her. Her hand reached out for his and she took her place beside him.

Reverend Mallory loudly cleared his throat, and began the vows. Carmen recited hers first. Damon silenced the voice inside his head that hinted at the fact, he might not be sure of this marriage. But there were so many people. So much money spent. Too much to lose not to get married.

"Damon, do you take Carmen to be your lawful wedded wife? Do you promise to love and cherish her, in sickness and in health, for richer, for poorer, for better, for worse, and forsaking all others, keep yourself only unto her for so long as you both shall live?

"I do." Damon adjusted his tie, secretly loosening it. The promises felt really big. He had a long history of preserving his own self-interests. He wanted that to be behind him now. He accepted the ring from Kurt and placed it on Carmen's finger.

"Do you together promise, in the presence of your friends and family, that you will at all times, and in all circumstances, conduct yourselves toward one another as husband and wife?"

"We do." He muttered as he searched his heart for certainty. Carmen's voice broke through his with full conviction.

Reverend Mallory smiled. "You may now kiss your bride."

Damon lifted Carmen's veil and looked into her eyes. He needed her. He needed *her* in order to become the man he wanted to be. She would settle him into a normal life, where he would go to work at his job as a car salesman, come home and eat dinner with her, and go to the grocery store on the weekend. Normal. He grabbed her around the waist and kissed her as a symbol to everyone, and to himself, that this was his new life.

Chapter 2

Carmen gazed out of the limousine's window and smiled to herself. Mrs. Carmen Harris rang pleasantly in her ears. They passed a group of girls jumping rope in front of a South Side apartment building as they slowly guided their way to the reception, to their new life as husband and wife.

She gently placed her hand on her stomach. "Look," she said softly, her mind filled with thoughts of her future family and perhaps daughters of her own.

"Mmmm?"

She looked over at Damon who was slumped back in the seat, his eyes closed, seemingly oblivious of his surroundings. To her disappointment, he had already removed his tie and unbuttoned his shirt. He could be worse than a little boy at times, especially when it came to dressing up. He had been complaining about that tux since the day he tried it on.

Carmen looked at his handsome face, appreciating his smooth chocolate skin. God had certainly been more than generous to him when it came to his appearance. His chiseled cheeks and jawbone crested into full lips that were crowned by a moustache. His eyes were deep and expansive. When she looked into them, she saw dreams come true. He was thirty-four years old, tall, and still naturally muscular, which he augmented with occasional visits to the gym—the kind of man that, when he walked into a room, women would briefly stop what they were doing to take him in and imagine what life with him would be like. And he had a quiet charisma that overtook anyone standing in his presence. At times, and without warning, he could hold her completely spellbound.

Damon's phone vibrated in his pocket and he reached down to retrieve it. Carmen assumed it was Craig since he was a "serial texter," constantly sending messages to Damon about the most meaningless things. She wouldn't have been surprised if he texted Damon and told him what he had for breakfast every morning. She rolled her eyes as she sat up in the limousine seat, "Can't he give you a break? It's your wedding day. I hope he's apologizing." She fluffed the billows of tulle that flanked her lower half.

Carmen had a low tolerance for Craig. He regularly dragged Damon out to clubs and bars around town and Carmen resented it. Not to mention, he tried to talk Damon out of getting married and backed out of being the best man at the last minute. In Carmen's eyes he was just plain rude. If she had her way, he would disappear down a Chicago manhole on a dark night and never be seen or heard from again.

"I know what today is, Carmen." Damon said without looking at her. Instead, he stared at his phone, smiling at the text message he had received. He feverishly began typing a response.

Carmen's mood changed quickly. She blew out a frustrating breath and gazed out the limousine window. "What took you so long to come out?"

"I needed a minute." Damon continued to press the buttons on his phone.

"A minute?" Carmen pressed on, with obvious inflection in her voice, "a minute for what?"

"Sometimes a man just needs a minute, Mrs. Harris." He flashed his irresistible grin. "Is that okay with you?"

She acknowledged to herself that he had a smile that could melt the coldest heart. And hearing him call her Mrs. Harris for the first time dissolved her irritation. She returned the smile in kind. Damon resumed texting and she returned her gaze to the world outside the window.

Ten minutes later the white limousine pulled up in front of *Banquets* reception hall. Carmen initially wanted to hold the reception at one of the fancy hotels downtown, but she had stretched the budget too far. Nothing against *Banquets*, it was very nice; but one of the fancy hotels would have been better. If a woman is lucky, and she hoped she was, she only gets married once. Why not go all out?

The driver opened the door and Damon crawled out, he turned around and held out his hand for Carmen. When they entered the lobby, Carmen could see through the double doors into the banquet area. The wedding planner was able to get the peacock feathers she ordered at the last minute, and they accented the large sconces on each table. The glow of the candles completed the look. Carmen told the wedding planner that she wanted a look of simple elegance and everything was beautiful. A single large teal bow draped the back of each white linen chair and tiny tea lights twinkled against the ceiling, like stars. A whisper of teal confetti splashed across each table. When she saw everything, she squealed with delight. In a moment she would enter, and the deejay would announce to the world that she was Mrs. Damon Lamont Harris. Her day was getting better by the second.

"Carmen!"

Carmen turned to see Cathy barging toward them with an annoyed expression on her face, "I don't have time for you, right now."

"Excuse us, Damon." Cathy abruptly grabbed Carmen by the arm and pulled her into the lobby bathroom. She violently pushed open the doors to all the stalls to make sure they were alone. The taffeta bridesmaid dress swished vigorously as she moved. The doors knocked back and forth on their hinges. She spun around and blasted Carmen. "Are you happy now? He's yours." Mock riddled her tone and facial expression. "You've got the ring to prove it." She folded her arms much like a teacher would when addressing a misbehaving child. "I don't know why you were so hell bent on marrying him. I mean he's fine and all—"

"Shut up, Cathy." Carmen's heart sank at the implication. Cathy had accused Damon of not loving her. It was a conversation that rattled Carmen's very soul and she refused to have it again.

"It's too late now. What's done is done." Cathy shook her head. "But you remember this day." She squinted and released her words with an arctic chill. "You remember what I told you about him. He didn't want to marry you. You know it, and I know it. And today just showed us how much we both were right."

Carmen gave Cathy a steely glare. "You're jealous." She snarled. "You always have been. You man-less, inconsiderate, disgusting little witch!" How dare you try to ruin the best day of my life? Why did you even come?"

"I came here to try to support my only sister. I came here hoping I was wrong about him, but face it Carmen…," she shook her head, again, as if in disbelief, "he didn't even want to come out of the room." Her voice raised an octave. "He was thirty minutes late…probably looking for an escape route."

Carmen lifted her nose to the air. "If you can't be happy for me, you know what you can do."

"As a matter of fact," Cathy said with a jerk of her head, "I was just leaving." She spun on her heels, walked out of the bathroom and slammed the door. A few seconds later, Carmen heard the doors close in the front lobby. Her bridal party was now minus one.

Carmen stood still. The heat in her body finally registered. Seconds later, her eyes misted. She turned toward the mirror and noticed the flushness of her cheeks and cursed the sheen of sweat that was on her forehead. She snatched a paper towel from the dispenser and tried to blot her face without removing her makeup. Why would Cathy try to ruin her wedding day? Who did that to someone? Especially someone's own sister. Sure, she would admit Damon never formally proposed, but she knew he cared for her. And sure, she would admit that at times he drank too much. Damon was just Damon. He was tough, but kind-hearted, weak and yet strong. Carmen admired that he had been trying so hard to change. He merely needed someone to show him the way. A good woman could settle him down. Cathy could never understand that. Every time a man showed some aspect of being human, of being made of flesh and bone, she ditched him. Carmen knew exactly what it took to make a man like Damon into the best husband a woman could have. In time, Cathy would see.

Carmen tossed the towel through the hole between the two sinks into the trash receptacle below. She grabbed another and wiped up the water that splayed the counter, tossing that in the hole as well. She leaned toward the mirror, wishing for more light and carefully smoothed the stray hairs she saw. Thank God for waterproof mascara.

Damon was still in the hallway. "Was that about me?"

"Don't worry about her." She soothed.

"I figured it was when she rolled her eyes at me as she passed." He took hold of Carmen's hand awaiting their cue. The deejay announced them. The doors flung open and

Damon kissed Carmen on the cheek. An onslaught of cameras flashed as they walked into the reception hall as Mr. and Mrs.

****

At eight minutes after midnight, the limousine driver dropped Carmen and Damon off at their brownstone. Damon had quite a bit to drink at the reception. More than Carmen felt was necessary. She had sent Kurt and her father to the church to retrieve his car and she saw it parked on the street a few doors down.

They slowly ascended the weighty concrete stairs to the front door. At the top of the stairs, Carmen took a moment and gathered up the layers of her dress that dragged the leaf-covered ground. She held as much of it as she could with one hand and reached into her bosom with the other to retrieve the key to the door.

Damon loudly slurred the lyrics to the last song played at the reception. Puffs of steam rose from his mouth and vaporized in the cold air.

Carmen was concerned about the neighbors. "Shhh." She crouched down in order to see the keyhole on the doorknob. Her teeth had started to knock together.

"Give me the key," Damon shouted and snatched it out of her hand with force, causing him to spin around on slick shoes and almost lose his balance. She reached out and clutched him by the collar of his jacket, steadying him before he fell down the stairs. Before she met Damon, she had purchased the brownstone in an up and coming area of the South Side known as Bronzeville. He moved in right after she suggested they get married. As of today, it was officially community property. She handed him the key, and after fumbling in the dark for a spell he finally opened the door and they stepped inside.

Damon removed his jacket and shirt and threw them on the sofa. Carmen walked over and picked them up. She scanned the floor for his tie. She felt for it inside his pockets...of course he would lose it. She rolled her eyes and followed him to the bedroom.

He wrestled with her as she tried to help him undress, insisting he could do it. He gave up when he couldn't get his pant leg off over his shoe.

She smiled at the confusion on his face and came to his aid. "Sit down." She guided him onto the bed, kneeled before him and removed his shoes. Before she could get his pants off, he fell backward onto the bed and began a gentle rhythmic snore. Carmen breathed in the scent of his body. It aroused her senses. She ran her hand over the silky fine hair that covered his shin before removing his socks and placing his legs on the bed.

She peeled off her pantyhose with a sigh of relief and headed to the bathroom to wash her face. Before getting into bed she tied up her hair and clicked off the lamp. The bed welcomed her tired body. As she relaxed, her mind replayed the events of the day. As far as she was concerned, there was no excuse for what Cathy did. None. She recalled what Damon said about his tardiness. "Sometimes a man just needs a minute." Maybe it was just pre-wedding jitters. She'd heard some men get them, didn't mean they wanted to call off the wedding. What did Cathy know anyway? She'd never been married. After a few minutes, she silenced her mind's chatter and let the thought settle in that she was now Mrs. Harris, and married to one of the sexiest men in Chicago; a man she loved very much. A feeling of elation rose inside her. Her heart expanded in pure joy. She smiled to herself, snuggled into her pillow and drifted off to sleep.

Chapter 3

Damon woke up with a slight headache. He walked to the kitchen and opened the cabinet above the sink where Carmen kept the Advil. He could hear Carmen in the shower. He was thankful for her. She came along at the lowest point in his life. He filled a glass with water and swallowed two pills. The coolness of the water soothed his dry throat. He thought back to that day—the day that changed everything. He was sitting in his Chevy Impala with the engine running, waiting for an acquaintance, Chuck—Downtown Chuck they called him, who was inside a store supposedly buying beer for both of them, but he was actually inside robbing the clerk. It just so happened, a cop pulled up as Chuck was running out the door with the clerk trailing behind him hollering for help, and it looked like Damon was the get-away driver. He spent eight months in jail for something that he didn't do.

By the time he was released, his siblings, and even Craig had lost their faith that he would ever be any different. It was the final straw of a long list of "inconveniences." His mother's questioning eyes hurt him the most. After that, he resolved to do better. He finagled his way into a job at a used car dealership and soon after he met Carmen at a gas station. Before long he was spending time with her and thinking less and less about the woman he loved.

He walked through the bedroom and quietly entered the bathroom. He peered into the shower. Her body was nothing like the tall, leggy ones that used to satisfy his appetite. She was a little rounder, a little earthier. He could have his pick of women, but he knew a woman like Carmen was hard to come by. He reminded himself that she was good for him. Without her, he feared he might revisit the mistakes of his past. "Do you want me to wash your back?"

"Thanks," she smiled and began soaping up her loofah.

She handed it to him. The white foam swelled in his hands and cascaded over his dark fingers as he covered her back with the soapy loofah. He hoped in time that marriage would melt the bitterness in his heart, the remains of losing his father so young. That it would help him overcome the belief that life isn't fair—that you could be blamed for something you didn't do, and the truth meant nothing when copping to the offense got you less jail time. That her light would stoke the glimmer of hope that he clung to. He smiled and handed her a towel. "Some night, huh? He dried his hands with the opposite end. "I probably had a little too much to drink. I didn't embarrass you, did I?"

"No. You didn't start dancing until the very end."

"I danced?" Damon's eyes widened, aware of his submissive relationship with liquor.

"It was pretty funny."

"Is that why my knee hurts?"

Carmen giggled. "Probably," she began drying her body. "I'll make breakfast in a few minutes."

Damon walked back out to the living room and turned on the T.V. He placed the remote on the cocktail table and picked up the bill from the wedding planner. There would be no honeymoon. They spent everything they had on the wedding. Damon's mind couldn't justify spending money to get married. He tried to convince Carmen to go to the justice of the peace, but she wouldn't hear of it. He wanted to spend the money *going* somewhere. Having lived in Chicago his entire life, it was a rare occasion that he had a chance to leave—once for a family reunion and once for a funeral. Even then, he ventured only far enough away that he could get there by car. Growing up poor on the South Side, his family couldn't afford to travel. They missed out, in his opinion, on one of the perks of getting married. As Carmen took care of all the intricate details that would make her day perfect, the wedding price escalated. By the time they got the bill for the wedding, there was nothing left. In fact, they still owed. His eyes scanned the bill in shock. Why did she order peacock feathers?

Carmen walked into the kitchen. Minutes later Damon could smell bacon and butter. He threw the bill on the table. He would put in extra hours at the dealership to help cover some of the wedding's expenses; a price he was willing to pay in exchange for the life he wanted. He now had an honest job *and* a wife—making him a legitimate man.

Chapter 4

On Friday night, Damon had finished eating his spaghetti dinner and was in the living room lying on their sofa clicking through channels on the television. Feeling the fullness of his stomach, he loosened the string on his sweatpants.

He and Carmen were coming up on their five month anniversary and being married was proving to be none too easy. He was trying to make the most of it, but he continued to have a sinking feeling in the pit of his stomach, as if he had done something wrong. He had always had reservations, but he felt certain that as time went on he would settle into it. He prayed he was right.

When he and Craig had argued days before the wedding, Craig told him not to go through with it—that he'd regret it later. He dismissed Craig since his life wasn't exactly the model for stable relationships. To think, at his age, he still believed sex should be one of a man's highest priorities in life. But now he wondered if he should have listened to him. Not about the sex part, but maybe, about the part that later he might regret it.

With Damon's reputation for being able to get almost any woman he wanted, Craig told him that he was convinced it was the way Carmen loved him physically. Assuredly, that could be the only thing that could get him down the aisle. Damon laughed outwardly, knowing that inwardly, that wasn't the reason. Carmen was an okay lover at best, and he had been with enough women to make the comparison. He had married Carmen for several reasons, several selfish ones. At the top of the list was the hope that marriage would rid him of the strange, abysmal feeling he couldn't describe, but felt on a daily basis. A few months in, it was still there. He wouldn't dare tell Craig that. Or anybody else for that matter.

He clicked through the channels a few more times, figuring out there was nothing of interest on. He fixed his eyes on a random spot on the floor and teased his thoughts. One after another came quickly until the dreaded one emerged—Rachel and Evan's wedding day. He recalled most vividly that hot afternoon. He passed out in his car outside the church, a half-empty bottle of scotch in his hand, while everyone else was inside. He was eventually awakened by someone tapping on his face. It was Evan, accompanied by a few of his handsome doctor groomsman, asking him if he was alright. His pride recalled how he must have looked; bloodshot eyes, soaking wet with sweat. Sad. Perhaps, pitiful. It took everything he had not to throw up on Evan's shoes as he answered "yes." He had missed the wedding. His heart would not let him go inside and watch her be betrothed to someone else. He was looking into the face of the man that had assumed the privilege of raising his son and taking care of the woman that should have been his wife. The fact that Evan provided a lavish lifestyle for both she, and his son London, ticked him off even more. Even now, every time he thought about it, he wanted to fight.

Damon had so many emotions running loose in his mind; he was beginning to think he might lose it. Fear over the choices he *had* made, and regret over the ones he hadn't, kept him awake some nights. And when he and Carmen fought over the Christmas holiday about spending more money on top of a still unpaid for wedding, Carmen won, which meant he had been putting in even more hours at the car dealership to pay down some of the debt. Seemed all he did was work and come home to Carmen and the T.V. He was bored and the pressure was mounting. He was trying to be the good husband, and had refused Craig's offers to hang out the way he did before he got married. It came to him in a flash. Maybe that's what he needed—a chance to unwind. A little bit of fun, a drink or two, and he might not feel as tense.

He threw the remote on the sofa and walked to the kitchen. Carmen stood at the sink washing dishes. "Hey babe…" he injected sweetness into his tone, "do you mind if I go out tonight? I need to unwind for a minute."

She turned off the water. "What's wrong?"

"Nothing's wrong. "I—I just need to get out for a minute." He saw the look of disappointment on Carmen's face. He smiled at her and with more sweetness to his voice added. "I promise I won't be out late."

Carmen sighed. "I know Craig's been harassing you about not going out with him like you used to. You've been real good about saying no and I appreciate that." Carmen turned the water back on and picked up a plate. "If you feel that's what you need, go ahead."

Damon walked to the bedroom and grabbed his cell phone off the night stand. He called Craig and told him he would meet him at the pool hall—one of Damon's favorite hangouts. He grew up in that place. It was as dear to him as his own heartbeat.

Damon dashed to the bathroom for a quick shower. He slid into his favorite jeans; the ones that were acid washed and sat low on his hips. No belt. He put on a white shirt and left the tail out. His favorite cologne was sitting on the dresser. He reached for it, but stopped short. Carmen was a good woman, but she was no fool. The *Ralph Lauren* might send her the wrong message. Besides, tonight that kind of attention was unwanted. All he wanted was a drink and a little camaraderie to relieve his stress. He placed the cologne back on the dresser.

After he was dressed, he walked down the hall and into the kitchen. Carmen was drying the dishes and putting them away. He kissed her on the cheek. "I won't be out long."

Damon walked out the door and down the stairs, headed for the pool hall. He decided to walk—the night air was crisp and it helped to clear his mind, much like smelling salts. With each block, he noticed the landscape changing. The manicured trees that lined the streets of his residential community disappeared. Beautiful brownstones were exchanged for storefronts that were the lifeline of a forgotten neighborhood: a beer and wine store that sold a few necessities like milk, diapers and lottery tickets, a fledging church, and a barbershop. Men and women congregated outside the doors on the street. Some greeted passersby and talked boisterously to their neighbors, some sold illicit goods, as Damon used to, to eager repeat customers. Others stood there with a soulless look in their eye that depicted a feeling he knew well—longing—and one he was trying to forget. A fire truck whizzed by blaring its siren and he covered his ears with his hands. He was officially on his home turf.

As he entered the pool hall, he smelled the familiar scent of alcohol. He heard a man talking loudly in the back and recognized the voice immediately. It was Craig. He was standing tableside, talking to one of the bar patrons while playing pool. Damon walked to the back and threw his leather jacket on a chair at the last available table. He greeted the patron with a nod and pulled a cue stick off the shelf on the wall.

Craig walked over to him. "How's married life?" He looked at Damon and began chalking his cue. The query felt awkward. Damon knew Craig resented that he had married Carmen.

"It's good. Perhaps you should try it." Damon flashed a smile showing all of his perfect white teeth as he lined up his shot, a smile that told many lies.

"Me?" Craig immediately rejected Damon's offer. "You know me better than that. I could never be satisfied with one woman." He shook his head enthusiastically, "Never."

Damon took the break shot with precision. He fixed his gaze on the table as the balls darted back and forth. Eventually one dropped in a side pocket. A wave of satisfaction crept across his face. Having come to the pool hall several nights a week as a little boy, he was a much better pool player than Craig. He looked up, "What about Samantha?" Craig had been seeing her off and on for the past several months. The few times Damon interacted with her, she seemed a bit standoffish.

"What about her?" Craig shook his head, watching Damon run the table. He emphasized his point further, "Like I said...I could never be satisfied with only one. In fact, after this game let's shoot over to the club. It's time I added one more to the stable."

"I don't think so, man." Damon shook his head, "Not tonight. You like to close down the place. I have to work tomorrow."

"Don't worry. I'll get you back home before you break Carmen's curfew." Craig pounded his fist to his chest. "Man up."

"This has nothing to do with me not being a man and more to do with me being an adult."

"You sure?" Craig raised his eyebrows mockingly. "Carmen's had you on a leash since the day you said 'I do'. Seems to me you come and go as she tells you to."

"It's not like that."

"Could have fooled me. A real man controls his woman, not the other way around." Craig held his hands up in remission. "I understand. You don't want to get in trouble." He continued mocking Damon with his tone.

Not wanting Craig to think Carmen was controlling him, Damon gave in. "I'm a grown man…I won't get in any trouble. We can go after we finish, but I'm not staying out late. I have to work tomorrow." Something inside nagged him a little after he agreed to go. Probably the look he saw on Carmen's face earlier. Bravado overrode the image. "But let me make myself clear, Carmen doesn't have me on a leash." Damon was stern. He hated the thought of Craig thinking of him as weak.

"If you say so."

He and Craig finished their game and drove across town to Shea's. Shea's was a Chicago nightspot they used to frequent quite a bit, *pre-nuptial*. They liked it, because even though the deejay played mostly hip-hop, it drew a mixed crowd, which satisfied Craig's broad appetite in women. He never met a nationality he didn't like. For Damon, Shea's provided ease. His thug days were long gone. He liked the fact that he could sit and enjoy music without the need to have a gun in his belt, in case he accidentally stepped on someone's gym shoes or caught the attention of their girlfriend.

As he and Craig scanned the parking lot looking for a place to park, he noticed a women walking into the club. Many of them wore tight jeans with high-heeled shoes; their hair painstakingly coiffed and makeup perfectly applied. He admired the effort they put in to get ready—the way Carmen used to. When they were dating, she always made sure she looked nice for him, especially in the beginning. Now in the mornings she seemed a foreigner, with her hair tied up in a rag and that big, frumpy nightshirt. He missed the way she used to look.

As Craig pulled into a parking space, a woman walking by flashed Damon a welcoming smile. His conviction grew deep. He was hesitant to go inside, knowing a club was no place for a married man. One that vowed to himself to stop repeating the mistakes of his past and to do the right thing. He wanted to be faithful to Carmen and be the man she deserved.

He glanced over at Craig. If he didn't go inside, he would mercilessly start teasing him again. It had been that way since he got married. Each time he declined to meet him for a drink or game of pool, Craig bombarded him with comments about him being afraid of Carmen and how she controlled him; all kinds of things that questioned his manhood. He had to go in.

He got out of the car, made a silent promise to himself and headed toward the door.

Craig elevated his voice above the music as he and Damon sat on the swiveling barstools. "Bartender, rum and coke for me and a gin and tonic for my man, here." Craig pointed to the women sitting next to him at the bar. "Another round of whatever these four ladies right here are having too." Damon spun around so that he could take in all the happenings in the club. People crowded onto the dance floor as multi-colored lights flashed across their faces. Damon spotted a girl that appeared to be over her limit. He chuckled as she attempted to find the elusive beat of the music. Sweat matted her blonde hair and bleeding mascara created dark circles under her eyes. He knew what that felt like; being out of control and having everybody there to witness it. On some level you know what's going on, but you're helpless to stop yourself. His heart held compassion as he watched her and he reminded himself to take it easy on the liquor, which had sometimes been his gateway to trouble. A few seconds later, a female companion came over to help her off the dance floor and sat her down at a table.

Damon looked over at Craig standing next to him, now flashing wads of cash. That was how he lured the women in. First, he bought them drinks, then he talked about how successful he was at his business, then he got their phone number, or if he was really *on* that night, he took them home. The desperate women, hoping for a chance to be Mrs. Craig Mincey, fell for it every time. Once he got what he wanted from them, they would never hear from him again. Only the ones he deemed worthy could remain in contact with him. If they knew what Damon knew, they would pass. Not only was he starting to wonder if marriage was overrated, but he felt sorry for any woman who might one day marry a man like Craig Mincey. He chuckled to himself. They might be better off in hell.

As the music thumped, it felt like old times. And just like old times Damon started to notice he was gaining the attention of two women who were sitting at a nearby table. One was the woman he saw in the parking lot. She arched her back and gave her hair a fluff before smiling at Damon and giving him a wink. Craig used his loud mouth and money to gain the attention of women. Damon on the other hand, drew women in like a magnet, without much effort at all. It had been the cause of occasional fights from jilted boyfriends, and it had even garnered him a few stalkers.

The woman walked up to him. Damon eyed her from head to toe. Her delicate skin gleamed against her black dress, her auburn hair grazed her shoulders and the push-up bra worked for her. "I'm Kim," she said. "What's your name?"

"Damon."

"Can I buy you a drink?"

Craig noticed her and diverted his attention away from the four wannabes. "Well...hello, Miss," he licked his lips as he looked her up and down, very snake-like. "What are you having?" he added, "If you say me, my work here is done."

"Apple Martini."

Craig smiled. He opened up the wad of cash he was holding and barked to the bartender. "Rum and coke, and an Apple Martini for this woman who's clearly taken leave of her senses. And another round for these ladies right here."

Damon apologized to Kim for Craig's boisterous behavior. "You'll have to excuse him. He's loud, but he means well...sometimes."

"He *is* a little loud, but I appreciate the drink." She accepted her martini from the bartender. She reached over and tapped Craig on the shoulder. "Thank you," she said, when he turned around. She posted her eyes on Damon's face. "Do you guys come here often?"

"I don't, but he still does." Damon eyed the delicate skin on her neck. Her perfume filled his nostrils.

She bit into the slice of apple. "If I wanted to see you again, how could we make that happen?"

Damon was determined not to let things get out of control, out of respect for the woman he married. He smiled at her. "Your offer sounds tempting, but I think I'm going to have to pass."

"Are you seeing someone?"

"You could say that?" He held up his hand and showed her his ring.

She smiled, grabbed her clutch off the bar and walked away.

Damon turned around, faced the bar, and sipped his drink. A few seconds later, he felt the tension leave his body. Watching Craig and his theatrics was always entertaining. The music, the gin and tonics—he savored the taste of freedom. It felt so good to be having fun again. Was this how marriage was supposed to be? No fun at all. Zero. Just bills and work? He thought a little responsibility was the missing piece to the puzzle of his life, but it was starting to feel like a noose around his neck. All Carmen talked about were the bills and other household or couple-y things, like towels. Sometimes, he had to strain to keep from falling asleep.

Jay-Z's *Problems* blasted from Craig's car stereo as they drove home. Thankfully, Carmen was a sound sleeper. Damon planned to sneak in and fall asleep on the couch, undetected.

When the car turned onto the street, Damon turned down the volume.

Craig mocked Damon as he got out of the car. "Boy…I'd hate to be you when you walk in that door. You'll be on punishment for six months."

"It's all good. Don't worry about me. I'll wake up to bacon, eggs and grits. What about you?"

"Meagan, if I'm lucky." Craig laughed as he looked at his phone. "I'm about to call her right now and ask her to meet me at my place."

Damon closed the car door and approached his front door. Craig rolled down the window. "Call me if she puts you out tonight and you need a place to stay." He laughed loudly and drove off.

Damon walked up the stairs to his front door and quietly put the key in the lock. His guilt had left him hours ago and he felt more like himself. The realization set in that he missed the times when life was carefree. When he came and went as he pleased and often drank too much. When he lacked a steady job, but had a lot more money. That was the man he knew. Not the caged, bill-paying, straight-laced man he had become—always coloring within the lines, following the crowd. Plain. Vanilla. Tonight, he saw a glimpse of his former self and it felt good. He liked excitement. He did not want to let it go.

Damon entered the brownstone surprised at how dark it was. Carmen had every curtain and blind drawn; he couldn't even use the moonlight to see. He quietly reached over and turned on the lamp and eased his keys onto the table by the door. The faint smell of jasmine filled the air.

"Where have you been? It's almost morning." Carmen stood up from the couch, startling Damon. He jumped two inches off the floor when he saw her.

Damon wanted to look away. "I was at the pool hall…I told you where I was going." He tried to sound confident, but being face to face with his wife caused his once dissipated guilt to return. The confidence he tried to project was barely noticeable.

"Are you going to start this again?"

"Start what, Carmen?"

"Hanging out with Craig….clubs…bars. Whatever the hell he does."

"I'm stressed out Carmen. All I do is work. You wanted the wedding and now I'm working hard to pay for it."

"Oh…it's my fault you're coming home in the wee hours of the morning? I missed something."

Damon backed down. "No…I'm sorry. It's not your fault. I was out a little late and I apologize for that."

"Are you going to start drinking again?"

"Nah. Those days are behind me. Promise."

"Then why do I smell liquor?" Carmen looked at him soberly. "Be careful Damon, if you want trouble, the streets are where you'll find it. And trust me. You won't have to look very hard."

Damon eyed her frumpy night shirt as she walked to the bedroom. He removed his leather jacket and crashed on the couch, attempting to get a few hours of sleep before he had to go to work.

Chapter 5

Damon began to take advantage of Carmen's good nature. Once he reconnected with Craig and a few of his old acquaintances, he began meeting them out for drinks or a game of pool several nights a week. Hanging out with his friends became his highest priority outside of work. He had tested the limits of his marriage, and he and Carmen had begun a tug of war. She began to tighten up the reins, requesting he report in often and come home at a respectable hour. He could find the truth in her words, but he would do anything to escape the monotony of his home life. He enjoyed laughing and talking with the guys. It made him feel more at ease. He had tasted the sweetness of the life he used to live and could not give it up again. The concept of being a good husband appealed to Damon, but he wondered if he was capable of such a thing. Maybe if his father hadn't died, he could have shown him how. Thug uncles and cousins shaped him into the man he was today. They were roamers. Gamblers and sharks; not the kind of men that would be home on a Saturday night. Like them, he craved the action and revelry. The last thing he wanted to do was hurt Carmen. He walked a thin line daily, attempting to please his wife, and at the same time, be true to himself.

Damon walked into the bathroom on Sunday morning. The newlywed phase was showing wear around the edges and he found himself in the throes of married life. The fact that he did not make a lot of money at the car dealership some weeks was pit against Carmen's elaborate wedding and it's still, unpaid expenses. Damon's sex drive had waned, he didn't know why; perhaps it was the frumpy nightshirt. The chores, the garbage, the list went on. The marriage was becoming real and the sinking feeling in the pit of his stomach was now a burning. Two weeks ago his stomach hurt so bad he missed work. He thought it might be an ulcer from the stress, but refused to go to the doctor.

He put Barbasol in his hands and lathered up. Shaving was one of the few things he had left that made him feel like a man. He'd heard some men got married for sex. He placed the cool razor against his chin. He didn't have to get married for that. That was the one thing that came easy for him.

Chapter 6

Carmen was in the kitchen on Saturday morning when she heard the doorbell ring. She could see the side of her sister Cathy's face through the glass pane on the front door. She opened it.

"What brings you here?" Carmen asked as she opened the door. Her tone was less than welcoming.

"Don't be nasty, Carmen. Can I come in? It's starting to sprinkle."

Carmen headed over to the sofa. She was eager to hear what brought Cathy to her house. They had not seen each other, and had only a few strained conversations on the phone since the wedding. The last one ended with Cathy telling Carmen she could not be around Damon knowing he fraudulently married her sister, and that it was best she stayed away. Carmen agreed.

Carmen lit a jasmine incense and placed it on the coffee table to mask the ash smell from the frequent fires she had lit in the fireplace all winter.

"And?" Carmen looked at Cathy in anticipation as she sat on the sofa.

"And what? Carmen, I just came to visit." She unbuttoned her jacket. "Are we going to get started again?" She looked around the living room. "Where's your husband anyway?"

"Out." Carmen responded, letting her sister know it was none of her business where her husband was, and perhaps she should get one of her own.

"Carmen look, I'm sorry for the things I said to you on your wedding day." Cathy straightened her back and scooted to the edge of the sofa. "But you have to know, I love you and the things I said were because of that. I know you love Damon, and I think he is a good guy deep down inside, but I still think you rushed the marriage. I don't think he was ready." She looked Carmen in the eyes. "And I'm here to tell you that I'm sorry, and while I support your decision, as your sister I'm still entitled to my opinion."

Carmen felt tears rising up inside. Being one year apart at thirty-one and thirty-two, Cathy felt almost like a twin to Carmen. She knew her better than anyone. Sometimes even better than Carmen knew herself. She possessed a keen insight into anything that affected Carmen and it proved a double edged sword. Carmen was appreciative of it when she needed advice, and resentful of it when Cathy seemed to know more about her than she wanted her to know. Carmen was glad that her sister had come. She was ready to move beyond their differences. She missed their Saturday afternoon shopping trips and late night phone calls. She stood up from the sofa. "Want some tea?" She asked her sister. Cathy nodded and followed her into the kitchen.

Cathy sat at the table while Carmen put a kettle of hot water on the stove. She retrieved her cell phone out of her purse and began scrolling through her messages.

"Cathy." Carmen caught her sister's attention as she pulled the kettle off the burner and poured hot water into a mug, tossing in a ginger flavored tea bag.

"Yeah?" Cathy looked up from her phone.

"Do you remember when we were little and momma would make tea for us on Saturday mornings?"

"Yeah, I remember. Kurt would be upstairs in his room."

"Remember how she would sit and talk to us, giving us her undivided attention? She treated us as if we were the most important people in the world."

Cathy's mood grew somber. She stared into her cup of tea. "Yeah, I think she focused her attention on us so we wouldn't feel the sting of not having daddy around. Some Saturday mornings he would come through the door, having not even been home from work on Friday. It was as if he was there…but not really…you know?"

Carmen sat at the table with her cup of tea. "Yeah…I think momma was trying to shield us from a lot of that."

"I never got it, Carmen. I never understood why momma would sit and take that from daddy or why he treated her that way. Hanging out in the streets night after night. Momma tried to keep it from us, but we knew. Talk in the streets was that daddy had another woman. Whether it was true or not, the whole thing was degrading…the way the neighbors stared at her with pity when she came out of the house—"

"Momma didn't care," Carmen defended as she carefully sipped the hot tea from the cup. "She held her head high."

"I know Carmen, but why? I can't figure out why she took that for all those years. Why she stayed."

"I think she did it for us. And she loved him."

"Well, in my opinion, that's too big of a price to pay. Even for us. There ain't that much love in the world as far as I'm concerned."

"Have you been to the new DSW yet?" Carmen quickly changed the subject to a more lighthearted topic—shoes. She was afraid that if she didn't, Cathy, knowing her the way she did, would be able to read between the lines and figure out that she had made the same mistake as her mother. But it was too late. An hour later as Cathy walked out of her sister's door into the cool March air she turned and looked at Carmen.

"Let momma's mistake be a lesson for you."

Over one cup of tea Carmen could tell her sister had seen right through her happy façade and figured out everything. Things weren't right between her and Damon. She knew it, and now it appeared Cathy might too.

Chapter 7

Carmen prepared dinner, as usual, and was glad that Damon was home early. It was a rare occurrence for a Saturday and she hoped a romantic evening would not be out of the question. All day she thought of him—of the two of them in bed together. Carmen and Damon's intimate moments were rare. She considered that Damon's lack of interest in her was due to the stress their financial situation had put on the marriage. Or, perhaps it was something physiological, and if that was the case, she had better get used to it. She knew Damon would never go to the doctor. Anyone who knew *him* knew *that*. She had prayed and asked the Lord to intervene, although it was appearing not to be one of His priorities.

After Carmen served Damon his chicken pot pie, one she made from scratch, they retired to their bedroom. Carmen sneered to herself as Damon flopped onto the bed with his clothes on. She hated when he laid on the bed wearing the clothes he had worn outside in the "germy" world all day. At his job, he touched and rode around with random strangers. It could not get any grosser than that. He kicked off his shoes and grabbed the remote. Lying in germs didn't seem to bother him at all. She moved beyond it and headed to the bathroom to take a quick shower.

A few minutes later Carmen returned to the bedroom smelling as fresh as the picture of the grassy meadow that was on the label of her new bottle of shower gel. She wore a matching bra and panty set. She tried to appear confident about her body and the few extra pounds she carried as she passed him and slid into the bed. He was watching *Survivor*.

Carmen sat up after a few minutes and repositioned her pillow behind her back. She turned to face Damon, "I'm glad you're home this evening." Her voice contained notes of sweetness. She gently guided her hand down his arm in a beguiling manner.

"Me, too." Damon slid his arm away from her touch. "I'm turning in early. I'm tired." He never took his eyes off the television.

Carmen expressed her displeasure with a forceful sigh. "That's what hangin' out all hours of the night will do. Wear you out." She banged her head against the headboard in frustration. "What's the big draw anyway?" She shrugged. "My father ran the streets for years. All that hard living gave him nothing but a face full of wrinkles and daughters who resented him."

"You're not going to start with me are you, Carmen?" Damon admonished her with his tone.

"Start with you?" Carmen squinted. Her posture grew erect and her tone, indignant. She took a deep breath attempting to calm herself. A fight definitely wouldn't get her what she wanted. "No, really, Damon. I don't want you to get upset, but please help me understand. We've been married for months now. You were okay in the beginning, but now I never see you. You're always out with your friends. What am I supposed to think?"

"You wouldn't understand."

Carmen turned to face Damon. Her face was serious. "Help me understand. I know that hanging out with your friends is important to you, but when you're married it creates a problem."

"Tell me about it," Damon smirked.

The fullness of her frustration erupted. "I'm trying to be a good wife here." Her voice escalated. "I cook. I clean.

I do everything to make a home for us. Why don't you want to be here with me?"

"It's not about you, Carmen." Damon was monotone. "I like hanging out with my boys. I grew up tagging behind my dad to the pool hall. It's what men do." Damon picked up the newspaper off the night stand and began to read it.

"Some men." Carmen shot back angrily. "The foolish ones." When Damon grabbed the paper, she knew the conversation was over. She lay down beside him. She had so much she wanted to say, but did not know how. Her senses told her quite possibly Damon wasn't feeling her in that way. She could tell by the way he looked at her. It wasn't the look of a man in love. It was sterile. Empty. She didn't want to believe Cathy. She didn't want to believe she rushed him into marriage. She decided to test her theory, hoping to prove it wrong. She leaned over and unbuttoned Damon's shirt, kissing him on his chest, praying he would respond. She was in luck. He placed the newspaper on the nightstand and turned toward her. He gently placed both of his hands on her face and bent to kiss her. Carmen could feel the pain of rejection and confusion melting away as they kissed.

Suddenly, he stopped. "I don't think I can, tonight." He rolled onto his back and stared up at the ceiling.

Carmen felt sick to her stomach. "Do you need to see a doctor?" Her tone brimmed more with criticism than concern. "This is not normal for a thirty-something year old man."

Damon picked up the newspaper and resumed reading it.

Carmen insisted. "You know we're eventually going to have to talk about this."

"I know," he said. It appeared he understood her frustration. "But not now, okay?

Carmen yanked open the top drawer of her nightstand, reached for her headscarf and tied up her hair. She fluffed her pillow with violence, and then mentally tried to soothe her lust and disappointment so that she could fall asleep.

Damon lay there for a few moments pretending to read the paper. He wanted to give her what she wanted. Not that she was a charity case, she wasn't. She was amazing. She nagged him a little, but she had every right to. He wanted to give her what she wanted because he felt guilty. Guilty for believing that she held the answers he was seeking. That she would stop the burning desire for *something* that he felt; only to find out she couldn't. And now, she was stuck in a marriage with him as he was desperately trying to give her the love she wanted. The love she deserved. Perhaps he just needed a little more time. He turned the light off and turned over on his pillow staring out the window, into the night. Eventually he dozed off.

He awoke the next morning to the sound of his buzzing cell phone. His eyes opened in a squint and he placed his hand in front of his eyes to block the sun. He didn't know why Carmen insisted on keeping the bedroom blinds open.

He felt for the phone on the nightstand as he tried to wake up. It felt like he had just fallen asleep. It was a text from Craig:

Meet at my house tonight. Poker.

Damon nervously scanned the room for Carmen. He stretched, yawned, and zeroed in on the sound of clanging cookware coming from the kitchen. Carmen was making breakfast. No matter how mad she got, she always cooked. He walked to the bathroom, took a shower and got dressed.

Carmen rolled her eyes when she saw him walk through the doorway. She plated up his food and slammed it down on the table. Damon scratched his head and sat down to see what was on the plate—grits, bacon and eggs.

"Thanks." He said as he picked up the piece of toast that had slid off the plate onto the table. He didn't know what else to say. He definitely wouldn't tell her about the text. He thought about staying in for the night. It was getting to be more of a chore to get out of the house. He decided he would let the day unfold and see where her mood would take them.

Chapter 8

Carmen ran errands for most of the day and didn't say much to Damon when she was at home. At least they weren't fighting. He tip toed around the house, careful to stay out of her path.

At around six o'clock he pulled off his running pants and slid on a pair of jeans, black T-shirt and a pair of Timberlands. He headed for the door while Carmen was in the kitchen.

"Be right back," he yelled, before quickly running out the door headed for Craig's house.

Craig lived in Hyde Park, an affluent suburb of Chicago. It wasn't far from Bronzeville geographically, but financially it was a long ways off. The houses in Hyde Park cost a lot more and Craig's house was no exception. Three years ago, he completed a full renovation on the house and tricked it out. The inside projected a minimalist feel with hard leather furniture and glass in every direction. It was wired from top to bottom with the latest gadgets. Control centers operated everything: lights, the sound system, and the flat screens. He had cameras and alarms everywhere— all compliments of his own technology company. The house was like some sort of high-tech fortress.

As Damon walked along the paved sidewalk, he thought about the conversation he had with Carmen the previous night. All the points she made were good ones. He did not admit it to her, but he was exhausted. He was no longer twenty years old. Late nights out and long days at work had caught up to him, true enough. Why didn't he want to be at home with his wife? Lately he had been doing everything he could to keep him distracted from thinking about the question. He felt guilty for sneaking out while she was in the kitchen, but he could not risk another confrontation. It was draining him even more. Not enough, though, to get him to stay home. He just didn't want to be there.

When he arrived at Craig's house, he could hear music through the door. He rang the doorbell and a few seconds later Craig's face appeared on the security monitor next to the doorbell. He buzzed Damon in.

He entered on the main floor of the massive three-story house. He walked towards the back of the house to the main living area where Craig was hosting his guests. It only took him a few moments to discover that poker was not the only thing Craig and his friends had on their minds. A woman walked past in thigh-high boots and a miniskirt. Damon reached up and scratched the back of his head. Several of her friends had accompanied her, wearing so little clothing it wasn't worth mentioning. It looked like a scene from a rapper's video. Liquor flowed freely, money sat on the table and the girls mingled about.

Craig was at the bar pouring himself a drink when Damon came in the room. He rubbed his beard and smiled when he saw Damon, and stopped short of filling his glass. He pulled his unlit cigar away from his mouth. "I was afraid you might not be able to get away tonight." Craig elevated his voice so that he could be heard over the music. "It's a school night." He mocked Damon, evoking laughter from the rest of the crowd.

"I come and go as I please." Damon defended his honor.

Craig scratched his newly grown goatee. "You sound convincing, anyway."

Damon sat at the bar. Should he play poker or not? It was a tough decision now that he was getting older. The gambling was getting classier and the stakes were getting higher. Back in his days on the block, he always had extra cash that he could use to gamble. No rent to pay and no car note. Life was good back then. Now Carmen counted every penny. The hundred he had in his pocket wouldn't last a hot minute on the table, but he would be explaining its absence to Carmen forever. He was never much of a card player anyway. Craps was more his game. He and Craig grew up shooting dice on the streets of the South Side—gaming older guys all night long and walking away with pockets full of money. Craig put his street smarts to good use. He went to college and now made more money than all of them put together running his own technology company, while Damon struggled to get by at the dealership.

Damon opened the ice bucket and dropped three cubes of ice in his glass. He scanned the bottles and selected a scotch with a name he couldn't pronounce. The Bulls were playing the Lakers on one of Craig's three small flat screens hanging above the bar and Damon halfway tuned-in. His thoughts captured the remainder of his attention. He replayed the events of the past several months and carefully considered how he got to this point.

As he sat at the bar lost in thought, he heard loud chatter coming from a table. He turned to see Wendell, a childhood friend, engaged in a lengthy debate with Craig and a few others that sat playing cards about the benefits of marriage.

"Wendell. C'mon. Let's be real." Craig studied his hand. He switched his cigar from the left side of his mouth to the right. "The only reason you're faithful is because you couldn't get any play if you wanted it. You ain't got it like

Damon. He has to beat 'em off with a stick. Ain't that right, Damon?"

Hearing his name, Damon tuned into the conversation from across the room.

"I don't need any *play* as you call it." Wendell said. He spread his cards on the table prompting the others to throw theirs down in frustration. "I have a wife and two beautiful children."

Craig egged him on. "You want me to believe that if any of the beautiful women in this house wanted you and Sheila would never find out…" he swigged his drink and a cat-like grin crept across his face, "you wouldn't take 'em up on it?" He placed his drink on the table, "In fact, pick out the one you want, I might be able to talk her into a little something." He picked up a one hundred dollar bill that was lying on the table and waved it.

"There's nothing that these women have that I want. I got everything I need at home and I don't have to pay for it. Sleeping with loose women is a good way to get burned…in more ways than one."

Damon looked around to make sure that none of the women could hear them. He was relieved to hear the sound of a blender and girlish laughter coming from the kitchen. He wasn't interested in the girls, but the way the guys spoke showed a level of disrespect. He had three sisters. No matter how unbecoming a woman was acting, she was still a woman and he felt that earned a little respect.

Damon watched Wendell. He seemed to be very much at ease, very comfortable in his own skin. He completely ignored the women and their stilettos and backless dresses. He didn't appear to be behaving himself or trying to resist, he genuinely seemed to have no interest and Damon was intrigued. He watched him from across the room as he sipped his scotch. What could make him so happy to be married? Damon knew Sheila and she wasn't all that. Had to be something else.

Craig would not let the matter go. "Wendell, are you telling me that you are approached by women and you refuse to take them up on their offers?" He ribbed him.

"All the time."

"I don't believe it. I don't believe you're approached by women and you turn them down just because you have a wife."

"It's a weak man that tries to satisfy his soul with carnality. Have you ever noticed that no matter how many, you still never seem satisfied? Have you ever thought about that?"

"Yeah, I've thought about it and I'm glad," Craig laughed. The guys joined him in full support.

"I wouldn't risk anything for what I have at home. I have a woman who loves me no matter what. Whether I have money, lose a leg, it doesn't matter. She'll be there. Can you say that about any of your women? Craig, if your business collapsed, where would all your women be?

Craig sipped his drink.

Wendell continued, "Having a woman that I love…that I'm building a life with…who loves me in return…" Wendell shook his head. "I wouldn't trade that for anything."

With no one in the room on his side, Wendell said, "Inside of every man is a certain yearning—a yearning to be whole; to feel complete. We've been conditioned to believe that what makes us men is having a lot of women, being tough, and all that garbage. But what truly makes a man, are things like character, honor, and the ability to give and receive love. My relationship with God and my family complete me. I know who I am, I know what I stand for and I'm completely satisfied with my life. I wouldn't even trade all your money for the life I have."

At this point, the girls had returned with daiquiris. The guys were fed up with Wendell and pretty much all agreed he was crazy. If he hadn't been such a long time friend he probably would have been asked to leave. They failed to accept what he said, but as Damon sat on the bar stool, the truth of Wendell's words pierced him deeply...he had described almost perfectly the feeling he had been looking for the entire time.

Chapter 9

Damon arrived at work at nine o'clock for the regular Monday morning meeting. As usual, the edict from the sales manager was that any female who came on the lot without a male escort was strictly Damon's. The sales manager made it a new house rule because Damon could usually get a woman to buy a car; sometimes with all the bells and whistles, including the extended warranty. Although the other sales representatives were slightly resentful of giving their potential sales to him, they had seen him work the ladies and knew the sales manager was right—his charisma was good for business.

"I don't know what it is you've got, but it can 'sho get a woman into a car," Cephus, one of the older and more seasoned sales associates said, and all the other sales representatives agreed. "I've been selling cars for thirty years and I ain't ever seen nothing like it."

Damon appreciated the comment, but he was still unsure whether his gift was a blessing or a curse. He had seen it work both ways. His friends seemed to enjoy it more than he did. They had debates about what made him so irresistible to women. Was it his looks or his physique? Was it his smile, personality, or thick, jet black hair? It seemed no one could put his or her finger on it.

A whistle came across the parking lot letting Damon know that a single female had walked on the lot. It was their code. The unsuspecting women never saw it coming.

Damon scanned the lot. To his far left, he saw a woman getting out of a luxury sedan, much nicer than the used cars he sold. He saw her legs first. Smooth, caramel, and long. She got out of the car and stood almost as tall as he was. A little over six feet with her high heels. She was wearing a floral sundress and a sophisticated sun hat. She clutched her bag underneath her arm.

"What brings you onto the lot today?" Damon inquired.

She looked over her shoulder and Damon recognized the look on her face. It was the look of a woman prepared to do battle with a pushy sales person. He knew it wouldn't be there long.

"I'm looking for a car for my daughter. She's going off to college." The woman said. Her voice was eloquent and sophisticated.

Seeing her, Damon wondered what her daughter looked like. The woman appeared to be approaching fifty and time was treating her quite well. She had the body, skin, and hair of a woman much younger. Damon eyed her sundress and imagined what was underneath. As she talked, he scanned her body, visually x–raying every inch of her. He knew a younger, tighter version had to be a sight to see.

"What are your daughter's needs and I'll tell you which models might suit her. Damon extended his hand and gently took hers. "I'm Damon. It's good to meet you. What is your name?

"Amanda." She removed her hat and began to fan herself with it. "Amanda Dale." The motion made a slight breeze that gently lifted her brown hair off her smooth chestnut shoulders.

Damon started around the lot and Amanda followed behind him in the hot sun. She listened to him discuss the features of each automobile. She asked so many questions it grew tiring. A woman this age had to have purchased another car before. He carefully and politely entertained each question, providing her with white glove treatment.

After three hours on the lot, she left having bought a Toyota Avalon, more car than was needed for a nineteen year-old college kid.

Chapter 10

Damon walked up the stairs to the brownstone. He knew Carmen was not going to be happy when he told her he was going out with the fellas again tonight. He vowed he would stand firm. With his hands in his pockets, he eyed the red bricks as he slowly ascended the stairs. He admired the regality of the building. He had come a long way. Here he was, married and living in a brownstone. A nice one at that. He and Carmen, in theory, should have a good life together. He couldn't understand why he was so miserable.

Damon opened the large wooden door to see Carmen sitting on the sofa. He darted his eyes away from her as he closed the door behind him. "Hey…how was your day?" She glanced up from her magazine. "Fine. And yours?"

"Made my quota for the month already."

"Congratulations."

Damon could sense the tension in Carmen's tone, and in her body language. The conversation between them was mechanical. It was as if she already knew what was coming.

"Carmen. I'm going out tonight, okay?"

She hurled her magazine at him. "I'm so sick of you." She growled. "Why do you even come home?" Deep frown lines peeled across her forehead. "Why don't you just stay out there? If it's better than being home with me, I don't want you here."

Damon walked into the bathroom to take a shower. He missed the early days when she didn't say much about him going out. Now she wasn't going down without a fight. He was used to the routine by now. Carmen would follow behind him as he dressed. They would continue to shout and then he would run out of the door. It always eased his conscious a little when he left after they fought. It gave him justification for leaving.

Damon walked down the street and whistled for a taxi. He took the short ride over to Chicago's South Side. Initially he planned to go the pool hall to meet Craig and the gang, but he took the cab past the pool hall to his mother's house. It had been a while since he had seen her. He missed the comfort, the constancy of home. As he exited the cab in front of her house, the sound of gun shots welcomed him home.

His mom heard the screen door slam. "I'm in the kitchen." She yelled.

Damon walked up behind her, grabbed her around her waist and hugged her.

"Mom, you know you can't leave that door open like that. Things have changed. It's not like it was when I was growing up."

"What are you doing here?"

"It's good to see you too, Mom."

"I didn't mean it like that. It's just that I hardly see you since you moved in with Carmen. Oh, excuse me…got married. It's still hard for me to picture you as someone's husband. There's nothing wrong, is there?"

Damon thought about the question. Nothing was wrong, and yet everything was wrong. He wouldn't burden his mother with his problems. He kept the truth to himself.

"My stomach has been acting up." He slid out a chair and sat down at the table.

"What are you worrying about?" Sharon raised an eyebrow curiously. "Carmen?" She sat down at the table across from Damon.

"Nah, probably something I ate." Damon rubbed his stomach, trying to divert his mother's attention.

Sharon stood up and walked over to the cupboard. She pulled down a bottle of Pepto Bismol and handed it to Damon along with a glass. He poured a dose before handing it back to her.

"Take it with you." She said. "You look like you're going to need it."

He swallowed what was in the glass and dropped the bottle in his pocket. After a few moments catching up with Sharon, he decided it was time to leave.

"I gotta' go ma." He jumped up from his chair.

"Yeah, I know. Grass doesn't grow under your feet for long."

Damon kissed his mother on the cheek and walked out of the kitchen toward the front door. He passed through the living room and noticed a photograph of his father sitting on a side table. He wished his father was still around. Perhaps he could give him some advice on how to handle the mess he was in; being married to a woman who was the best thing that ever happened to him, but whom he didn't love, the woman he loved was married to someone else. Two sons by two different women, one he rarely saw. Child support payments. The attempt to be an honest man who made an honest living and work a 9 to 5, that was more like 9 to 9 and offered inconsistent pay.

Damon grabbed the Pepto out of his pocket and took a second dose as he stared at the picture. Why did it have to be that on one fateful night, a stranger entered the dimly lit bar and argued with his father over the most trivial of things, and in the end, his father lay, cut open in a pool of his own blood? The patrons too drunk, too shocked and too scared to help. The authorities took their sweet time coming to the bar, which they nicknamed Friday Night Fights, because of its reputation for drunken violence. By the time they got there, the stranger had disappeared, never seen or heard from again, and his father had died at the scene. Damon thought of the man that changed their lives forever on that night. Where was he? What was he doing? Did he ever think of that night? Did he ever think of the pain and anguish he had caused his family? Did he know that a boy had lost his father? Did he care? The anger rose up into the back of his throat bringing up the Pepto Bismol. He swallowed it down and walked out the door.

He decided to skip the taxi and make the walk all the way back to his brownstone. It would give him an opportunity to burn off some steam. He felt like a chained animal, gnawing on his own foot to get free. The pain sometimes seemed unbearable. The pressure was on him to make Carmen happy, fix the finances, make himself happy, and be a good father. His feet struck the pavement with anguish. He arrived home at a decent hour, surprising Carmen, who was watching the news. She looked at him as if she could tell something was bothering him.

"Are you okay?" she asked.

"Yeah."

He walked to the kitchen, poured himself a glass of milk and went to bed.

Chapter 11

"You looked as if something was bothering you last night. What's going on? Do you need to talk?"

"No, Carmen. Can I get these last few minutes of sleep?" Damon snapped, placing the pillow over his head to block out the sunlight coming through the blinds. Carmen was usually up before Damon to be at her job at the insurance company by eight o'clock. Being a car salesman and working later into the evening, Damon got up a little later. He found her early morning interrogation quite annoying.

She snatched the blanket from around his lower body, "Get up! We need to talk."

"Carmen, can't you see I'm trying to sleep." Damon snapped and yanked the blanket from her grasp. "Close the door and the blinds behind you on your way out." He repositioned the pillow over his head again, attempting to block out her voice and the light from the sun.

"All right." Carmen responded in a way that surprised Damon. The frustration and anger in her tone was missing. He was a little shocked she gave in so easily, but sleep prevented him from pondering it seriously. The past several nights he had been up dancing with his racing thoughts. He needed the extra hour to get him through the day. He was happy to hear Carmen slam the door on her way out and he drifted back to sleep.

An hour later, he was awakened by his alarm clock. He sat up in bed in a cold sweat. He had been having a terrible dream and was glad the clock went off. He sat on the bed for a few moments looking around the room and trying to get his bearings. Perhaps all of it had been a dream, including his marriage. As he brought things into focus, the reality of his situation returned. He saw Carmen's nightshirt hanging on the doorknob. He shook his head and headed for the shower.

***

At work, Carmen found it difficult to focus. She pondered the idea of a marriage counselor, but was fairly convinced Damon would never agree to it. She thought about trying a new hairstyle, purchasing a new wardrobe, including some sexy lingerie, and losing a few pounds. Her mind sank deeper in thought, and her cell phone startled her when it rang. She almost jumped off the chair. She looked at the Caller ID It was Cathy; the last person in the world she wanted to talk to at that moment.

"Yes, what is it?"

"I called to check on you. For some reason I had this weird notion to call you. I know you're working. Are you okay?"

"I'm fine, thank you."

"What's with all the formality?"

"What is it, Cathy?" Carmen snapped. "I'm working."

"Carmen, are you and Damon okay?"

"Here we go."

"No…I mean really."

"Cathy, we're fine." Carmen raised her voice somewhat, remaining cognizant of her surrounding co-workers. "Why can't you mind your own business? It would make things a lot easier for all of us."

Cathy was quiet for several seconds. Carmen continued, "I have to get back to work. I'll talk to you later."

"Carmen. Wait." her voice was soft and remorseful. "I saw Damon out the other night at Shea's."

Carmen was quiet. How humiliating to know Cathy had seen her married husband hanging out in a club for singles. She acted as if it didn't matter.

"And?"

"And I felt you should know."

"I know my husband goes out with his friends occasionally. Thank you. Goodbye." Carmen hung up the phone. Her eyes welled up and a solitary tear dropped to her lap. She wiped away any traces of it and went back to work.

For the rest of the day, in between her customer service calls, her mind drifted back to the conversation she had with Cathy. At the close of her workday, she drove home. Sitting at a stop light she caught a glimpse of herself in the rearview mirror. She looked different. Worn. Prominent bags had formed under her eyes and her hair had lost its luster. She tilted her head toward the mirror and made a makeshift part with her hands. Her normally thick locks had lost some of their bulk and she could see way more scalp than she normally did, peeking through in spots. *Damn you, Damon.* The nights she'd spent awake, and the days worrying about the condition of her marriage and having no idea what to do about it, were taking their toll. Considering life without him in it tore at the edges of her sanity. She stopped by the liquor store to grab a bottle of Cabernet before heading home.

When Damon entered the door with takeout, Carmen was sitting on the couch in front of the T.V., burning an incense and sipping her second glass of wine. He fetched two plates from the kitchen and joined her on the couch. He fixed Carmen a plate and handed it to her. Carmen assumed he was buttering her up and was reluctant to take it from him.

She braced herself, and then peppered her tone with defense. "What's this about?"

"It's not about anything. I thought you might've been hungry."

"Thanks." She relaxed her guard a little. How was your day?" She walked over to the portable bar, retrieved a wine glass and sat it on the table in front of Damon before sitting back down.

Damon waved his hand and declined the wine. "I received a voice message from a lady I sold a car to several weeks ago stating there was a problem with the car. Kinda' strange…" Damon dipped a dumpling in sauce and crammed it in his mouth, "since the car is only a year old. It was part of a rental car's fleet and they usually keep those in good condition." He questioned aloud, his mouth full of food. "I'll call her tomorrow. Other than that my day was great." He swallowed the food in his mouth. "We'll have a little extra money this month."

Damon appeared to be enjoying the dumplings so Carmen took a bite. The rich buttery flavor filled her mouth. She relaxed into the sofa and savored Damon for the few hours she had him that night. His charm engulfed her and the time she spent in his presence almost made up for the time he was away. She completely forgot about Cathy seeing him at Shea's and about going to a marriage counselor. She wished she could stay in that moment with him forever—him, her and Chinese dumplings for the rest of her life.

Chapter 12

Damon dragged himself into work the following morning.

As he walked through the double glass doors into the dealership he saw Cephus polishing the window of one of the showroom's cars. He looked up at Damon. "Man, you look like the last place in the world you want to be is at work." He released a chuckle before spraying cleaner on the window and wiping it.

Damon forced a smile as he walked past Cephus and trudged up the stairs to his office. It was a small, cramped space with makeshift, paper thin walls that were covered in gray fabric that stopped a foot shy of the ceiling. The flimsy construction allowed him to hear everything going on around him at all times. Every call made to a wife or mistress, every sale made, lost, or stuck in between, he could hear. If he focused in on it, he would go mad, so he had learned to block it out. He sat down at his desk and began deleting the noise from his consciousness. He scanned his desk for the Post-it note on which he had written Amanda Dale's number. He found it stuck to the back of some errant papers on his desk. He picked up the phone to call her.

"Mrs. Dale?"

"Yes."

"This is Damon from the dealership."

"Oh...hello, Damon. Yes...I—I called because the car is running funny."

"What do you mean running funny?"

"I don't know. I can't describe it. It runs funny. Could you come by and take a look?"

A frown appeared on Damon's face. "The car is still under the manufacturer's warranty and you upgraded it, so whatever it is, just bring it by and the service department can take a look. You won't be charged a thing."

Amanda was insistent.

"Well, I don't know a thing about cars. What if it quits while I'm driving it? Could you come and take a look?"

Damon hesitated. Something didn't feel right, but he appreciated her business, and hopefully the business of all her socialite friends that had kids going off to college, so he agreed to stop by. He prided himself on giving the best customer service to his clients.

"I don't normally do this, but I'm looking at your address and you don't live far. I can come on my lunch hour."

"Thanks, Damon. I really appreciate it."

Damon hung up and moved on with his workday. At noon, he prepared to leave the dealership. He planned to get to Amanda's house, look at the car quickly and spend the remaining time having a quick bite to eat at the Subway nearby. An hour was just enough time. On his way out, he ran into Cephus and told him about the dream he had the previous morning. In the dream, he saw a princess. Without speaking, she beckoned him to follow him into the forest. When he caught up to her and reached out to grab her, she turned into a large serpent. The serpent took a swipe at him and he woke up. Upon hearing the dream, Cephus asked Damon if Carmen was one of them ole' Geechee women. He warned him she might have put a root on him. Damon wasn't exactly sure what *Geechee* meant, but it sure didn't sound anything like Carmen. She was good to the core. He looked at his watch as he headed out the door on his way to

Amanda's. Now he only had forty-five minutes before he had to be back to work.

Mrs. Dale lived down the road in a historic neighborhood. When he pulled up in front of the stately brick Tudor, he saw her walking down the tree-lined driveway to meet him. She was barefoot, wearing a spaghetti-strapped pink floral dress and was carrying and stroking a large grey cat.

He turned off the engine and opened the car door. As soon as his foot hit the pavement, she greeted him. "Thanks for coming. The car is in the back." He eased the car door closed, plastered on a smile and followed her to the rear of the house.

The car was sitting in front of the three-car detached garage. She put down the cat and handed him the keys. He jumped in and gave the car a start.

He turned his ear toward the dashboard to listen carefully. "Sounds fine to me," he told her, when he heard nothing but a smooth running engine.

"You don't hear that?"

"No. Don't hear a thing. What do you hear?"

"That noise. That clicking, popping sound."

"I don't hear it, but again, if there's a problem with the car Mrs. Dale, your warranty will cover it. Give it a couple days and if you continue to hear it, or if there are any other problems, bring it by. I'll have our service people look at it. If they can't fix it, I'm sure we can work something out.

"Are you hungry?" She quickly interjected. "I made lunch. It's my way of thanking you for doing this." She smiled, "My feelings will be hurt if you don't accept my hospitality."

Damon looked at his watch. Time was ticking away. He had less than thirty minutes to drive to a restaurant, pick something, wait for it to be prepared and drive back to work and eat it. It wasn't possible.

"As a matter of fact, I am hungry."

"Come on in." She smiled again as she walked up the stairs to the side porch. She reached down to pet the cat on the head before walking into the house.

Damon followed her inside. The house was full of antiques. Something was missing from the atmosphere. It didn't have the feel of a home—that warm, connecting energy wasn't there. The house had more of a museum quality. Everything was neatly arranged and meticulously kept, probably the work of a housekeeper. The only thing you could hear was the creaking of the dark wood floors as they walked and the ticking coming from the grandfather clock somewhere in one of the large rooms. She led him to the kitchen where a croissant stuffed with tuna salad sat on a white china plate decorated with floral embroidery. It was accompanied by a side of potato chips and a handful of bright red strawberries.

She invited Damon to wash his hands at the kitchen sink and he sat down at the table. He thanked her sincerely as he picked up the sandwich and took a bite. Mrs. Dale approached his chair from behind. She sighed deeply and placed her hands on his shoulders proceeding to give him a massage. Damon stopped chewing.

"What are you doing?" He asked. He was puzzled but remained calm.

"I don't know…I'm guessing you might be tense from all that labor you do." She continued to massage his shoulders.

"I don't do labor at my job." Damon sat the sandwich down on the plate.

"You don't fix cars?"

"Nope. Never." Damon was now aware of the scheme she was running. He stood up. "I'd better go."

"Wait," she said and blocked the doorway with her taut frame. "Don't go. All right you've figured me out. Ever since I saw you at the dealership, I haven't been able get you out of my mind."

Mrs. Dale picked up the plate that held the tuna salad sandwich and walked out of the kitchen. Damon watched her hips sway as she walked. Her dress hugged her lean body. She seductively gathered up her long brown hair and gently rested it on her left shoulder.

Damon stood alone in the kitchen. How far was she willing to go? Not to mention, he loved tuna, and that was the best tuna sandwich he had ever tasted in his life, and he only had two bites of it. He knew better, but in a moment of weakness, he followed her and that sandwich out of the kitchen.

He walked slowly down the hallway. The planks yielded a quiet groan with each step. At the end of the hallway was a bedroom. When he entered, he was struck by the tall pedestal-like queen bed. It was very formal and much too neat to be a bed. It looked more like a platform. By the looks of it, and her elaborate scheme to get him there, he concluded she wasn't getting much action.

Damon scanned the room for the sandwich. He found it sitting on the dresser on the other side of the room next to Mrs. Dale, who was standing in front of the sun-drenched window. She had dropped her dress and stood there wrapped in only a towel and a pedicure. Damon walked over to the dresser, grabbed the sandwich off the plate and took a bite. The savory spices and the creamy texture pleased him. He began scanning her from head to foot. He focused on her long legs, which seemed almost twice as long as her torso. His mind exploded with possibilities of what they could do together.

She walked over to him and began unbuttoning his blue shirt revealing his muscular chest. He finished chewing his bite and swallowed hard. How wonderful it would be to indulge her in her little game of cat and mouse. Perhaps he wasn't in such a bad situation after all. Whenever Carmen had made advances, he was uninterested. He wondered if there was something physically wrong with him, but as he stood in the room thinking about all the things he could do to Mrs. Dale, and knowing that women her age were at their sexual peak, he got the answer to his question. Everything was working just as it should be. He could feel his desire for her expanding as blood raced to every part of his body. He was relieved that he was fine physically, but frightened that for some reason Carmen didn't do it for him.

Suddenly, they heard the back door slam. Mrs. Dale ran over to the window and saw her husband's white BMW in the driveway.

"We're screwed," she whispered. "That's Dale, my husband."

Damon noticed she referred to him by his last name. Where he came from, that was a symbol of earned honor and respect—the mark of a true boss.

They urgently scanned the room for a hiding place for Damon. At the last possible moment, he dropped to the hardwood floor and shot underneath the bed, thankful for its platform like nature. There was not an inch to spare between him and the bed's underside.

As he lay there giving thanks, Damon saw her husband's wing-tipped shoes pass by, a few inches from his face.

"What's going on?" Her husband asked. His tone was intimidating.

"Nothing, Dale." The sweet drawl in her voice was a clear diversion. "What are you doing here this time of day?" She asked.

"I was on my way to an offsite meeting and I had to use the bathroom. What's that smell?"

"Oh, that? I was eating that sandwich. It's Tuna."

"Not that. I smell something else."

Damon quickened. Was it his cologne? Or perhaps his senses had detected his presence in the room, much like a dog picking up the scent of another male dog.

Dale probed further, "Why are you wearing a towel in the middle of the day?"

"Can't a girl take a bath? It's hot out."

As their dialogue continued, Damon's heart began to pound. He crossed his fingers that Dale would not figure them out, pull up the bed skirt and thrust his face under the side of the bed to find him. He felt at a disadvantage since he couldn't size him up. Was he tall? Short? Muscular? Does he keep a gun in his nightstand? Damon's armpits began to itch and droplets of sweat populated his forehead. Any chances of an intimate moment had passed, even if Dale left. On a fear scale, he was at ten! Definitely a mood-killer. All he could think about was getting out of there. Amanda tried to distract him further, "Dale, since you're here," she beguiled, "Why don't you wash my back for me?" Damon saw her towel drop to the floor. He was disappointed that he had missed the opportunity to see what was underneath it. And, even more disappointed he would be trapped underneath the bed listening to Dale having his wife for an afternoon snack, and to top that off, he would be late getting back to work.

After a few moments of kissing, Damon heard Dale decline her tempting offer. He sighed with relief as he heard Dale urinating in the toilet. She had effectively thrown him off the scent. Damon counted the minutes until he saw Dale's shoes walk past the bed and out the bedroom door. He listened as he walked down the hall. Damon peered from under the bed and saw Amanda standing at the window.

"Amanda," he said with quiet force. At this point, calling her Mrs. Dale seemed ridiculous. The event had definitely placed them on a first name basis. Amanda pressed her finger to her lips urging him to be quiet. She watched out the window as Dale got in his car and drove down the driveway. Damon crawled out from under the bed with dust in his hair and dust bunnies clinging to his shirt.

"Oooh!" Amanda said with laughter bellowing from her throat. "I need to clean under there."

Damon rolled his eyes. He didn't appreciate her casualness. Where he was from you could be killed by messing with someone's wife. He walked out of the bedroom, through the kitchen and out of the side door. The door slammed behind him causing the cat to shriek loudly and leap from the porch. It scurried underneath to safety.

Shaking off the dust and the fear, and allowing his blood pressure to return to normal, Damon walked down the driveway, buttoning up his shirt. When he looked up, he saw a young woman walking toward him. When Amanda came to the car lot that day and told him she was buying a car for her daughter, he had imagined what a younger version of Amanda might look like and he had been right. She was absolutely gorgeous. With her small waist and wide hips, Damon felt she was cheating herself by not ditching her college career for a Paris runway. She approached him with a confused look on her face.

"Can I help you?" she asked.

"I'm Damon…from the dealership. Your mom asked me to come by and look at your car. It's making a noise or something." Damon shook his head, recalling what had just happened.

"I'm Amber. And there's nothing wrong with my car," she snickered, seeming to know what her mother was up to. Damon eyed Amber's rose-colored lips as she spoke. The day was hot and she, like most young girls in June was scantily clad. Her halter and cut off jean shorts barely covered anything. If only he could replay the events of what transpired in the house. He would remove Amanda, insert Amber, and Dale would be deceased. That would have been a nice lunch.

"Nice to meet you, Amber. I'd better be getting back to work. If you have any problems with the car, please don't hesitate to call me." He handed Amber his card. He had escaped tragedy and was able to conjure up a lie to tell his boss on his way back to work.

Chapter 13

The next morning Cephus burst into Damon's office interrupting his morning's paperwork. Damon slowly looked up.

"There's someone here to see you—a young girl."

Damon hopped up from his chair hoping it was a referral from a past client. Perhaps he would make a sale and start the day off right. When he descended the stairs, he was surprised to see Amber. She was bent over, looking inside the gold Accord that was parked on the showroom floor. The salesmen had noticed her jean shorts.

"Hello, Miss Dale." Damon said. "The service department is around back."

"I told you the car is fine."

"What can I do for you, then?"

Amber shrugged her shoulders. "I just wanted to…you know…stop by." She ran her finger seductively along the car's door.

Damon read the flirty look on her face and didn't want trouble. "If there's nothing wrong with the car, I'm not sure why you're here."

She walked up to him. "I thought maybe you and I could go out sometime and…" Amber gently bit the side of her rose-colored bottom lip, "get to know each other better."

"I don't think so, Amber."

"Oh, come on Damon. Don't be that way." Amber wrapped her arms around his waist while his nosy co–workers looked on.

Damon grimaced and uncoiled Amber's arms from around him. He grabbed her by her wrist, and hurried her toward the back of the dealership. He cornered her in the dark hallway by the vending and ice machines. He noticed Stan lurking at the front of the corridor, probably trying to figure out why Amber had come. He moved closer to her so that he could not be heard above the humming ice maker.

Amber smiled widely and tried to kiss him.

He pulled away. "Stop it!" Admittedly, she was beautiful, but he had enough of the Dales: momma, daddy, and now, baby included. His words were firm. "You have to leave."

"I know you're not giving me the brush-off." Amber retorted quickly and placed her hand on her hip. "I saw you coming down the driveway buttoning your shirt the other day. I know what you and mother were doing inside the house."

"What? Your mother and I weren't *doing* anything."

"Yeah?" She pointed her finger in his face. "How many service guys you know come to the house on their lunch hour and leave buttoning their shirt. How 'bout I tell daddy what your little house call was all about?"

Damon knew he had better play his cards very carefully. Amber, in her determination to get her way, could make things bad for all of them. Her incorrect assumption could get him fired, or worse. The last thing Damon needed was to get beat up for something he didn't even do. He tried a softer approach.

"Amber," he said, flashing his irresistible smile. "You are beautiful and you have no idea how much I would love to go out with you." He whispered softly in her ear. He wasn't lying. "But the truth of the matter is, as beautiful as you are I know I wouldn't be able to give you all the attention you deserve."

Amber had a confused look on her face.

"I'm married," Damon consoled. "He held up his hand to show her his wedding band. It was the first time he had found comfort in saying those words. When Amber heard that, she walked down the corridor and out the dealership doors, hopefully for good.

Having thwarted catastrophe again, Damon returned to his office. In his zeal to sell cars and get a bonus for the month, he had neglected his paperwork duties. He would spend the morning catching up.

An hour later, he was paged over the intercom by the dealer receptionist. "Damon, you have a guest in the lobby."

He hoped this time, it wasn't Amber's father. He pondered, briefly, what to do. The only way out was through the showroom floor. Could Amber possibly be that spoiled? Would she tell her daddy a lie just because she didn't get her way?

He stood up and walked out of his cubicle. His face brightened when he beheld Rachel, his son's mother, standing at the bottom of the stairs. "I see you have decided to trade in that junk of a car for a real car," he said jokingly referring to her new Audi coupe.

"Dream on." Rachel joked. She was a vision in yellow slacks and matching summer sweater. She always had taste, but when she married Evan, she was able to afford high-end designer clothes that were tailored to fit her beautiful figure perfectly. She always looked as if she had stepped off the pages of a fashion magazine.

"What brings you here?"

"It's London."

Panic manifested on his face. "What's wrong with him?"

"There's nothing wrong." Rachel spoke in a sure tone. She pulled out three of London's school pictures and handed them to Damon. "I wanted to drop these off."

Damon smiled in admiration as he looked at the pictures before tucking them in his wallet.

"Do you have a few minutes to talk?" Rachel said in a serious tone.

Damon nodded his head and lead Rachel up the stairs to his office. He was nervous about what she might say. Even though they disagreed on just about everything, they had maintained their friendship. She was always open and honest with him, and he was always careful not to piss her off too much. She sat down in his extra chair and began to explain the reason for her visit.

"London is getting older and I think he needs to start spending more time with you."

Damon was pleased to hear Rachel say that. He had two sons; London, and Jamal, who was from a previous, short-lived relationship. It was back during his wilder days. He unleashed his animal magnetism on many unsuspecting woman, and on one careless night eight years ago, he slipped up and got one of them pregnant. The child's mother had since wised up and moved on, wiping Damon from she and her child's memory, leaving Damon paying child support for a son he barely knew.

"I've always been available for him, Rachel. You're the one that made me beg you to let him stay with me."

"I know, and I'm sorry for that, but in my defense, your lifestyle in the past hasn't been conducive to nurturing a little boy. Now that you're married and a little more settled, I feel more comfortable.

"Settled, huh?" Damon wanted it to be the truth, but he knew he was missing the mark completely.

"Yeah…I think Carmen is good for you, Damon. Anyway…Evan was playing with London the other day and London kept saying that Evan was his father. And while Evan loves him like his own child, he came to me and said that London seemed confused about the nature of their relationship, and that he needed to know, and be clear about, who his real father is."

Yet another reason that made it harder for Damon to hate Evan. He was a good man and he had given both Rachel and London a good life. If it wasn't for the fact that he stole the only woman Damon had ever loved, perhaps he and Evan could have been friends.

"He wouldn't have to be confused if we were still together." Damon said. He looked directly into her eyes, attempting once more to feel her out and determine if she still might have feelings for him.

Rachel stood up and grabbed her Louis satchel off the desk. "You and I have been through this Damon. It will never be. That part of our life is over." Her voice carried over the thin walls of the cubicle for all to hear. "I'll bring London by this weekend."

Damon walked Rachel down the stairs and to the front door of the dealership.

"Rachel?"

"Yeah."

"Thanks." Damon opened the door for Rachel and followed her through. "It means a lot to me. I know you haven't trusted me much in the past. And, I'm sorry about what I said. I would never want to jeopardize our friendship. Are we cool?" Damon extended his hand.

"Yeah, we're cool." Rachel smiled as she shook his hand before walking away.

Damon eyed Rachel's yellow outfit as she got into her car. Her shapely figure conjured up nights when they used to make love. No other woman made him feel the way she did. He smiled and waved to her as she drove past him and out the parking lot.

Chapter 14

Rachel pulled up in front of the house on Saturday morning. Damon stood in the doorway, eager to greet his son. Rachel barely got London's seat belt off before he tore up the stairs to Damon. "Daddy," he screamed and hugged Damon around his legs. Carmen appeared next to him. Rachel approached them and handed London's duffel bag to Carmen.

"There's cough medicine in his bag, Carmen." He's just getting over a cold.

Damon teased her, "Why are you giving instructions to Carmen? Ya'll think I'm not capable of giving him his medicine." He looked at London, "See how women do us, little man?"

Carman unzipped the bag, "I'll take care of it."

Rachel started back down the front steps. "Instructions are on the bottle. I'll pick him up tomorrow morning." Rachel waved over her shoulder. "Have fun you guys. "I'm going shopping."

Carmen and Damon escorted London inside. Carmen took his duffle bag to his room and he and Damon took their place on the sofa while Carmen made pancakes. They finished eating and were watching television when Damon asked Carmen to excuse them for a minute. He took London to his room and sat him on the bed.

"Your mom tells me that you and Evan are getting pretty close."

London kicked his legs one at a time and grinned. "Yeah." He found a lose string on the edge of the blanket and started pulling on it. "We have a really good time together watching T.V. and playing ball and stuff like that."

Damon looked in his eyes. "Which one of us is your father?" London frowned at Damon causing him to reconsider his question. This was no time to get competitive, after all Evan took care of London without Damon's financial help. There was no reason not to like this guy. "I mean…do you know what a biological father is?"

"No, but I have two daddies."

Damon scratched his head. "Two daddies?"

"Yeah…you and Evan. My friends only have one, but I'm lucky…," he held up two fingers, "I have two."

Damon tickled London underneath his arm and he laughed out loud. He was still too young, yet. He'd try again in a year or so. "Two daddies it is, then."

***

Rachel came by early, too early, and picked up London so he could go to Sunday school. Damon yawned as he sat on the sofa in the living room reading the Sunday newspaper. He had just finished the eggs and toast that Carmen had made for breakfast. In the past, he would rip out the sports section and toss the rest, but lately he enjoyed lingering over the paper on Sunday mornings. He perused the business and world sections. Half the stuff he didn't fully understand, but he found it interesting anyway.

Carmen walked into the living room and sat a cup of tea down on the small table next to him. "You should think about talking to my Aunt Renee," she stood over him with her arms folded.

"I'm good. I don't need to talk to anyone." Damon picked up the cup and took a small sip, carefully testing the tea's temperature.

"It's vanilla bean."

He had begun to look forward to the cup of herbal tea that Carmen would make for him on Sunday mornings. He enjoyed being surprised by the new flavors she would introduce him to. He knew it wasn't exactly macho; if the boys knew he drank herbal tea he would never hear the end of it. Especially from Craig. He still had bourbon for breakfast.

He savored the rich flavor of vanilla until Carmen rudely interrupted him.

"Something's bothering you and I don't know what to do about it.

Damon looked up from his cup with an eyebrow raised.

"Aunt Renee might be able to help you…" Carmen shrugged, "work through things."

Carmen's Aunt Renee was a psychotherapist and the last person on earth Damon wanted to see. Where he came from, people who needed a therapist were crazy, and if they weren't crazy, they would be after a few visits with a head shrinker.

"No thanks, Carmen." Damon raised his voice at her and gave her a stern look. After which he resumed reading his newspaper. He hoped his few words would send a message to Carmen to leave him alone. She snatched her breakfast dishes off the cocktail table, went to the kitchen and slammed them in the sink.

Damon could hear her filling the sink with water. Realizing he had hurt her feelings, he got out of his comfortable position on the sofa and walked into the kitchen. He placed his plate in the sink and kissed her on the back of the neck.

"Let's go into the city today." Carmen said, as she turned off the water.

"And do what?"

"Shop."

"With what?"

She turned to face him. "We've been so good with our money lately and we've paid off some bills." Her voice grew eager. "Let's treat ourselves to something."

Damon was a little concerned. Shopping downtown could be pricey. He didn't mind Carmen treating herself to a little something, but he wasn't trying to break the bank either. Damon scratched his head, "Maybe…if we find something on sale."

After Carmen finished the dishes she and Damon drove downtown. Damon was getting nervous about spending money. They were starting to make headway on the bills and he felt as if he could breathe a little better; at least in that area. The marriage thing was a whole other issue. He privately joked that he might have to pawn Carmen's wedding ring to pay for their purchases. He was still upset over all the money they had spent on that ridiculous wedding ceremony, but he wanted to make Carmen happy; at least for today. He felt he owed her that. He hadn't been the most available person. He had remained closed off to her, still in disbelief that he agreed to get married. He was angry with himself and tried not to take it out on her, but from time to time his resentment showed.

***

Carmen was excited about the day. Spending time with Damon always filled her heart with joy, but as they walked through town her upbeat and happy demeanor started to change. She began to feel uneasy and on guard. She saw beautiful women dressed to the nines, which normally wouldn't have been a big deal, after all, it was Chicago—a city of very affluent people. But, it was the way that many of them looked at Damon when they walked past. The clandestine, come hither looks they gave. The way they eyed his creamy chocolate skin, and his fitted T-shirt that stretched delightfully over his perfectly chiseled chest and arms. The way they eyed his jeans that sat low on his hips, offering a hint of bad boy–ness that assured them a night of pleasure. His deep eyes and dark features beckoned them, one after the next. Their blatant advances made Carmen feel as if she was invisible. By the time they got to Bloomingdales, her insecurity had reached its peak.

She pulled a form fitting dress off the rack and checked the label for the size. The label showed it was a twelve, but it looked awfully tiny when she held it up to her body. Perhaps she had gained a little weight. "Damon?"

Damon looked across the aisle into the men's department spotting a manikin wearing a pair of designer jeans and a fitted T-shirt. "Yeah, what is it?"

"Do you think I look okay?"

He furrowed his brow, the manikin still vying for his attention. "What kind of a question is that?"

"I don't know? Do you like the way I look?"

He started towards the men's department. "You've gained a little weight. That's normal."

Carmen hung the dress back on the rack and followed him. "What do you mean normal?"

"A lot of people gain weight when they get married."

"You didn't."

Carmen knew she had been guilty of letting herself go. Perhaps that was the reason he was so distant. The women she saw that day were a sample of the women she knew he could have. She wanted to believe that he loved her so much that her looks didn't matter to him, but who was she kidding? She made a vow to herself to return to her premarital fabulousness. She would lose a few pounds and cover her prematurely graying hair. Maybe a vitamin would bring back its fullness. Since she had vowed to lose weight she decided to skip buying clothes. Damon bought the jeans and she found a nice pair of sandals on sale and bought those instead.

Chapter 15

Craig stayed to finish his drink and was one of the last ones to stagger out of the club after it had closed for the night. Damon had refused to go with him so he went alone, as he did quite often. He was pretty much a regular. He walked out the door and scanned the parking lot looking for his red Lexus. He walked over to it knowing the last drink had pushed him to the edge of cognizance, but figured he would take his chances and drive home anyway. He giggled as he clumsily shuffled through his key ring trying to identify the one that would get him into his car. He had several keys on the ring, including the ones to his truck and motorcycle and tonight they all looked alike. He noticed a long scratch going down the side of the car door.

"I'm high," he laughed out loud. "This ain't even my car." He scanned the dimly lit parking lot, which was now almost empty. That was the only red Lexus he saw. He scratched his head in confusion. He stumbled to the rear of the car to check the license plate and saw more scratches, and, the car appeared to have a mysterious lean. "What?" He whispered slowly. When he brought the trunk into focus, he saw the word *bastard* carved into it. He staggered backwards a few steps to get a view of the license plate. It was his car! Adrenaline rushed through his veins. It became clear why the car was leaning. He approached the passenger side. He was horrified to see slashed tires, and his thousand dollar rims were mangled. He screamed when he saw a huge dent in the passenger side door. "What happened to my car...I can't believe this." Then he sensed someone standing behind him. When he turned around to see who it was, a fire-like pain seared his face and his eyes slammed shut against his will. He couldn't even pry them open. His nose began running profusely and he fell to his knees in agony. *Pepper Spray*. He writhed in pain on the ground, blowing snot from his nose and coughing loudly. He scooted up against his car for protection. "Hello," he pleaded. He had no idea who it was that attacked him or his car, or if they were finished. He couldn't see a thing. He felt afraid for the first time in a long time and lay there in silence. He thought of what it must feel like to be blind. "Please don't hurt me."

After a few moments, he heard the sound of high-heeled shoes walking away. Whichever one of the many women he had dissed in the past, they were smart enough not to speak in order to remain unidentified. He heard her get in her car and drive away.

Craig fumbled for his phone and pulled it out of his pocket. He was thankful for voice-activated dialing since he couldn't even open his eyes to see his phone. "Call Damon," he yelled angrily into the phone.

"Did you say call library?" The irritating voice of the phone feature replied.

"No," he whined, "call Damon."

"I'm sorry, did you say call secretary?"

Craig was tempted to hurl the phone across the lot. He took a deep breath, calmed down and accessed the feature again, this time with a clear voice. "Call Damon."

"Did you say Damon?"

"Yes."

"One moment please…."

He sighed with relief as he heard the phone dialing Damon's number.

***

Carmen and Damon were jolted awake by the sound of the ringing phone. Damon patted the nightstand randomly, feeling for it. When he picked it up, he could hear Craig's frantic voice on the other end of the phone.

"Damon, I need your help."

Carmen sat up. She gathered her nightshirt in the center of her chest, near her heart. She eyed every word coming from Damon's mouth trying to decipher who was calling.

"Craig? It's three o'clock in the morning. Carmen and I were sleeping."

Hearing Craig's name, Carmen rolled her eyes and fell backwards on her pillow. She sat up again, fluffed her pillow with three punches, let out a grunt and fell back down again.

Damon fought through sleepiness and focused in on what Craig was saying.

"I know, man, but I need you. I have been viciously attacked in the club parking lot. I'm blind. I can't even see well enough to get home."

"Do you need me to call 911?"

"No, but I'm in pretty bad shape. Please hurry."

Damon jumped out of bed. He explained to Carmen that Craig had been jumped at the club. He quickly pulled on his sweat pants and a hoodie, pocketed his phone and ran out the door. Who would do something like this? It must have been someone's husband. Craig could be unscrupulous when it came to women. He didn't care if they were married or not. He would stop at nothing to get them in bed. Damon always said his luck would eventually run out.

As he pulled into the parking lot he spotted Craig's shiny, red Lexus in the corner of the lot. Craig was lying beside it with his eyes closed. Damon parked next to him. He got out and helped him off the ground and into his car.

"Do you need to go to the hospital?" Damon asked Craig. He scanned his body and was relieved when he didn't see any blood anywhere.

"No, I'll be alright."

"Who did this, man?"

"I didn't see the person, but I think it was Samantha?"

"I didn't know Samantha was hooked up with anybody."

"She wasn't." Craig continued to wipe his running nose.

"Wait a minute." Damon was confused. "You mean a chick did this?"

"Yeah and I think it was that bitch, Samantha. I was looking at the damage done to my car and when I turned around, she sprayed something in my face. I think it was pepper spray. I couldn't see a thing, but I'm pretty sure it was her. I could tell by the sound her heels made as she walked away. Take me to her house." Craig demanded.

"To do what? I know you are not thinking of putting your hands on a woman. Besides, you aren't even sure if it was her. You're going to assault a woman that you can only identify by the sound of high heels. All of your women wear high heels." Damon shook his head. "I'm taking you home, man."

Damon drove Craig to his house and helped him inside the front door. A loud beeping pierced the air with full on annoyance. Damon carefully followed Craig's instructions to disarm his high-tech security system. He stated it required speed *and* accuracy. It was a series of letters, numbers and spaces. Damon pressed a wrong button on his first attempt, and missed a dash on the second. He gave his full attention to Craig's nasally voice, which could barely be heard over the intensely loud beeping reminder that time was running out. He could feel moisture in his palms as he made the third attempt. All he needed was for the cops who regularly patrolled the neighborhood to arrive at the scene, guns drawn. They might not even believe that Craig lived there. He had been arrested before; it was no fun.

The third attempt to enter both characters and numbers worked and silence welcomed them. Damon led Craig into the kitchen. His gait seemed surer and his speech was losing its slur. Damon hoped it was a sign that sobriety was moments away. He guided Craig over to the sink where he turned on the faucet and slowly lowered his head. He moaned gently as the cool water doused his face. "Can you reach in the second drawer on the island and hand me a towel?"

Damon opened the drawer to find a row of neatly folded towels, he chuckled to himself when he saw Craig's last name, *Mincey,* monogrammed on them. He walked over and handed one to Craig who covered his face with it, and softly pressed it to his eyes. He pulled it away to test his vision, looking left and then right. A few seconds later he placed his head under the faucet again. After he flushed his eyes a second time, Damon helped him onto a chair.

"Now, tell me what happened again?"

Craig blotted his eyes with the towel. "I was getting in my car when I felt someone behind me. When I turned around they sprayed pepper spray. I ducked, but I wasn't fast enough."

"And you think it was Samantha?"

"I know it was." He blew his nose on the towel.

"Let's say it was…do you think you deserved it?" Damon had issues in the past with women, and had hurt quite a few, but Craig took doggish to another level. He was just wrong when it came to women. He used them for sport and Damon thought he had earned a little of what he had gotten.

Craig attempted to focus his eyes on Damon. They were the color of blood oranges. "There you go getting a conscience on me?"

"I'm just saying…" Damon stood up and held out his hand. "C'mon. Let's get you to bed." He helped Craig off the chair and led him down the hall to his bedroom. As they entered, Craig told Damon he needed to throw up. Damon helped him into the bathroom and waited outside the door. When he finished, Damon helped Craig into the bed and took his shoes off, where he fell asleep fully clothed.

Chapter 16

Carmen walked through her mother's front door. She was sitting on the couch in the living room with her face buried in the bible. When she saw it was Carmen, her look of surprise was immediately replaced with joy. The corners of her mouth immediately rolled up into a smile. "I'm glad you stopped by."

Carmen noticed the subtle scent of collard greens in the air.

"Where's Damon?"

"I don't know," Carmen replied. Her voice was laden with disappointment.

"Cathy thinks you two are having problems. That true?"

"She talks too much." Carmen snapped.

"She does. But is it true?"

Carmen shrugged her shoulders. "Something like that."

"C'mon in the kitchen." Her mother responded. "I'll make you some tea."

Carmen trailed behind her mother into the tiny kitchen. The tall ceilings of her brownstone made her mother's kitchen feel almost claustrophobic. Carmen thought back to when she was a little girl growing up. That same kitchen seemed such a magical place with its bright blue walls and yellow flowered curtains. Back then, the ceilings seemed as tall as the sky. Having grown used to the spaciousness of her brownstone, now they felt as though they would crash in on her at any moment. An already tense Carmen found it hard to relax as she sat at the table in the small kitchen. Her mother prepared the tea and poured her a cup. She sat staring at the table.

"Baby?" Gert said in a slow and soothing voice as she sat next to Carmen at the table.

"Yeah, Mom."

"Looks like you're carrying a mighty big weight on your shoulders. Might be too big to carry it by yourself. Anything you want to talk about?" As Gert stirred her tea, her spoon clicked against the dainty china teacup. The familiar sound transported Carmen back to being a little girl and sitting with her mother and sister at the same table on Saturday mornings. Many times, her father would just be coming in.

"Momma, why did you put up with Daddy all those years?"

"It sounds as though you're asking me for advice." Gert looked Carmen square in the eyes. "I loved your father, Carmen. Still do. We always had an understanding."

"Humph," Carmen smirked as she folded her arms. "And what was that?"

"When I married your father I had a full knowledge of the kind of person he was. He drank. He gambled. He loved running the streets. In fact, that's where I met him. How could I have expected him to be any different? Initially, I was disappointed...I think every woman wants to come first in her man's life, but I learned to love him and accept him for who he was."

"Why, Momma? Why did you put up with it?"

"I knew he was a good man. He provided for us without complaint. He's never raised his hand, or spoken a cross word to me. And, I always knew that he loved me and you girls. He would die for us and that was all I needed to know. I was willing to give my love freely to him without any conditions." Gert took a sip of tea from the tiny cup. "You young girls marry men with the intention of changing them. You can't…it's impossible. I don't know what's going on with you and Damon, but if you're trying to change him, you're setting yourself up for heartache. Only Damon can change Damon. And, if he's not willing to do that, you're going to have to accept him for who he is. You can't have peace any other way."

Carmen heard the front door open. Seconds later, she heard Cathy shooing away her mother's cat. She burst into the kitchen.

"Momma…you and that stupid cat. I can't stand that thing."

"Leave Buttons alone. As many cats, dogs, and gerbils as I put up with when you were growing up. You owe me." Gert raised her cup. "Want some tea?"

Cathy rolled her eyes and plopped down on the chair. Her mother walked to the stove, grabbed the teapot and filled a cup with tea. She placed it on the table.

"It's not herbal." Cathy snapped.

Gert gave Cathy a stern look. "Next time, bring your own."

"What's wrong with you?" Cathy asked Carmen.

"Nothing."

"Marital problems?"

"Leave me alone, Cathy."

Gert intervened, "Cathy…stop it. Your day is coming soon."

"Not me. I'll probably never get married."

Carmen couldn't resist. "Let's rephrase that…no one will probably ever marry you."

Cathy laughed. Gert did too.

"You'll probably die an old maid." Carmen said. "No sensible man would subject himself to the punishment."

"Men love me…in fact, I have a date tonight."

A key in the back door interrupted their conversation. Seconds later, their father walked into the kitchen. Had it been dawn instead of dusk, it would have been exactly the same as it was when they were young, but the years had shortened his time away and he usually made it home before dinner. Now he and Gert spent their evenings watching television in the living room and making up for lost time.

"Somethin' wrong?" he asked when he saw the three of them at the table. His tone lacked emotion, but Carmen knew him well enough to know he was genuinely concerned about them. That was just *his* way. She recalled that he always had difficulty displaying emotion and never quite seemed comfortable with so many women in the house. He was a complicated man, much like her husband.

"Everything is fine." Carmen could feel the distance between them. As it had been most of their lives, they exchanged few words.

"Why don't I go back out and grab us something for dinner, Gert. You girls want anything?"

Carmen spoke up, "No daddy, I'm fine. I'd better be getting home to Damon anyway and Cathy has her first and only date with this new guy."

Cathy shot Carmen a cross look.

"All right." Her dad responded. "Gert, I'll be right back."

Their father walked out the door. Carmen and Cathy stood up to leave.

"You girls are going to have to forgive him, you know."

"Momma?" Carmen had a question that had been plaguing her for a while now. She felt as though her mother had opened the door for her to ask it, knowing there had been rumors. "Do you think there were ever any other women?"

"Not sure. It's crossed my mind a time or two. My only saving grace is that most of the time he was so drunk he barely made it home. I'm sure that kept him honest some nights, even when he didn't want to be. I choose not to dwell on it. What we have is good right now. That's all that matters."

Carmen kissed her mother goodbye and walked out the door to her car. She was still so confused about Damon. Her mother's words rang in her head. She wanted so desperately for Damon to change and she was disappointed that he hadn't. When she dreamed of being married as a child, it looked nothing like her current situation. In fact, her current situation looked a lot like her mother and father's marriage. Carmen tried to wrap her head around the fact that although she promised herself as a little girl that she would not grow up to be like her mother, she was making exactly the same mistake. The thought of her marriage ending up like her parent's marriage terrified her. Would she just adjust to it after while? Would he, like her father, thirty years later decide that it was now time to put her first? Her stomach churned as she drove home. Once there she went straight to the kitchen, poured a glass of wine, sat at the kitchen table, struck a match and lit an incense.

Chapter 17

Carmen was sitting in the living room when Damon walked in the house carrying three bags of groceries. With both hands full, he barely made it in the door. The look he gave Carmen asked her for help, but she remained unstirred on the sofa and continued to sip her chardonnay. He walked past her to the kitchen and began putting the groceries away. She leaped off the sofa and followed him.

"I'm not going anywhere tonight, Carmen, so there is no need to start in on me." The smell of jasmine was strong.

"Start in on you?" Carmen felt her actions were justified. "As your wife, don't you think I have a right to want you home with me? Every woman wants to be first in her man's life."

Damon walked about the kitchen and continued to put away the groceries. "You are first in my life."

"No, I'm not. You put your friends before me. What's going to happen when we have a family?"

"A family? What do you mean a family?" Damon placed the tomato he was holding on the table. "I already have two kids."

"What about me? I want children Damon, but I refuse to raise them in the same kind of house I grew up in. With an absentee father, who's never around and only good for paying the bills. And you don't even do that by yourself."

Damon could tell this was a battle he couldn't win. Carmen was enraged for some reason. Perhaps it was the wine. He walked over to her and tousled the ends of her hair that lay on her shoulders. He noticed it was now all black. The usual bands of grey were gone.

"Babe." He said softly. "We've talked about this before. My hanging out with my friends has nothing to do with you. I like being around them. It's how I relieve stress. I like listening to music and talking with the guys. You might think it's about women, but it's not. I just like hanging out. I can't explain it."

Damon understood women enough to make the assumption that Carmen was concerned about other women, but in reality it was the furthest thing from his mind at this point. He never had an issue getting women— it was a constant that never left him. Because of that, he never really gave it much thought. When he was out with the guys, he might offer an occasional look of admiration if the situation warranted, but more times than not his mind was more preoccupied with his current loss of freedom. And, he was trying to honor his vow to her.

"What do you do when you're out?"

"We've been through this, Carmen," Damon said as he continued to play with her hair. "I like your hair like this."

"What do you do when you are out?" She repeated.

"It depends… play pool, have a drink, watch the game…" Damon reached for her hand and entwined her fingers with his. "Can we just have a quiet evening watching television tonight?"

As Damon embraced Carmen he could feel his phone vibrating. He reached down into his back pocket and turned it off. He was confident it was Craig sending a text, asking if Carmen had issued a pass for the night. Instead of being caught in their tug of war, he decided it was best to turn it off and retire to the sofa with Carmen for a boring Saturday evening at home. They watched a movie on Lifetime and went to bed a little past midnight.

The next morning, Carmen awoke early and began shaking Damon. She pulled on his arm.

"Damon!" She tried to rouse him. Go to church with me this morning."

Damon growled and turned over, barely disturbed from his hard sleep. Carmen shook him and repeated her request; this time tapping him on the face.

"Damon, wake up. Let's go to church."

Damon shoved her hand away, annoyed. "You're kidding me, right?"

"No, I'm serious. Let's go." She shook him again.

"If you want to go to church….go." Damon raised his voice and surprised himself. He quieted back down. "I'll take a pass."

Carmen jumped out of the bed and began getting dressed for church as Damon rolled over onto the pillow.

"I might as well be married to myself." She mumbled as she rummaged around the room. She deliberately knocked things over and made as much noise as she possibly could so that Damon could not fall back to sleep. The details of the condition of the marriage were becoming all too clear to Damon. She wanted someone far from the person he really was. He was unsure if he could ever be the person she wanted him to be.

Chapter 18

Craig had been calling Samantha all day leaving psychotic messages on her cell phone voicemail and answering machine. One moment he was cursing and threatening her. Another moment he begged to see her. After the eighth attempt, at nightfall he drove to her apartment unannounced. He sat in the parking lot on the hood of his badly damaged car and whistled up to her window. The light was on and she was moving around in lingerie. She was wearing his favorite piece. In the past, she would run to the window and greet him. This time, he was being completely ignored. He was determined to make her bow down to him and come to the window. After what she had done to him, he had to retain some sense of dignity.

He waited and waited. He called. He whistled. But, she refused to come. After about an hour, he grew furious and entered her apartment building. He ran up the stairs and began pounding on Samantha's door.

After a few seconds, she opened it. "What is it?" She demanded. She cracked the door and Craig stole a glimpse of the purple silk camisole she was wearing. The rest of her body remained tucked behind the door. He was convinced she had on the matching bottoms and he grew eager to enter.

"Stop playing games, Samantha. Let me in." Craig tried to sound forceful.

"You're trippin'. Goodbye Craig." Samantha attempted to close the door, but Craig blocked it with his foot.

"Who's in there?" Craig demanded.

"Nobody's in here." Samantha was quick to answer in an annoyed tone. "I don't have to answer to you. Do I need to call the cops?"

"Call the cops?" Craig pointed to his chest. "On me? Right. I know that was you who maced me, Samantha."

"Boy, please. I have no idea what you are talking about...but...I do know this.....you've got about ten seconds to get away from in front of my doorway." She swung her dyed honey blonde hair with bronze highlights off her shoulders. The door opened a little further giving Craig the full view he wanted. "Like I said...goodbye." She shoved him backwards and slammed the door in his face.

He knocked again, gently this time. The tone in which he beckoned her to the door was a lot softer.

"Samantha....C'mon. Don't be like this." His voice was tender.

Samantha flung the door opened and screamed in his face, "Goodbye." She slammed the door, again.

Craig leaned up against the wall and banged it with his head. He was stumped. This wasn't the first time he had been caught cheating, but usually when he came crawling back he was always accepted. Samantha broke the mold. Not only did she exact the ultimate revenge by demolishing his car, she added insult to injury because she wasn't taking him back right away. Craig refused to accept defeat. He needed a different approach. He decided he would regroup, come up with a different strategy and try again later.

As he walked down the hall, he noticed a man walking toward him. Craig looked him up and down in an attempt to size him up. Decent looking, he thought. And, then it dawned on him. This was who Samantha was wearing the purple number for. Craig burned inside as he approached him.

"Are you going to see Samantha?"

"Who wants to know?" The stranger replied as he brushed past Craig, almost ignoring him. Craig caught a whiff of his cheap smelling cologne.

"A friend." Craig injected confidence into his voice. The stranger continued to walk down the hall. He stopped at Samantha's door and knocked. She opened it and let him in.

Craig tore down the stairs of her building and to his car. He peeled out of the parking lot with images of Samantha wearing her lingerie and commingling with the stranger flashing before his mind's eye. Craig summed him up as a chump. Although the suit he wore was top notch, the cheap smelling cologne said everything.

Chapter 19

Carmen drove straight home after work. After changing out of her work clothes, she went to the kitchen to begin dinner; she was going to fry chicken. She peeled a few potatoes, set them up to boil for mashed, then snapped some green beans and put them on the stove. She had worked through lunch and was starving. She couldn't wait to eat. Her first thought was to only make enough for herself, but she didn't want to be selfish or spiteful. She needed a blessing from God more than ever right now. She made sure there would be enough for Damon to have something to eat when he got home. After the food finished cooking, she fixed her plate and sat down in front of the television to watch a Lifetime movie. It was the cutest love story about an older woman and a younger man, who against all odds, found a way to be together. Carmen longed for someone to love her like that.

The movie ended and she plodded into the kitchen to return her plate. She poured herself a glass of wine and the telephone rang. She looked at the caller ID. It was Cathy. She walked to the living room and sat down on the sofa.

"How was your one and only date with *what's his name*?" Carmen clicked the T.V. off with the remote.

"His name is Stan." Cathy responded, totally ignoring Carmen's jest.

"What kind of a name is Stan?"

"Well, it's Stanley…and, I like him. I mean I really, really like him."

Excited that Cathy might have potentially found someone she liked enough to change her evil ways, Carmen probed more deeply.

"Tell me about him?"

"He's a geologist."

"A what? I mean what does he do?"

"Like I said, he's a geologist."

"There are no rocks or stones or whatever in Chicago. How does he make a living?"

"He teaches at Northwestern."

"Wow. Classy." Carmen was shocked. Although Cathy was attractive, tall and slender, her craziness preceded her by a mile. Carmen wondered how she managed to pull a college professor. He must be nerdy or worse, she thought. "What does he look like?"

"He's nice looking. He's a little older, but I think you'll approve of him."

"How much older?"

"He's forty."

"Hmm...when do I get to meet him?"

"You will, eventually, when the time is right. I don't want to mess this one up, Carmen."

It appeared she was falling fast and Carmen didn't want her to make the same mistake she had made. With Damon she fell fast—hard—and fast. "Maybe you should take things slow. You just met the guy. You have lots of time." There was a short pause between them.

"Carmen, why do you think I have such difficulty with relationships?"

Carmen pulled the phone away from her ear and looked at it. This was so unlike Cathy's neck jerking, know-it-all; *I don't need a man* behavior. "One thing that might help is if you were a little softer. Don't be so aggressive. Men like to know that they're in control. That's just the way they're wired. Let them take the lead sometimes."

"Thanks, Carmen. I don't want to blow this one. I think he might be a keeper. But, it's hard for me, you know? Hard for me to let a man control me."

"Then don't. Being softer is not about being controlled. Sometimes strength is silent."

"You were always better than me when it came to relationships, with the exception of the one you're in now."

"You had to go there, didn't you?"

"Carmen, wait…I'm—"

Carmen hung up the phone. She tossed the receiver on the sofa. She loved her sister, but her constant comments were wearing her down. She understood her marriage was a mess; she didn't need to keep hearing it. A ray of hope still flickered in her heart.

Carmen looked out the window; it was now good and dark. She looked at her watch. Damon had been off work a few hours, and as usual, was late coming home. Where is he tonight? She wondered. The pool hall? The club? Her thoughts were interrupted as Craig and Damon walked in the door, laughing. Although Carmen was glad that Damon was home, when she saw Craig, she wished they had stayed out together. She remained in her relaxed position on the couch continuing to enjoy her wine. She didn't even try to hide her loathing for him.

"Mrs. Harris." Craig greeted Carmen with a smile. It reminded Carmen of the Cheshire Cat. Long after he had disappeared, chaos would remain.

"Craig," Carmen greeted him with a nod, but without a smile.

"Carmen, guess what? You are not going to believe this. Craig's in love." Damon laughed out loud. "And the women he's in love with ambushed him and took him out the other night. Remember the call?" He closed the door behind him.

"How could I forget?" Carmen looked at Craig. Her smile was still *AWOL.*

"Let me get this straight Craig, man." Damon continued. "You go to her house and she won't let you in. As you're leaving, a guy comes to her door. You try to threaten him…and when *he* knocks on the door, she lets him in." Damon giggled with mockery. "I just want to make sure I'm clear."

"First of all, man, check your facts." Craig grew serious. I'm definitely not in love. She's trying to play hard to get. She wants me. If she didn't care, she wouldn't have jacked my ride up the way she did."

"And let's not forget that she jacked you up, too." Damon said, still laughing.

"Yeah you're laughing, now. We'll see who gets the last laugh." Craig scratched the back of his head as he sat down." She'll be eating out of my hands."

Carmen stood up from the couch. Here he was, a grown man—the CEO of his own company, still talking about conquering women. Carmen found the whole situation nauseating. "Yeah, Craig. It sounds like it. She'll be eating out of your hands." Carmen added sarcastically. She exited their presence, headed toward the bedroom.

***

Damon looked across the room at Craig and noticed he was in deep thought. He had never seen Craig this way, especially not over a woman.

"Craig?" He snapped his fingers. "Are you all right?

"I'm good. I just need a new strategy. She'll come back. You'll see."

"You don't sound real confident. This is not the Craig, I know."

"Something about Sam is different. I don't know what it is, but she's not like all the others."

"Yeah, she fought back. You're not used to a woman standing up for herself. I think that's what has you so caught up."

Craig scratched his head.

"Damon, what made you do it? What made you get married?"

Damon peered down the hall to make sure Carmen had closed the bedroom door and couldn't hear their conversation. He was pleased to see the door closed and the light was out. He knew it only took seconds for Carmen to fall asleep once her head hit the pillow and their privacy was assured.

"I spent a lot of years being childish and irresponsible. I went to jail and got two women pregnant. My future looked bleak—"

"Yeah, you were kind of out there. That was during the time I was building my company. I wanted you to come and work with me, but you were too unreliable back then."

"When my immaturity cost me the woman I loved, and the chance at the family I wanted, I wised up. Unfortunately, it was too late for me to reclaim what I'd lost, but I vowed to grow up and start acting like a man. It was time for me to face my challenges instead of running away. So I cleaned myself up, found a decent job and here I am."

"Yeah, but are you happy? Do you think you made the right decision marrying Carmen?"

"Carmen is a good woman. I'm not sure what the future holds for us, but I'm here and I'm trying to make it work."

"Sounds to me like she's not the one. You and I both know that when a man has found her…he knows."

Damon was uncomfortable with Craig's questions. "How did this conversation jump from talking about you to talking about me? The real question is, what are you going to do about Sam?"

"I don't know, man," Craig said, shaking his head. "I just don't know."

Chapter 20

Carmen spent all day Saturday preparing an elaborate feast for Damon. She had opened one of her favorite bottles of Chianti and had been drinking it the entire afternoon while she prepared dinner. She was making all of his favorite foods. After checking the roast, she began toasting the bread crumbs to top her macaroni and cheese. She spread them evenly in the pan and placed the pan in the oven. Then, she started on the icing for the German chocolate cake. It was like Christmas in July. The sights and smells reminded her of the times she spent in the kitchen with her mother during the holidays, preparing elaborate family meals. When Carmen cooked, she was the most happy. Just like her mother, she poured all the love she had into her food. She stopped for a moment in the hot kitchen and stared out the window. She wondered if the meal would succeed in getting Damon to open up and talk about the rift in their marriage. They had tried to continue on, touching on the subject, but never fully giving it the attention it warranted. Carmen felt it was time. As she sipped her glass of wine, tears began streaming down her face. She realized that she was so much like her mother, who was tolerant and steadfast, and now she was in the same predicament, married, but alone. She couldn't understand what was so powerful in the streets that constantly pulled him away from her. Perhaps he wasn't being pulled. Perhaps he was seeking refuge there. She wondered what was it about her that could be so terrible that he couldn't stand to be around her. She wiped her face and cracked the kitchen window hoping to let some of the heat out only to discover the air outside was even hotter. She closed the window and began icing the cake.

The table was perfectly set, the candles were lit and Carmen sat staring at the floral tablecloth, waiting for Damon. He got off work at five o'clock on Saturdays. It was now six thirty. Carmen, feeling the effects of the wine, started to laugh at how ridiculous she had been hurrying to have dinner ready for him when he came home. She had tried to time everything just right. With Damon, that was impossible. She never knew when he was coming home, and more times than not, it was way past dinnertime. What was she thinking? She enjoyed a good joke and continued to sit at the table. She poured another glass of wine.

Damon arrived twenty minutes after eight o'clock. Carmen looked at her watch with disapproval.

"Where have you been?"

"I stopped by Momma's after work." He avoided eye contact. "She's getting older you know, and she never locks her door. I get worried about her sometimes."

"I spent all afternoon cooking for you."

"I'm sorry. Why didn't you call me?"

"Would it have made a difference?" Carmen said dispiritedly. "Sit down; let me fix you a plate."

Damon was glad to see that Carmen had prepared several of his favorite dishes. As he ate, he eyed the German chocolate cake that sat on the counter. He wondered if perhaps Carmen might be poisoning him at the moment, but everything tasted so good, he felt it was well worth the risk.

After several moments of silence between them, Carmen began.

"Damon. I prepared this dinner hoping that we could talk."

"About what?" Damon jammed a forkful of food in his mouth. He licked a few morsels from his fingers and wiped his hands.

"Our marriage."

"What about it?"

"It isn't one."

Damon thought long before answering. He knew Carmen was right. The whole situation was unfortunate, but he didn't know where to begin in finding a solution.

"Carmen, we just need to give it a little more time. Trying to understand each other might help."

"I understand you, Damon. You want to have your cake and eat it too—like a selfish little baby." Carmen's voice was escalating.

"What are you talking about?" Damon's attitude was one of defense. He agreed to talk, but now Carmen was getting personal.

"The streets, Damon. That's all you do. You're never here. We rarely do anything together. It's like I'm married to myself."

Damon frowned. He glanced at the bottle of wine to see how much was missing. Carmen continued.

"I cook, I clean…"

"Yeah, and you continually remind me of it. If you're going to complain about it, don't do it." Damon yelled.

"What?" Carmen screamed. "You don't appreciate all the sacrifices I make. You're selfish, Damon, just plain old selfish. You think the world revolves around you. Well, I've got news for you. It doesn't. I pay the majority of these bills. I keep this house in order while you hang out with your friends all night, doing God knows what. But, you know what? You'll get yours," Carmen threatened. "The streets are going to claim you just like they did your father."

Damon jumped to his feet. He felt that this time Carmen had gone too far. Wishing his father's fate on him was unforgivable. She had no right to reference his father's death in that way—to deem him responsible for his own death. Damon felt it was the ultimate in disrespect. He walked over to her and looked into her eyes with a steely glare. In that moment, the anger, resentment and regret over marrying her over took him. He grabbed his keys off the table and took off.

Damon hit the streets, walking to the pool hall where he hung out with his father as a little boy. He thought about how disrespectful Carmen had been to his father and to him. After all, he had been trying so hard to do the right thing by her. Maybe he missed the mark, but he was giving it everything he had and she hadn't even noticed. He felt she had no appreciation for it and it made him furious. Back in the day, he would have left her in a trail of smoke. She should have been glad he had stayed with her this long.

He arrived at the pool hall and took the front stairs two at a time. He walked in and sat at the bar.

"Roscoe." He called to the bartender. "Gin and tonic. Double."

Roscoe finished drying his glass and threw the damp, dish towel over his shoulder. He made Damon's drink and topped it off with a wedge of lime.

Roscoe nodded to the far left corner. "Your boys are back there," making reference to Craig and Wendell. Damon figured they would be, but was hoping they weren't. Tonight he wasn't in the mood for company. Damon turned around to see Craig wearing his favorite jeans and sweater, chalking up his cue in the back. Damon raised his glass to acknowledge him. Craig nodded back and Damon turned back around on his bar stool. After he finished off two doubles and had ordered another, he realized he was still sober. When he noticed the drinks weren't overriding his anger, he decided to keep his money. He spun his stool around to watch the patrons. In the back, he noticed that a couple of girls had joined Craig at the pool table. Wendell sat on the side. The girls had obviously picked up on his married vibe and were ignoring him. Wendell seemed cool with it and was watching Craig in his classic game of *get the girl*. Several times Damon saw Wendell shake his head. Damon concluded it was either disbelief or disgust. With Craig, either was possible.

After a few moments of watching them, Damon panned to the right side of the room. That's when he saw her—tall, slender, and yet very curvy, which Damon found ironic. Typically one was sacrificed for the other. He found a woman was either slender or curvy—rarely both. She was a vision of perfection. Naturally beautiful with minimal makeup and a behind that would make some men surrender their checking account number upon the initial introduction. Damon was intrigued and continued to watch her as she moved about wearing white pants and a gold, sequined, halter top that glistened against her dark skin. He noticed her strapped, high-heeled shoes matched her halter-top. Damon had never seen her in the pool hall before and he was curious about the way she was dressed. She looked like she belonged in a trendy, upscale night club, but he could tell by the magical way she handled the cue that she was right at home. He continued to watch her as she ran the table against her male counterpart. Damon couldn't figure out who he was to her, but he could sense the distance in their interaction and assumed he was a friend or brother.

After several moments of staring at her intently, he could feel his body chemistry change. As she leaned over the table to make what looked like an impossible shot, she tossed her head full of jet black, curly, ringlets out of her face so that she could get a better view. That's when she noticed him watching her. Embarrassed, Damon turned back around to the bar and ordered another drink.

Several moments later, he turned back around to see her declining another game. She grabbed her shawl as if she was leaving for the night. Instead of exiting, she walked over and sat next to him at the bar.

"Corona, please." She said to the bartender.

Roscoe eagerly opened a bottle and placed it in front of her.

"It's on the house," he smiled. "Anything else?" He winked, and for a split second Damon thought he saw his tongue hanging out.

"No thanks." She smiled at Roscoe. His flirting was obvious to both of them. Didn't matter that he was old enough to be her grandfather.

Damon stared blankly at his wedding band as he caressed his drink and thought about what Carmen said to him—that she could even form her mouth to say what she said about his father.

His unknown acquaintance was undaunted by the symbol of his nuptials.

"I'm Candy." She extended her hand.

"I'm Damon." He shook it.

"You from around here?"

"Yeah. Well, not now. My wife and I live in Bronzeville, but I grew up around here."

"Me too. 61st street. I still live here. South Side 'til I die." She chuckled.

After a few moments of silence, she spoke. "You look as though something is bothering you. Anything you want to talk about?"

Damon was afraid that Craig and Wendell might have spotted him sitting at the bar talking to Candy. He sat there feeling uneasy and didn't dare turn around and make eye contact with them, when suddenly, he felt someone place their hand on his shoulder, giving him a firm, hard pat. He almost leapt off the chair. It was Wendell.

"Let me talk to you, man." He turned to Candy, "Excuse me Miss." Wendell pulled Damon off the barstool and over to the door. "Whatever you're thinking about doing...don't. It's not worth it. I guarantee you'll regret it in the morning."

"I have no plans of doing anything except going home to Carmen after this gin wears off a little."

Craig approached, interrupting their conversation. He extended his hand to Damon and shook it.

"She's beautiful," Craig said in a strong voice. "Good luck and Good night."

Craig and Wendell left the pool hall and Damon returned to his seat next to Candy at the bar.

"Friends of yours?"

"Yeah."

"I recognize the tall one. He owns his own business, doesn't he?"

"Yeah. He does pretty well."

"I thought so. Anyway, are you going to tell me what's bothering you?"

"Nah. I'm all right. Just life, that's all...it can be like that sometimes."

Candy reached into her purse and pulled out a piece of paper. She used a pen that was sitting on the bar to write her phone number and address on it. She stood up and leaned into him, placing her hand on the bar stool between his legs, almost touching him. She was dangerously close. Damon could feel his heart start to pound.

She whispered in his ear, "One night with me and you'll forget all about your wife." She folded the piece of paper, placed it in his coat pocket, tapped it twice and walked out.

Damon sat there thinking. It was a better idea to go home, but he was still furious with Carmen. He stood up, tossed back the last of his drink and exited the pool hall. He swayed momentarily at the top of the stairs. His anger had delayed the effect of the double gins he'd ordered. He steadied himself before reaching in his pocket. He pulled out the scrap of paper Candy had given him. He knew exactly where the address was. He descended the stairs, walked down the block and headed over to her place.

Damon dizzily walked up the four flights of stairs to Candy's floor. He scanned the doors and located apartment number twelve. He knocked on the door softly and waited. A few seconds later, he attempted to knock again, but the door creaked open before he got the chance. He looked around before walking in.

Her place was small and dark. She had attempted to decorate it with modest furnishings that looked more like hand me downs. There was an old patchwork quilt that draped the sofa, and a few doilies adorned the side tables. Some sort of jade-green fish netting hung over the lampshades. When she turned on the light, it caused a weird pattern to reflect onto the walls. There was an open box of takeout on the table and the stale smell of it filled the room.

"You want a drink?"

"No, Thanks." He knew he had already had enough.

"This way." She said, and Damon followed her into her bedroom.

Chapter 21

As Candy removed her earrings, Damon looked at the unmade bed. There was a dingy cast to the sheets and a stain that looked like coffee. He had gotten used to the way Carmen kept house. He loved the way the sheets at home always smelled like the lavender scented fabric softener Carmen used.

"You got anything?" Candy asked.

Was she asking about drugs or condoms? He had been out of the game for a while and couldn't tell. Back then, it was a commonly asked question. Usually somebody always had something—pills, a little weed; maybe even something harder. He had left that life behind and carried a record with him. It was a place he vowed he would never revisit. He decided he had better clarify. "Protection?"

"Yeah."

Before he married Carmen, he always carried a condom in his wallet for moments like this. "No," he answered. "You?"

"No," she said as she grabbed him by the jacket and thrust her tongue into his mouth. Sheer force threw them onto the bed.

Damon could feel his manhood returning. Every inch of him pulsed as she undressed him and ran her mouth over his body. He thought about Carmen and her goodness, knowing it was only a fight, but her words ate into him. He could feel a cascade of emotions bursting forth. The reminder of the loss of his father, the lack of control he was feeling, and the discontentment with his life welled up inside him, and he allowed the sensations he was feeling in his body at that moment to overcome him. He eased into that familiar place. A time when life was carefree and he was free to live the way he wanted to. This was who he used to be.

He undressed her and kissed her all over. His ego swelled with power and control as her slender frame arched in response to his touch. His confidence returned as he found himself filling that familiar role; giving women what they wanted, and he getting what he wanted in return. Shortly, he would leave her. His guilt surfaced again, and he blocked it out. And, when it appeared she could no longer stand it, he united with her.

The sounds she made caused him to feel like a man again. A few seconds later, he rolled onto his back having let go of months of frustration and anguish. As his heartbeat began to normalize, he thought of Carmen. This time, he couldn't contain his guilt. He looked over at Candy.

"I have to go," he said.

"I know." She covered her breasts with the dirty sheet. "We should do this again, sometime."

Damon slid on his jeans and looked around anxiously for his socks, "Yeah," he said.

He put on the rest of his clothes and avoided eye contact as he told her he would call her. He left her apartment and headed back to the brownstone.

***

The sun peered through the blinds, shining directly on Damon's face. As he turned over, he pried his encrusted lips apart. A rank taste assaulted his taste buds, and his head throbbed with every pump of his heart. His mind quickly searched for a cause. He called to mind the night before.

He had fought with Carmen. She enraged him. He'd walked to the pool hall, had one too many drinks and stopped by Candy's on his way home. His mind flashed through images of things he did with the stranger—her mouth all over his body, his on hers. Various positions. Months of tension had been released. He sat up, his back erect in the bed. Although Carmen had pissed him off, he knew he was dead wrong to betray her in that manner. It was amazing how rational a sober mind could be. He turned to see her sleeping peacefully on the other side of the bed. He wondered how he could have done what he did; how he could have let that happen. He had been trying so hard to do the right thing, and in a momentary lapse in judgment, he had turned back into his old self. He continued to sit there, watching Carmen as she slept. He considered waking her, apologizing, and begging her for forgiveness, but considered it best to sweep the entire night under the rug and forget about it.

"Why are you staring at me, weirdo?" Carmen said in a slow, sleepy voice. His glare had stirred her from her deep sleep.

"Nothing, babe. I apologize for running out last night. Go back to sleep."

Carmen turned over and continued her slumber. Damon slowly got out of bed and walked to the shower. He hadn't bathed since the incident and was glad his secret remained undetected. He lathered himself remorsefully. He filled his mouth with water trying to wash away the taste. The disappointment he felt was overwhelming. Not only had he let Carmen down, more importantly he had broken his promise to himself. As he showered, he vowed, once again, that he would not be who he was in the past. The man who did whatever he wanted to do without regard or consideration for another. The man who avoided responsibility for his actions, and blamed everything on everyone else. Instead, he would be the man he knew he could be; the man his mother always said he was. If he had to give up drinking, he would do it. Whatever it took.

Chapter 22

For the next several weeks, Damon stuck close to home. Carmen's heart and mind found peace as she considered that her marriage might survive. Damon still remained distant emotionally and physically, but he was home and she felt that was a start. She was thankful to God and attributed it to her recent, regular visits to church. She was glad things were turning around for them, and on her way to work she called her sister to brag about it.

Cathy answered the phone. She dragged out the word, "hello."

"Are you up?" Carmen asked.

"Yeah," Cathy yawned." Just barely."

"I'm just checking in...to see if things in your world are going as great as they are in mine. How are things going with Stanley?"

"It's all good." Cathy moaned as she stretched. "Things are good. He's gone a lot with work, but I'm starting to get used to it."

"Uh, Oh," Carmen said with a teasing tone. "Ya'll are getting serious? Is he marriage material? What's his place like? You don't want to marry a slob."

"I haven't been to his place yet." Cathy said. She yawned again.

"What do you mean, yet? You've been dating him for a couple months."

"Yeah. He always comes to my place. What's the big deal?"

Carmen was silent, trying to piece things together.

"Wait a minute Cathy. Something doesn't add up. He's out of town a lot and you've never been to his place?"

"Yep."

"Girl...that man is married!"

"Married!" Cathy shouted. "He's not married. We spend too much time together. He's at my place all the time."

"I don't care. Maybe his wife is a stewardess or a doctor at the hospital. You know a highfalutin professor like that could pull a doctor. Maybe she works third shift.

"Anyway," Cathy said changing the subject. "How's *your* marriage? Maybe we should talk about that."

"I'm so glad you asked," Carmen gloated. "My man is trying to be the perfect little husband. Comes straight home from work. I have no complaints. I told you that you were wrong about him."

Carmen could hear Cathy running water.

"Time will tell." Cathy said dryly. "Look, sis, I just want you to be happy. I'll make a deal with you. I'll stop nagging you about Damon on one condition...the minute he stops being the perfect little husband, as *you* called him, and treating you the way you deserve to be treated, promise me you'll be outa' there."

"I Promise. Now, will you shut up about him?"

"You promised, Carmen."

Carmen ended the call as she pulled into the parking lot. She pulled a tube of burgundy lipstick out of her purse and, looking in the rearview mirror, touched up her lips before she got out of car and headed upstairs to her desk.

***

Carmen cooked a quick pot of chicken and dumplings for dinner. She had let the drumsticks thaw in the fridge all day and used buttermilk biscuits to make the dumplings—

her momma's recipe minus some of the butter. After she cleaned up the kitchen, she popped a bag of microwave popcorn and she and Damon retired to the sofa in the living room to watch the movie Damon had rented on the way home. It was a sci-fi thriller and they were on the edge of their seats the entire time, thoroughly enjoying every scene. Right when Captain Logan had pulled his gun and was about to open the door to the closet where the ship's crew had contained the terrifying alien baby, Damon's cell phone started ringing and vibrating in the kitchen. He ignored it. The movie was just too good. He didn't want to miss a second of it, but the phone kept ringing. It would stop and then it would start up again. By the number of times it rang, Carmen could tell someone was really trying to get in touch with him.

"Who is that?"

"I don't know, Carmen. I'm in here with you, watching the movie." Damon shrugged. "It's probably Craig wanting me to come to the pool hall."

"Would he call that many times?"

"It's Craig, remember?" Damon grunted as he got up from the couch and headed toward the kitchen. He grabbed his phone off the table and opened it. He had two missed calls and a text message. He didn't recognize the number right away. He read the text.

Can U get away?
Call me,

Candy

Damon felt a pang in the middle of his stomach. That explained his missing business card holder. He and Carmen had torn the house up looking for it. He always kept his holder with him—he would never miss an opportunity to sell a car. When Candy was pulling off his clothes that night, it must have slipped out of his pocket. He turned the phone off, flipped it closed and put it in his pocket. He had no choice but to ignore her. Hopefully, she would get the message. He returned to the living room and joined Carmen on the couch.

"Who was that?" She asked.

"Craig. I'll call him tomorrow. What did I miss?" Damon scooped a handful of popcorn from the bowl and focused in on the movie, trying to act as normal as he could.

Chapter 23

Damon quietly opened the door to his mother's house. He tip-toed into the kitchen and stood there undetected. He watched his mother while she stood at the stove. He couldn't believe that he had entered the house and she didn't even know he was there. He quietly walked over to her. Then he grabbed her aggressively around her neck and twisted one arm behind her back.

"Let go of me, Damon." Her voice was calm. She continued stirring the pot of beans.

Damon relaxed the grip on her arm. "Mom, you've got to start locking the door. This is the South Side."

"Damon, I'm not a child. Do you see those knives right there?" She nodded toward the butcher block of knives that sat next to the stove. She used them often and kept them razor sharp.

"If I hadn't detected your cologne right away, you would have felt one of those piercing your eye socket. Lucky for you, you've worn that same cologne since you were in high school."

Damon flinched when he thought of how a good idea could have gone bad. He was reassured of one thing; his momma didn't play and even though she was getting older, she still held some of the fire she had when he was growing up.

"Sit down. Let me fix you a plate." Sharon began plating up greens, sweet potatoes, and fried chicken. "Damon, I'm 57 years old. I raised you, your brother and your sisters. I fed you. I clothed you. And, did it single handedly once your father passed on. Where would you get the notion that I can't take care of myself? I work every day and pay these bills and take care of this house. Did you ever consider that?"

"It's not the same, Mom. I know you can take care of yourself, but physically, you're no match for a man. I could have been anybody coming in here."

Sharon placed her hand on her hip. "Yeah, and you would have needed a pirate's patch for your right eye." Damon could tell that she really believed what she was saying. Sharon sat at the table. She pulled the rubber band off her salt and pepper ponytail and scratched her head to release the tension as she watched Damon enjoy his food.

"Damon, I've been meaning to talk to you."

"About what? You never call me."

"You know I hate those voice mails. And all that stupid crap you got on that phone...songs and silly mess."

"Call me on the home phone. If I'm not there, Carmen will tell me that you called."

"How's she doing anyway? You never bring her over here."

Damon stuffed his mouth with chicken and stabbed at his sweet potatoes. His mom continued.

"Damon I've been around the block enough times to know how a man acts when he cares about someone. The two of them are usually inseparable, and normally the man is always eager to show off his new bride. You barely make mention of Carmen. What's up?"

"Nothing's up." Damon said, making a loud noise as he sucked greens out of his teeth. He looked at Sharon. "What did you want to talk to me about?"

Sharon stared at him intently, as if she was trying to figure out what he was keeping from her. He quickly dropped his eyes to his plate.

"I've met someone," she said.

Damon dropped his fork.

"I'm telling you now so you don't go off half-cocked on some illusion that you have to protect me, because I can't protect myself. Your father's been gone for a while now. It's time."

"What did Cheryl say?"

"All of your sisters are fine with it...and your brother, too. I know how much you loved your father, and I knew this news might not be as easy for you to hear. Maybe you're so protective because you're the baby."

"I'm the youngest." He corrected her. It sounded better than being the baby. He picked up his fork and resumed eating, but stopped short of finishing. He noticed his food was getting cold and the news Sharon gave stole his appetite.

Sharon leaned into Damon. "Something's bothering you. I can tell. You haven't been yourself for months." She touched his hand. "Whatever you're facing, God's already given you everything you need to navigate this life. You're only defeated if you believe He's not bigger than your problem."

"I'm good, ma. Really."

Sharon smiled as she conjured up memories from the past. "When you were a little boy and I would take you out in your stroller, people would stop, stare, and play with you so much that I could barely get where I was going. There was something about you that was special...and there still is. They loved you at school, the doctor's office, the playground. Everywhere we went you drew attention."

Damon gently slid his hand away from Sharon's grasp. He shifted in the chair as Sharon kept speaking.

"Your future can be as bright as a star. The only thing stopping you...is *you*."

Damon's mind flashed back to that night with Candy. He had almost forgotten about it, but his mother's talk brought it center stage in his mind. If he was so special, why did he keep making one mistake after another? The only thing his 'specialness' had gotten him was the affection of women. That always led to trouble.

Sharon interrupted his thoughts. "Let me get you a piece of carrot cake. I made it for Ronald, but I'm sure he won't mind."

"Oh, now it's Ronald's food?" Damon raised his eyebrows in mockery.

Sharon ignored his reference to the food. She sliced the cake and put it on a plate. "Damon, deep down inside you know who you're capable of being. That's why you left your old gang behind. There's a power in you that's more than you can imagine from where you sit right now. I've seen it in you, since you were a little boy. When you understand that, your whole life will be different." She lovingly winked at him. "Become the man you want to be."

Damon could feel tears welling up in his eyes. He quickly looked down at the slice of cake sitting on the plate. He jammed a forkful in his mouth hoping that as he swallowed, it would carry the lump of emotion in his throat down with it.

"You finish your cake. I have to go and get dressed. Ron is coming by shortly. You can stay or go if you want. It's up to you."

Damon quickly finished his cake and ducked out the back door. When his mother came back to the kitchen, she noticed he had placed his dish in the sink.

Chapter 24

Craig pulled up to Samantha's and waited impatiently in the parking lot as he always did for her. Samantha was a high-maintenance kind of woman. Her hair was always perfect; freshly dyed and flat ironed. Her legs were always silky smooth. Always the freshest clothes. He had never even seen her with a chipped nail. She made it look easy, but Craig had sisters. He knew that a woman who looked like that spent a lot of time on herself. He loved it and hated it at the same time. He opened his CD case, looking for a CD to distract himself from the annoyance of having to wait for her. He smirked as he reminded himself that it definitely was not a habit of his to be waiting for a woman.

As he flipped through the case, Samantha exited her apartment building wearing a lavender dress, catching his eye. She looked beautiful in lavender and wore it often. It complimented her bronze skin and hair extremely well. As she descended the staircase, the wind flirted with her dress allowing Craig the opportunity to see the musculature of her glistening legs. He was overcome with desire for her. In fact, he burned with it, and had been for the past several weeks. She was all he could think about. Every conversation, every thought ultimately became about her. He was in crisis. He kept wondering over and over why Samantha was treating him the way she was. By now, he should have been forgiven. That was the usual pattern, but Samantha was breaking all the rules. He replayed the events of their courtship again and again. It had begun like all the others. He wined and dined Samantha at the fanciest restaurants and surprised her with well-contemplated gifts. When she had given in to him, he placed her on the shelf with his other trophies. And, while she was definitely a prize, gorgeous and independent, it wasn't enough to get him to choose her over the others. He hadn't anticipated Darlene—the latest of his conquests, doing what she did. One night, after they made love, she rummaged through his things while he was in the shower. She found business cards and brochures for the catering business Samantha ran out of her restaurant, including receipts for purchases Craig had made for her business. In a blind rage, she showed up at Samantha's restaurant and barged into the kitchen where Samantha was standing at the counter in her apron, slicing vegetables. As Samantha sliced away, Darlene proceeded to tell her that her dream guy was just your average, run of the mill, no good man. And while she was working long hours building her business, Craig was spending time with her, and she suspected it wasn't just the two of them—there were more. After that incident, Samantha was done. And Craig, now sorry for his loss, was trying to do everything to make it up to her. For some reason he discovered, after the fact, that Samantha was the only one he wanted to keep.

As she walked over to the car, Craig pulled the Tiffany box out of his glove compartment and placed it in his suit coat pocket.

"You look beautiful, Samantha." He said as she got in the car.

She smiled. "Thanks. You look quite handsome yourself. Where are we going tonight?"

"Dante's."

"I've never been there. It's too rich for my blood. Who did you pay to get the reservation?"

"Nothing but the best for you." Craig reached down and placed his hand on hers. He was thankful she didn't pull away.

Samantha and Craig arrived at the restaurant and valeted the car. They entered the restaurant, which was known for the most elegant dining in town. They followed the waiter past the potted palm trees toward their table. The waiter pulled out a chair and Samantha sat down. He placed her napkin on her lap and opened a menu for her. "Thank you," she said. Craig sat down opposite her.

Samantha painstakingly perused the menu. When the waiter returned, Craig attempted to order for her, but she insisted upon ordering for herself. First, the choice of wine was made—Cristal from Louis Roederer, one of the priciest ones on the list. Then she ordered two appetizers, one was caviar. She followed those with a full rack of lamb that the waiter insisted she had to try. Since she was a chef, she was all over that. Lastly, she ordered a desert that didn't look like much on the plate, but the waiter said it was more than worth the price. The chocolate was from Belgium, of course. Craig's seething thoughts of the excessive bill were being pacified by the constant visions of the sexual pleasure he would have with her later on that evening back at her place. It didn't matter that the meal would cost as much as the monthly note on his Lexus.

Craig didn't like to lose, and at this point, he was ahead. He was glad that after several weeks of trying to get her to go to dinner, she finally accepted. He chalked the meal up to being the cost of doing business. It was a small price to pay to get what he wanted, which, right now, was Samantha on a platter. He was so consumed with thoughts of what he would do with her later, he barely ate. After she finished eating the equivalent of his car note, she excused herself to the ladies room. When she returned to the table the waiter had removed her plate and a tiny blue box sat in its place.

"What's this?" She said as she sat down.

Craig smiled widely, "Open it."

"Craig, you didn't have to do this. It was nice enough that you bought me dinner."

Craig considered the irony of knowing that what was now in her stomach had cost more than what was in the box, but when she opened it her eyes sparkled and he was pleased. They left the restaurant on good terms, laughing and enjoying each other's company. Craig was convinced taking her to dinner had worked and he was back in her good graces.

When they got back to her place, he pulled into the parking lot and parked the car. He turned the car off and pulled the key out of the ignition. When he opened the door to get out of the car, Samantha stopped him.

"I don't think so Craig." Samantha's voice was gentle and contemplative.

"What?"

"I don't think it is a good idea for you to come in. Thanks for dinner. I really appreciate it. I've always wanted to try that restaurant."

"Sam, are you telling me you are not going to invite me in?" He struggled not to show his anger.

"Pretty much, thanks again. Have a good night." Samantha exited Craig's Lexus. He scrambled to get out of his door.

"Can I at least walk you to your door?" He asked as Samantha navigated the graveled parking lot in high-heeled shoes.

"Won't be necessary," she yelled back, throwing her hands up in the air, gesturing goodbye. "Thanks, again."

Craig got back into his car. He didn't know what to think. He was still barred from her place. He did all the right things that should have gained him access, but he failed. Not only did he fail, he had been set back a piece financially, and he sat in his car empty-handed. Now what? He vowed he would get her back. If she went to dinner once, she would do it again. His resolve was now even stronger.

Chapter 25

It had been two weeks since Cathy had seen Stanley. She found herself anxious as she waited for him to arrive. She never thought she could like a nerd. She teased him about his horn rimmed glasses and nutty-professor persona, but it attracted her to him all the more. She stood at the mirror and brushed her hair, thinking about what Carmen had said. Maybe it was a little strange that she hadn't been over to his place. She hadn't thought anything about it until Carmen had mentioned it. Could he be married? Even though he spent the night with her regularly?

A knock at the door jarred her from her thoughts. She made her way to the front of the apartment. When she opened the door, Stanley wrapped her in his arms, catching her off guard. He was early and she was still in her robe and pink fuzzy slippers.

"How was your trip?" Cathy said. She reveled in his delight over seeing her.

"It was fine." He kissed her with smiling lips and entered the apartment.

Cathy smelled his cologne as he passed her. "Yeah, digging for rocks. I guess that can be kind of boring." She teased him.

He gave her a serious look. "I've told you I do a lot more than dig for rocks. I'm one of the most respected in my field."

"I didn't mean to offend."

"I teach, I do research, I write…I do a number of things."

"Sorry." Cathy saw an opportunity. The door was open. "Do you have anything at your house that might give me a better feel for what you do at work? I'd love to see some artifacts or something."

Stanley frowned. "I have journals that I can bring you that will give you an idea of what I do, but since you're always making fun of it, you might find them boring."

"There's nothing at your house?"

"What do you mean? "

"I'm just saying. Why don't we ever go to your place?"

"It's just a small bachelor's efficiency. I'm not comfortable there."

"What color are the walls? Does it have a kitchen? If you don't like it, let's find you a new place. You don't do anything else with all that money you're making."

Stanley tugged at the belt around Cathy's robe and opened it. He eyed her breasts. "Can we talk about this later? I've had a long trip and all I could think about while I was away was getting back to you. And this is what I do with my money." He kissed her and pulled a small wrapped box out of his pocket.

Cathy wrestled it out of his hands. She opened the box to find a little sparkling display of affection. It was a necklace, a small heart encrusted with diamonds. She smiled at Stanley and headed toward the bedroom to thank him for his thoughtfulness. He eagerly followed her. He picked her up playfully and tossed her on the bed.

"Allow me to give you a proper thank you, scientist." She pulled him down on top of her.

He looked into her eyes. "You are so very welcome."

A little while later, Cathy came out of the bathroom and stood in the bedroom doorway. She looked at Stanley lying on the bed. Her face was still flush.

She slipped on her house shoes. "Stanley, let's go to your place tonight."

Stanley sat up and pulled his T-shirt over his head. "For what? I told you I don't like being there."

"Or do you mean someone else is there?"

"What's that supposed to mean?"

"It means what I said." Cathy snapped. "If there's no one else living there, there's no reason why we can't go to your house." She smiled willfully. "I can't wait to see it."

"We're not going to my place and that's final."

"What?" she yelled, she didn't appreciate being spoken to like a child. "You know what? Get out! Get your things and go. Right now." Cathy moved around the room snatching up Stanley's belongings. She scooped up his collared shirt, belt and shoes.

Stanley grabbed the box he had given her earlier off the nightstand. He ran over to her in a desperate attempt to smooth things over. "Let me put this on you."

Cathy snatched herself from his embrace. "I mean it Stanley. Just go." She dropped his clothes and grabbed the necklace from his hands. She turned toward the mirror and put it around her neck.

Stanley picked up his belongings off the floor. "You don't mean that." His voice was calm. "All because you can't come to my nasty little place?"

Cathy could hear the patronage in his voice. She remained quiet as he kept talking. "All right. I'll go. But you know you're being silly, right?" He put on the remainder of his clothes and slid into his soft soled shoes.

Cathy admired her new necklace in the mirror and wondered how much it cost. She had no idea. She worked at the post office. She had never had the money, or the man, that could treat her to such nice things. The necklace caught the light through the blinds and shimmered brightly.

Cathy's demeanor relaxed as she continued to admire it in the mirror. Stanley headed for the door.

"I like the way it looks on you."

"Shut up, Stanley, and get out," Cathy said, with a smile. After seeing how beautiful the necklace looked on around her neck, the level of her anger dropped several notches.

Stanley walked out of the bedroom. As soon as she heard him close the front door, the phone rang. She walked over and picked it up, looking at the caller ID. It was Carmen.

"Hey." She answered.

"Hey, yourself. What are you up to today?"

"Nothing. Stanley just left. We had a fight. I tried to get him to let me come over to his place. He still won't. I can't figure it out.

"I can," Carmen replied.

"He's not married, Carmen. It's too obvious. He knows that's the first thing I would think of."

"Yeah, you keep thinking that."

"I spend too much time with him." She said with conviction.

"Yeah, she's probably an ER doc. They work long hours."

"Nah, it's gotta' be something else."

"Now look who has relationship problems."

"I don't have relationship problems."

"If dating a married man isn't a problem, I don't know what is."

"He's not married."

"I hope you're right…let's go shopping today. Damon is God only knows where. I ain't sitting around waiting for him. Not today. I'll be by around noon."

Cathy ended the call, still reflecting on what Stanley was keeping from her.

Chapter 26

Carmen sat on the sofa reading a magazine she had picked up while out shopping with Cathy. For a few months now, she had been reinventing her image. She had lost a little weight, and now she made it her business to keep up with the latest trends in fashion, hair and makeup. Initially, she did it to garner the attention of Damon. Now, she just liked how she looked. She was growing more confident every day. Why did she let herself go in the first place?

Damon entered the brownstone looking a little off.

"What's wrong with you?" Carmen inquired.

"I don't feel right. I think it was something I ate."

Damon sat down at the opposite end of the couch. Carmen continued to read her magazine.

"What are you reading?"

"*Essence*"

"Are you cooking tonight?"

"Don't I always cook?" Damon could clearly read Carmen's tone; she wasn't in the best mood. He found her that way on many occasions the past couple months.

"I probably won't eat much, anyway."

The growing tension between them stood front and center in Damon's mind again. Their conversations were becoming stiff. Impersonal. He was trying as best as he could to be a married man, but deep down, he was miserable with her. He didn't want to be, but for some reason, no matter how hard he tried, he just couldn't change his mind.

"Carmen. You know that I'm really trying, right?"

She rolled her eyes as she stood up. "Don't make me your charity case, Damon." Carmen walked into the kitchen to start making dinner. After a few moments, Damon came and stood in the doorway, leaning against the doorjamb. He removed his jacket and threw it on the kitchen table. He felt his temperature rising. He removed his T-shirt and threw it over his shoulder. He folded his arms and found a more comfortable position with his back against the wall.

"Face it, Damon. You don't love me."

"What are you saying? I'm here, aren't I?"

"No, Damon. You really aren't. Your body might be on occasion, but your heart and mind are far from here." Damon walked over to Carmen and wrapped his arms around her waist. Her hair smelled like something that had been burned. She had been to the salon earlier and the curling iron that was a little too hot had left behind its mark. It was a far cry from the way Rachel smelled. Hers was a scent of freshness and purity, a very clean smelling scent. Damon found it almost angelic. Realizing his thoughts had wandered, he brought his attention back to the conversation with Carmen.

"Baby, I know it hasn't been perfect, but most marriages aren't. I'm here...and I'm trying. You have my word on that."

"You don't get it, Damon. Your word isn't enough. Trying isn't enough. You don't love me."

Damon looked Carmen in the eyes. All of a sudden, a searing pain shot through his stomach with an intensity that bent him over. He broke out in a cold sweat as a rush of heat flooded through his body. Carmen handed him the kitchen towel she was holding. He blotted sweat from his forehead before pressing the towel to his mouth. "All of a sudden, I don't feel so good," he grumbled. "I need to lie down for a minute."

Damon headed for the bedroom. Not only was his stomach upset, but he noticed he was getting chills. He had no idea how to make things right with Carmen, or with his life for that matter. And now, he was coming down with something. He wished that life would give him a break. He wrapped the blanket around him; it seemed he couldn't get warm. Exhaustion sneaked up on him and he fell asleep.

A little while later, Carmen placed a plate on the bedside table and left the room. The aroma roused Damon from his sleep. He sat up in the bed and ate as much of the homemade beef stew as his appetite would allow, pondering how Carmen was one of the best things that ever happened to him, and trying to figure out how he could find peace within, and at the same time, not let her get away.

Chapter 27

Damon sat alone in the living room on Friday evening. He assumed Carmen was out with Cathy. He had finally managed to shake off whatever he had caught and was feeling more like himself. He noticed it had been a few weeks since he had spoken to Craig and surprisingly, he appreciated the break. Whenever he was out with Craig, things happened that he didn't feel good about—perhaps he drank too much or flirted more than he should. More importantly, he would be dog tired the next morning at work. It was as if Craig was stuck in some bygone era. The years were advancing, but he was not. Damon was ready for a change. He hadn't seen or spoken to Wendell in a long time. He decided to give him a call. After three rings, he answered.

"Wendell...its Damon."

"Hey, Damon, what's up?" Wendell added with a chuckle. "What did Craig do now?"

Damon laughed. "Haven't seen him. I'm kind of wondering what's going on with him."

Craig was their mutual friend and they were both closer to Craig than they were to each other. Whenever they hung out together, Craig was usually there. Right now, Damon didn't want to hang out with Craig. He needed someone objective to talk to. "I was just thinking... sometime...if your wife will let you out, maybe we could go and grab a beer or something like that. I still like hangin' out with Craig, but he wears me out sometimes. You seem a bit mellower. Just let me know, you know, if you want to hang out sometime."

"First of all, my wife doesn't have to give me permission to go out. She's out with the kids tonight, though, so if you wanted to go tonight, that would be good." He laughed and Damon joined him. "I can be at the hall by seven-thirty."

Damon hung up the phone. He looked forward to hanging out with Wendell. Wendell seemed to be at peace with his life. Why did he have it so good? Damon hoped he would share his secret.

Damon went to the bedroom, changed out of his work clothes into jeans and a sweater and headed for the pool hall. As he walked along, he noticed how quiet the streets were. It puzzled him at first, and then it dawned on him that school was back in session. He was amazed at how much noise the kids made at night.

A few moments later, he reached the pool hall. When he walked in, he saw Wendell sitting at the bar. He was ordering a beer from the bartender and was about to pay. Damon walked over and joined him.

"Put your money away." Damon said. "The beers are on me tonight. It's my treat." Damon placed a twenty on the bar and asked Roscoe to start a tab.

Wendell smiled and nodded, expressing his appreciation for Damon's generosity.

Roscoe slid two beers down the bar.

"Where is your wife tonight, anyway?" Damon asked as Wendell gulped his beer.

He recovered his breath from swallowing deeply. "Mother-daughter sleep over. It's like that when you have children. There's always something going on. I've even slept over night with the girls before. It's a trip when you think about a grown man at a sleepover, but you'll do anything to make your kids happy; even sleep on someone's floor."

"Wow, I can't even relate. Rachel used to barely let me see my son. I've never been involved with him like that. I guess her current husband does all those things with him." Damon could hear his own regret in his voice as he spoke.

Wendell placed his hand on Damon's shoulder. "I feel for you, brother. Not being able to be in your son's life has to be rough. I don't know what I would do if I couldn't be involved with my girls. You handling it okay?"

"Not much I can do about it now except make the most of the time I'm with him."

"Here, here." Wendell raised his glass and he and Damon clicked their mugs together. "What's Craig been up to?" he asked.

"You know Craig. He's still crazy. Now all of a sudden, he's really into Samantha. I don't know if you remember her."

"Tall? With the blonde hair? Wears purple all the time."

"Yeah, that's her. She's done something to him, man." "Flipped his world upside down. I have a feeling that's where he's been. I've never seen him like this."

"Oh, he must be in love."

"I don't know what's wrong with him. I just hope he doesn't catch a stalking case." Damon played with the edges of a paper napkin that sat on the bar.

"Yeah, I've been there too."

"What?" Damon stopped playing with the napkin. He was surprised to hear that. Wendell always seemed to have it all together. He wanted more details. "You? Stalking?"

"Yeah, my wife." He corrected himself, "Well, before she was my wife. I was strung out. She would get mad and break up with me over something stupid I had done. I would hide in the bushes outside her house to see if another guy was there. I'd follow her to work. Sick, man.

Jonesin.' She never called the cops, but she threatened to."
Wendell laughed, "Several times."

Damon laughed.

Wendell looked confused. "You were never like that
over Carmen?"

"Not really."

"Wow. Lucky you. My wife? When I first met
her...shoot man, I was just like Craig. Distracted, confused.
I didn't think I could live without her. I was sick when we
were apart. She finally pitied me enough to marry me."
Wendell said with a proud smile. "We've built a great life
together. I love her more than life itself. And my kids,"
Wendell grinned from ear to ear, "the two of them have me
wrapped around their fingers and I wouldn't trade it for
anything. Sometimes I feel like the luckiest man in the
world."

Damon sipped his beer. It was a far cry from the way
he was feeling. He deciphered from Wendell that one of the
keys to being happy was that you had to love the person.
He was missing that key ingredient. He wondered what
else?

"Man," Wendell continued. "Craig needs to get his life
together. Settle down and surrender his life to God. That's
where his peace lies. It's not in the conquest. Every time he
gets what he wants, he only wants more. That's a hole only
God can fill. He needs to fall in love, get married, and find
someone to spend all that money on. I guarantee you, he'll
be much happier."

After about an hour of talking, Damon's cell phone
rang. When he flipped it open, he saw it was Candy's
number. His eyes grew wide as he looked at the display.

"Is everything, okay?" Wendell asked, seeing Damon's
expression.

"Yeah, it's Carmen, cuing me that it is time to come home." Damon flipped his phone closed and settled the tab. He thanked Wendell for meeting him. He had enjoyed the conversation. No macho talk, only real talk about real feelings. He asked Wendell if they could get together again in the future and Wendell agreed. He walked home from the pool hall that night with the realization that things might never be right with Carmen. He never felt the feelings Wendell described for her. He also acknowledged Rachel still had a grip on his heart.

His life was a mess. The last thing he wanted to do was hurt Carmen. He never told her about his one indiscretion with Candy. He wanted to close that chapter of his life. Damon felt bad for what he did and it seemed life wouldn't let him forget.

Chapter 28

Damon approached his mother's house through the back yard. He didn't feel like walking all the way around so he cut through the neighbor's yard, like he often had when he was a young boy. A deliciously sweet aroma flowed forth from the kitchen, which probably meant Ronald was nearby, or soon would be. He entered his mother's kitchen through the back door. He was surprised and glad to see his older brother, Ike, leaning against the kitchen sink eating a freshly baked chocolate chip cookie.

"Hey!" He greeted his brother with a tender embrace. He rarely saw him since his promotion to District Manager moved him to Grand Rapids. "What brings you here?"

"I'm here to scope out this new cat mom keeps talking about." Ike resumed his comfortable stance against the kitchen sink and popped the last piece of cookie in his mouth. Have you seen him yet?" He dusted the cookie crumbs off his hands.

"Not yet. Don't want to."

"I know what you mean, man, but it's been a long time for her. She was so busy working and raising us without daddy. I don't ever recall her dating anybody. Do you?"

"No, I can't. I'm sure she probably had a little something here and there. She probably just didn't let us know about it. Where is she anyway?"

Ike looked toward the ceiling. "Upstairs." He shrugged, "Well, she has my full support." He grabbed another cookie. "She's still fairly young you know. We can't expect her to grow old alone."

Damon was silent.

"How's my girl, Carmen." Ike's tone was warm and his wide smile revealed blazing white teeth against his dark skin. "She and Diane always did hit it off. She asks about her all the time. About both of you. How are ya'll? Married life treating you good? Mom says she hardly sees you and I know I never do."

"It's all good." Damon lied. "Are Diane and the kids okay?" Damon took off his leather bomber and threw it across a kitchen chair. "I might try to make it up there soon."

"We'd love that." Ike licked his fingers. "It's not that far, you know."

"Yeah, I know. With work and stuff, it's hard to find time. I'm coming, though. You can bet on it. I'll bring Carmen with me."

Sharon descended the stairs and entered the kitchen. She smiled when she saw her two boys talking.

"Wow, how the years have flown by." She walked over to the counter and retrieved a spatula from the top kitchen drawer. "It seems like yesterday I was pulling you two apart and making you sit at opposite ends of the table so that I could get some peace. Damon you would be at that end huffing and puffing and wiping tears." Sharon pointed, "Ike you would be at that end grinning from ear to ear." You loved tormenting your little brother. Now, look at both of you. All grown up with families of your own." Sharon started removing cookies from the cookie sheet and gently placing them on a plate.

"Yeah, Momma, we're men now." Ike teased and flexed his bicep. "You make sure Ronald knows that, right Damon?"

Damon still wouldn't comment.

"I miss having all of you here. Ike, since your job moved to Grand Rapids, I never see you. Damon's not far, but he claims he's so busy. Doing what, I don't know. She lightly slammed her hand on the table. "I want all of you here for Thanksgiving this year. No excuses. Pat, Cheryl, all of you..." She looked at Damon sternly, "And Carmen. I'm not taking no for an answer."

Damon and Ike glanced at each other, wondering what had provoked her mood.

"Will Ronald be here?" Damon asked.

"Yes, and so will you." Sharon added in a final tone.

"In fact, that's who I was talking to on the phone upstairs. He is on his way here, now. Isaac is going to dinner with us. Do you wanna' go?"

"Naw, I was just passing though."

Sharon twisted her mouth and rolled her eyes. "You're not fooling me, Damon. I want you here, Thanksgiving."

Damon headed out the back door. He could hear Sharon's voice trailing.

"Do you hear me, Damon?" She shouted.

He heard, but he sure didn't want to.

Chapter 29

Carmen arrived at her mom's house. She had driven there without calling first, but found comfort in knowing her mom would always be there when she came. Her mom never went anywhere. When Carmen thought about it, it was kind of sad, but she was still comforted in knowing Momma would always be there. Carmen opened the door to see Gert sitting on the sofa reading the bible.

"Look at what the cat drug in." Gert said with a warm chuckle.

Carmen sensed someone walking up behind her. When she turned, she saw Cathy. "Speaking of cats," Cathy said, barreling past Carmen into the house. "Where is that nasty thing, anyway?"

Carmen rolled her eyes in disappointment. She was hoping she and her mother would have a chance to talk, alone. "What brings you here?"

"Do you think you have a moratorium on Momma's house?" Cathy puffed. "I can come here if I want."

Carmen looked out the door. "Where's your car?"

"Stanley dropped me off to run over to the university. He said he would only be a minute and didn't want me to wait."

Carmen sat down next to Gert on the sofa.

"That was courteous," Gert said.

Carmen looked at Cathy. "Courteous, or sneaky?"

"Let it go, Carmen. Just because your love life is tore up doesn't mean mine has to be." Carmen ignored Cathy. It was obvious she was in a mood to spar with someone.

Gert got up from the sofa. "I'll make you girls some tea." She headed toward the kitchen and Cathy followed.

Carmen could hear them talking in the kitchen. She hoped Stanley would handle his business *ASAP* and return to retrieve the witch so that she could talk to her mother.

When they returned, Gert was carrying a tray holding three tea cups, a box of Earl Grey, and a tea pot filled with water. She placed the tray on the cocktail table and filled each cup with water before sitting down on the sofa.

"Mom, Damon's mother's cooking Thanksgiving dinner. Are you cooking this year?"

"Of course I'm cooking. What year have I not cooked?" Gert's eyebrows shot up. "You'll have to do double duty. Go there first and then come here, or vice versa." She turned toward Cathy. "Are you bringing Stanley?"

"Yes. I guess it's time y'all met him." A car horn began blowing outside of the front window. "Gotta' go," Cathy said. "See ya'll later."

Carmen released her breath when she heard the door slam behind Cathy. She took a cup of tea off the tray, hoping the bag had steeped long enough, and took a sip.

"It takes some kind of mood to deal with her some days." Gert said. "I feel sorry for that man." She walked over to the window and slowly pulled the curtains back. "I will say this, though..." she hesitated trying to get a glimpse of Stanley in the car, "I question the intentions of a man who won't come to the door and meet a woman's family." She added slowly. Her tone was full of skepticism. "We'll see what Thanksgiving brings."

Gert released the curtain panel and returned to the sofa.

When she sat down, Carmen posed a serious question. "Mom, how did you know that daddy loved you?"

Gert looked her in the eyes. "I could feel it. From his heart to mine. He didn't even have to say it." Why do you ask?" she added with a soft frown.

"He doesn't love me." Carmen shook her head in defeat." I thought my love for him would be enough for the both of us, but I can't do it by myself anymore." Her eyes filled with tears. "The way he looks at me, Momma. The look in his eyes is so sterile. The whole thing was a mistake."

"You're still in the newlywed phase." Gert comforted. "The beginning of a marriage can be tough. It takes time to figure this stuff out. He's trying to figure you out and you're trying to understand him. He's got his habits, you've got yours. It can be a tumultuous time."

"I'm not happy Momma," She shook her head in deep contemplation. "I don't know what to do."

"Well, if you're not sure, don't do anything. Maybe he just needs time to adjust. Taking a wife can be a huge responsibility for a man."

"I know, Momma." Carmen headed for the door.

"You be careful driving, Carmen. You haven't been drinking, have you?"

Carmen was shocked by her inquiry. She hadn't realized that other people had noticed her affinity for fine wines.

"No, Momma."

Carmen walked out of her mother's house. It was dark. She didn't want to go home, but she had no place else to go. It felt so empty there. So lonely. She was desperately trying not to hear the solution to her problem. She didn't want to face the fact that her marriage was over.

Chapter 30

Damon could feel the uncomfortable distention in his stomach as he walked up the stairs to his mother's front door. It was Thanksgiving. He had stopped by Gert's house, where she insisted he eat with Carmen, Cathy and their father. He wanted to resist, saving room for dinner at his mom's, but Gert was a better cook than Sharon. Once he got started, he couldn't stop. He ate two plates of turkey and dressing, black eyed peas, greens, and macaroni and cheese, leaving no room for Sharon's German chocolate cake. It was his favorite and she made it on every holiday or special occasion. She was going to be furious.

He waited a moment, knowing his mother's house would be full of people. He looked in the window. The house was packed full of immediate, and some extended family. He wished he could have stayed outside, alone. Once he was inside, he would have to put on the air of being okay, and he wasn't. He took a deep breath and rang his mother's doorbell.

Sharon flung open the door. "C'mon in, baby." She greeted him. "Hand me your coat. She held out her hand. "You're always late, but today I honestly thought you weren't coming." She grabbed him by the hand. "Come with me. I want you to meet someone."

Damon's mother led him into the living room to meet Ronald. When he saw Damon, he stood up from the sofa and extended his hand. Damon sized him up; looking for evidence that he wasn't worthy to be with his mother, and for an excuse to immediately throw him out.

"Damon," Ronald grinned. "It's good to finally meet you." Ronald's hand was warm and soft and Damon gripped it firmly, almost yanking his arm.

"What's up?" Damon said with a nod. Sharon frowned at Damon's less than friendly welcome and went to go hang up his jacket.

"Your mother tells me that you and your wife live in one of those fancy brownstones over in Bronzeville." Damon could tell Ronald was trying to make small talk. "That's a nice area."

"We like it."

"Is your wife here?"

"She'll be here shortly. She's at her parent's house." Damon studied Ronald, again. His mocha skin was smooth and shiny. His temples were grey and his pink lips unfolded around gapped teeth. His appearance was bland; not like his father's. His dad's jet black hair, chiseled chin, smooth caramel skin and full beard gave him a striking appearance. Ronald was just ordinary. The only thing you might remember about him was his grey temples. Big deal.

A call coming from the back of the house saved Damon from the conversation.

"Is that Damon Harris?" Dianne struggled to get through the crowd.

Damon turned around to see his sister-in-law, Dianne, Ike's wife.

Her delicate arms appeared from beneath her red wrap. She embraced him and intently placed a kiss on his cheek. "Where's Carmen?"

"She's on the way." Damon smiled. Dianne was the epitome of class. Ike kept her laced in the finest outfits and jewelry. She had an elegance and sophistication you did not find in most women. Her warmth and sensuality seemed to fill the room and Damon found it very attractive, even on his brother's wife. He loved his brother enough not to get too close to her, though. He made sure that whatever feelings she evoked in him stayed neatly tucked away.

After a few moments of catching up, Diane joined the family in the kitchen.

Damon found the crowd too much. Too much noise, too many people. He reached in the pocket of his jeans that always sat low on the hip and popped an antacid in his mouth. He hadn't been feeling well lately, and knew he would pay severely later on that night for overeating. It seemed as though every couple of weeks something was plaguing him. If it wasn't a rash or sore throat, it was fatigue. If it wasn't fatigue, it was stomach problems. He regretted letting things bother him so much that it affected his health. When he looked up and saw Carmen walk through the door, he popped two more antacids in his mouth. Now the charade would begin—parading her through the house, acting as the happy couple. He started belching, one after another and feared he might not be able to keep his food down.

He walked over to her. "Thanks for coming," was all he could think to say. He took her coat and threw it over his arm.

"No problem. Mom was glad you came by."

"It was good to see her too. It had been a while."

"Stanley came by after you left. Really nice guy. I think I might have been wrong about him. He's absolutely crazy about Cathy. You can tell."

"Good." He changed the subject. "After dinner, I'll be ready to go."

"Yeah, me too."

They walked through the house making their empty introductions then sat down at the table with the family for dinner. Damon picked at his plate hoping Sharon did not notice he was not eating.

Joy and love filled the room, but to Damon it felt like a cage. He and Carmen listened as people offered advice and told corny newlywed stories. They conjured up a few happy ones of their own. They left that evening, went home and to bed in total silence.

Chapter 31

Cathy sucked down the last of her morning oatmeal and ran to her bedroom to pick up her cell phone before it stopped ringing. She was delighted it was Stanley. The day before, he had left on a business trip. Before she went to bed the previous night, she left a message on his answering machine with her Christmas gift wish list.

"You get my messages?"

"Yeah, all three of them." He laughed. "I guess I'm Santa, now."

"I just wanted to give you some options. You don't have to get all three of them, Stanley, although I wouldn't be disappointed if you did."

"I'm sure."

"Just pick one. You're going to love what I'm going to get you." Cathy's voice gushed with the element of surprise.

"Well, don't spend too much. I'm not very picky."

"You'll love it. I promise." She insisted. "Call me when you get back."

"Will do."

Cathy hung up the phone. She was so excited about Christmas. This was her favorite time of year. She had painstakingly anguished over what gift she would give to Stanley. He could buy pretty much anything he wanted for himself and he was a bit quirky. The normal rules didn't apply. She was afraid he would find a sweater or shirt unremarkable. A telescope would be better, but she settled on a series of hardback books she had seen in the window of a bookstore she was walking past near the University one day when she was out with Carmen. They were all on some aspect of geology. One volume was on gemstones. Another covered volcanoes and other natural disasters, and one provided a history of the greatest geological findings from the past 100 years. Books that would make most people cry from boredom—ones people would probably refuse to read, even if they were paid. They were perfect for Stanley. Tomorrow she would drive over to the bookstore, purchase them and get them wrapped up before Stanley returned home from his trip. Then she could spend the next few weeks up until Christmas torturing him with the wrapped box.

After spending all day lugging mail at the post office, she hurried over to the store to buy the books she had seen. She drove around the block several times trying to find a parking spot. The pitch black Chicago winter sky made the bitter chill feel even colder. She finally spotted someone pulling out of a space a few doors down from the bookstore. *Perfect.* She pulled in and parked. She reached in her purse and pulled out her gloves. As she was putting them on, preparing for her short jaunt to the door, she looked into the window of the little Vietnamese store she had parked in front of and saw a tall man that looked exactly like Stanley. Same grey coat, same grey Kangol. She squinted to get a better view, only to be horrified. He had told her he would be out of town, working on a project with colleagues until the weekend, and now he was standing right before her. She put her car in reverse, backed up and screeched out of the space. As she drove away, she called him on his cell phone and he answered.

"Sweetheart, I was just thinking about you."

"Hello, Stanley. How's your trip going?" The car's accelerator raced as the gas pedal gave way under her foot.

"Everything's going fine. I'll have things wrapped up toward the end of the week."

"Really?" Cathy's tone brimmed with irritation and sarcasm.

"Is everything all right? You sound as if something's wrong."

"Nope. Nothing's wrong. Call me when you get back." Cathy hung up the phone and dropped it on the passenger seat.

Again? Now, she would add Stanley to her relationship graveyard. And, to think, this time she liked the person enough to change her evil ways. She wanted to be softer for him. She wanted to be a woman that a man could love for a change.

She would to have to tell Carmen that she had been right about him. The thought made her sick to her stomach. She decided she would wait a while before she would tell her it was over between them. After all the fuss she had made about Damon, it was just too big of a crow to eat.

Chapter 32

It was Saturday morning. Cathy carefully brushed the last coat of ruby nail polish on her pinky toe and capped off the bottle. She heard a knock at the door. She knew it was Stanley. He had called her minutes before and told her he was on his way over. She was glad he had finally arrived. It was time to get it over with.

She removed the cotton from between each toe and tossed it in the trash can on her way to open the door. She still had on lingerie. It wasn't intentional, but she knew that breaking up with him while wearing lingerie would be downright dirty. She smiled to herself as she opened the door and let Stanley in.

"Where were you this week?" Cathy asked. Her tone was somber.

Stanley frowned. "Buffalo. You know that."

"Right." She paused. "All week?"

"Yes, all week. Why?" He removed his coat and tossed it on the sofa.

Cathy circled him. She looked him up and down. A sneer appeared on her face.

"You have an attitude about something." Stanley said. "What's all this about? You know my job takes me away quite a bit."

Cathy moved to the other side of the room and remained focused. Knowing men could be crafty liars, she was careful not to lead him in any way. She needed to catch him red handed. If he were to sniff out what she was doing, he might come up with a cover too quickly.

"What did you do on Tuesday?" Cathy probed. She picked up a brush that lay on a console table, next to the door.

"I don't remember," Stanley shrugged his shoulders. "Who cares?"

"I do. Tell me what you did Tuesday night."

"I think I went to dinner with Bob and the guys."

"Tell me the truth, Stanley." Cathy stood in front the mirror and brushed her hair.

"That is the truth." Stanley forced.

Cathy turned toward him and hurled her brush across the room, grazing him on the ear. She had a temper. When she lost it, she usually grabbed the closest object and sent it crashing into a wall. This time, she was so mad she threw the brush directly at him, hitting her target.

He lunged toward her, grabbed her by the wrist and pulled her close. She could feel his breath on her face. His eyes threatened her. She could feel the grip of his hand start to burn her wrist. She tried to break free but couldn't. She grew concerned at his display of aggression, but not enough to make her back down.

"Tell me the truth or get out." She said. Calm, determined, and serious. She was out of patience with men, especially ones that were liars. She stretched out her long slender arm, extended her finger and pointed toward the door. She didn't think words were necessary.

Stanley dropped to his knees, his hands clutching at the see-through lace of her black night gown. "Cathy...baby...wait, wait, wait. Okay, you got me, but it's not what you think. I'm in the process..."

"Get out," Cathy growled, enunciating every letter in the phrase.

"Please, let me explain."

"What? That you don't love her. That you're staying because of the kids. Oh, and I forgot, you don't even sleep in the same bed with her. Real original. Get out, or do I need to call my brother to escort you." Cathy could feel her temper rising even higher. Not only was this fool married, but he expected her to go along with it. She looked at the vase that Stanley had given her when they first started dating. He had made such a big deal about the fact that it was made from a rare type of Alabaster. He had found it in Egypt while on assignment. Cathy only cared about the fact that the creamy color matched her living room's decor perfectly.

She picked up the vase. In seconds, it would be in scattered pieces on the floor.

"Don't do it, Cathy." His voice pleaded and he shook his head in frustration. "I'll leave. I hope you'll eventually give me the chance to explain."

Stanley picked up his coat off the sofa and walked out the door.

Chapter 33

It was Christmas Eve. The dealership was closed. Damon drove forty-five minutes north of the city to an outlet mall to do some shopping. He picked up toys for his nieces and nephews, Emeril's cookbook for his mom and a gold charm bracelet for Carmen. While he was standing in line waiting to have his purchases wrapped, he received a text from Craig. He, Wendell and a few others, were meeting at the pool hall later that evening for a game of pool and a drink to celebrate the Christmas holiday.

After paying for his gifts to be wrapped, Damon returned to his car and loaded his packages. He smiled deeply. It felt good to be doing something for someone else. Blessing his loved ones was more important than his dwindled bank account.

He drove back to the brownstone. The only space he could find was several doors down. He parked the car and walked down the block toward the house. He could smell the smells of Christmas. Cinnamon and butter filled the air. He smiled as he walked past a group of off-key carolers. In his old hood, they would have been robbed before they pulled out their song sheets. Hell, he might have even been one of the robbers.

Damon unlocked the door and entered the brownstone. There was no sign of Carmen so he placed the gifts underneath the tree and headed back out the door and down to the pool hall on foot. He wouldn't stay out late, after all, it was Christmas Eve and he knew that a husband should spend Christmas Eve with his wife.

The smell of beer greeted him as he walked through the pool hall doors. He saluted Roscoe and walked to the back where Craig and Wendell were already playing pool. He pulled up a chair and joined them.

"Where've you been?" Craig asked. "I haven't heard from you in a while."

Damon slung his coat on the back of his chair. He briskly rubbed his hands together, puffing them with warm air from his mouth trying to get the feeling back. "Where've I been...where have you been, is the question?"

"Around."

Damon felt he knew the reason Craig had been scarce. He was probably spending every waking moment chasing after Samantha, and the ones in between, scheming about how to get her back. "How's Samantha?" He probed, almost teasing.

"It's all good." Craig said through beer and bravado.

"Carmen?" Craig challenged.

"She's fine." Damon directed his attention to Wendell. He was ready for an honest conversation. "How you doing, man? How are the kids?" Damon said as a grin crept across his mouth.

"The kids are excited, I'm broke and Sheila's mad that I spent too much money on the girls...she's really going to be mad when she sees what I bought *her*."

Damon laughed. "What did you get her?"

Craig rudely interrupted them. "Wendell, are you talking or playing pool?"

Wendell bent over to make his shot. "Scrooge."

Damon laughed, again. Craig was finally showing some vulnerability to a woman. Samantha had changed him. He wasn't hanging out as much and was downright grumpy. Damon felt she was just what he needed.

It was good to see Craig. Damon admitted to himself that although he appreciated the break, he had missed him.

After several games of pool and a few beers, Damon exited the pool hall into the cold, dark night. There were a few patrons on the street. He squinted up at the street light to see how bad it was snowing; his hair was already wet with snow. He pulled up the collar on his jacket and started down the block at a determined pace. As he turned the corner, he saw someone walking toward him. He immediately recognized the jet-black head of curls being tossed vigorously by the wind. Sure enough, as she moved closer to one of the street lamps that peppered the block, he could clearly see it was Candy. He was thankful her attempts at contacting him had stopped. When he thought about it, he still felt awful about what he had done, but he was glad she had moved on.

They moved closer to each other. He expected to see her beautiful face, but when he focused in on her, her eyes were hollowed out with dark circles underneath. She had sores on her face and looked sickly thin.

"Damon?" she inquired, as if she was surprised to run into him.

"It's me. What's up with you?" He frowned. "Please tell me you're not on that stuff." He pulled up his collar as the wind swept across his face. He had seen many of his childhood friends get hooked on drugs. Beautiful woman, even ones as pretty as Candy.

"No, Damon, I wish that was all it was." She looked directly at him. "I have AIDS."

Damon's eyes blinked. He didn't believe what he was hearing.

"I tried to get hold of you, but you didn't return my calls. I did manage to track down a few of the guys I had been with." Candy looked down solemnly at the snow-covered ground. "They were pretty upset when I told them.

One of the guys beat me up pretty badly. At that point I stopped trying to contact people. I started praying that anyone I was with didn't get it. There were so many guys and I was always so drunk." Her eyes filled with tears, but then brightened a little. "But the other day, I ran into one of the guys and he told me his test was negative. I'm so sorry that I might have put you at risk. You've been to the doctor recently, right?" Anxiety riddled her tone. "You're fine, right?"

"Yeah, girl, I'm good." Damon forced a cocky smile.

"Good." Candy said with a sigh of relief. She wiped her face with her mitten. "You take care of yourself." She said as she walked away. "Merry Christmas."

"Yeah, same to you."

Damon stood underneath the street lamp and watched Candy continue down the block.

He was frozen in place. His eyes fixated on her back as snow swirled around his body. A wave of despair swept over him when he thought about the message she had given him, and although he tried to deny it in his mind, his gut readily accepted the truth.

Damon walked the rest of the way home in the bitter cold. He replayed Candy's news over and over as he walked down the dark, silent street. Her words, her face, and her body kept flashing before him. He thought about the errant illnesses he had been plagued with over the past several months that seemed to appear and disappear without cause. He had been tired a lot, always blaming it on his marriage problems and the stress of everything. He was numb as he walked up the stairs to the brownstone. He could feel the heat coming from the door and all he wanted was to see Carmen. He needed the comfort of seeing her in that big frumpy nightshirt. He needed to feel her curled up against him on the couch.

He opened the door and called out to her, but she didn't answer, which was unusual. Carmen was like old faithful. She was always home in the evenings, and always had dinner ready like a good wife. Damon had grown to depend on it. He suspected she was out doing some last minute Christmas shopping which would buy him some time to sort through his thoughts. He sat down on the couch in the quiet brownstone and stared at the Christmas tree lights as they blinked off and on, absorbing everything. He was deathly afraid of the news Candy had given him. How was he going to tell Carmen? He wouldn't. Not yet. He might not have it. His emotions swung from acceptance to denial and back again.

After a few hours had passed, he tried to reach Carmen on her cell phone, desperate for her comfort, but she didn't answer. He sat on the couch for a little while longer. Carmen was never out late. Was she hurt? In an accident? As he sat on the sofa, he was overcome with a compelling notion to check the closet. He ran into the bedroom and violently flung open her closet door. It was empty. Only two hangers remained. They chimed, like bells, as they swung back and forth, gently knocking against one another.

In shock, Damon took three steps back and sat on the bed, staring into the closet. He fell backwards and stared at the ceiling as the events of the night sank in. As the realization went deeper and deeper, a shroud of sorrow enveloped him. He had made mistakes in his life, one bad choice after another. Hustling the streets when he was younger was a mistake. Losing Rachel and London was a mistake. Perhaps even marrying Carmen was a mistake. But, Candy? Now, that was a mistake of epic proportions.

Perhaps she had cost him his very life. He assumed the fetal position on the bed and sobbed. He could taste the bitter pain of regret mixed in with the saltiness of his tears. His teeth tore at the blanket and his fists balled up into his chest. He cried until he had no more tears to give.

Chapter 34

Not knowing what to do, and having been dealt two impossible blows on the same night, Damon called Rachel, the only woman he had ever loved. He needed the comfort of a woman's voice, even if it was just on the other end of the phone.

"Merry Christmas, Rachel." He said when she answered. He struggled to sound enthusiastic. "What's London doing?"

"Up. It's way past his bedtime. He's too excited to sleep."

Damon nearly melted at the sound of Rachel's voice. Their history together overwhelmed him. Even though there had been bad blood between them after they broke up, and even though he wasn't exactly "warm and fuzzy" toward her husband Evan, their relationship had blossomed into a friendship. As she spoke, he dreamed he could have her in his life the way he wanted. Had he, none of this would have happened. But, a close friend was all she was. And tonight, he needed her. Rachel as a friend was better than no Rachel at all.

"Rachel, I have something to tell you."

"What is it?"

Damon paused. He couldn't bring himself to say it. "Tonight, as I was walking home..."

He fell silent again. He called Rachel because he needed someone to talk. He couldn't call his mother—at least, not until he had more information. But, even with Rachel, how could he bring himself to say it?

Rachel interjected. "What's up, Damon, my family is waiting for me."

"Carmen left me."

"What?" Rachel said with obvious disbelief.

"Carmen left me. I came home and she was gone."

"Damon, I'm so sorry. Where did she go? Have you tried to call her?"

"Yeah, she didn't answer her phone."

Damon heard Rachel exhale deeply into the phone.

"Something else happened." He paused for a moment. "A few months ago, I was unfaithful to Carmen—"

"Surprise. Surprise."

"It wasn't like that, Rach. It was just once. I'm not trying to excuse what I did, but Carmen and I were really going through a rough patch. Obviously, I didn't know how rough. I never thought she would leave me."

"I'm not surprised, Damon. Carmen is a good woman. No woman wants to be married to someone who's been unfaithful."

"She doesn't know about that."

"You sure?"

"I'm sure. Anyway, I just bumped into the girl I had been with on the street and she...," Damon tried to contain the shakiness in his voice, "she told me she has AIDS."

Rachel gasped quietly on the other end of the phone. After a few seconds, she spoke.

"You've got to get tested."

Damon said nothing.

"Do you hear me, Damon? I know you hate going to the doctor, but you need to make an appointment. I'll go with you. The sooner you know, the sooner you can put this whole thing behind you."

He had a serious case of white coat syndrome, but knew she was right. "Thanks Rachel. I know I haven't been the easiest to get along with, but you've still managed to stay in my corner. I appreciate that."

"You're my son's father." She hesitated, "And I consider you a good friend as well."

Damon thought of London. He shuddered at the thought of what a positive test would mean for him. "I'm scared, Rachel."

"I know."

Chapter 35

It was Christmas Day. Damon awoke not feeling well. He was tired. He acknowledged that he hadn't slept soundly. He secretly prayed that was all it was. He walked to the kitchen and poured himself a glass of milk. He placed a few slices of toast in the toaster and pulled the jelly out of the refrigerator. He didn't have much of an appetite, but felt he should try to eat something.

He walked to the living room and sat the plate and glass on the table. The house was eerily quiet, so he turned on the television, wanting the noise to keep him company. So this was how it would be living alone. He had never lived alone before. He was certain he wouldn't like it.

He clicked through the channels. *It's a Wonderful Life* was playing on two different stations. He had seen it several times as a kid. He recalled lying in the bed and watching it with his mother. The sports highlights on ESPN seemed a better choice.

After two bites of toast, his stomach began to rumble. He threw the bread back on the plate and lay back on the sofa. He looked up at the ceiling. *This can't be happening.* He recalled what his mother said and had always taught him about God. He remembered Sundays in church as a little boy and thinking of how big God must be to handle everyone's problems.

The words came slow and with uncertainty.

God, I know I haven't spoken to you in a while. I know I haven't been to church, but I need you right now, God. I need you to make this whole thing...

The phone rang. Damon sat up on the sofa and looked around for it. He walked over and grabbed it off the dining room table. It was his mother.

"Merry Christmas, baby."

"Merry Christmas, Ma."

"Are you and Carmen coming over today? I'm cooking sweet potatoes."

"I'll probably stop by a little later. I don't know where Carmen is."

"What do you mean you don't know? It's early. Did she run to the store?"

"I don't think so…"

"Well, where is she?"

"I said I don't know. Look, we can talk about it later, okay?" Damon was curt.

"Do you need me to come over there?"

"Nah, I'll stop by, later. Ike and 'em coming down?"

"I don't think so. He'll probably let the kids play with their toys all day. Pat, Cheryl and Mona will be here with their kids, though. "

"Okay, I'll stop by. I picked up a few things for the kids."

Damon hung up the phone and dialed Carmen's cell phone. He wanted everything to be back to the way it was. Even if it wasn't perfect, it was comfortable and familiar. He would definitely trade being married to someone he didn't love for being HIV positive. As the thought bounced through his mind, he languished. How could he tell his family something so terrible? What would they think of him? How would they act toward him?

After several rings, her voice mail picked up. He left her a message apologizing for the man he had been. Sincerity bled through his words as he pleaded with her to let him know she was all right. He hung up the phone and lay back on the sofa again, staring at the ceiling. A few minutes later, he received a text from Carmen.

It's over, Damon. I want you to be happy. I finally am. You can keep the brownstone. Once the divorce is final, I'll have my name removed from the lease.

Divorce? The words jumped from the screen. Everything was happening so quickly.

He trudged to the bathroom. After he showered, he stood in front of the mirror brushing his teeth. He stared at his face and opened his mouth. The white coating on his tongue was still there. It had been there for a few weeks, now. He tried brushing his tongue, but the coating wouldn't budge. He needed to talk to Carmen. He would go to the doctor as soon as he could to get confirmation of what he already knew. And he would have to tell Carmen what he had done, knowing she had been nothing but good to him. She definitely didn't deserve this.

Chapter 36

Later on in the afternoon, Damon went outside to start his car and scrape the ice off his windshield. He came back in the house and took a moment to warm his hands at the radiator. When they were sufficiently warm, he loaded the gifts in a shopping bag, went to the closet and found a rarely donned hat and placed it on his head. He loaded his trunk and headed for his mother's house. On the way over, he called Rachel and asked to speak to his son. Normally on Christmas, he picked him up and spent time with him. Today, he didn't feel like it. He couldn't look him in the eye not knowing what his future held.

He spoke gingerly to London on the phone, choking back tears the entire time. London told Damon about the gifts Santa had brought him the night before. The Nintendo Wii Santa had brought via Evan Kilgore, M.D overshadowed the truck and basketball Damon had given him. It was all he talked about. Damon was slightly jealous, but he had more important things on his mind to give it too much attention.

After he listened to London, he told London to give the phone back to Rachel.

"Merry Christmas," she said.

"Same to you." He wasn't feeling so *Merry*.

"How are you feeling?"

"Okay, I guess."

"I found a physician for you. His name is Dr. Lipkin. He's not far from you. Do you have a pen?"

"Hold on, let me pull over." Damon guided his car onto the side of the road. He located a pen in the car's console and picked up an old Auto Trader that was lying on his seat. Rachel gave him the number and he wrote it down.

"You will call first thing Monday morning, right? This is nothing to play around with."

"I know. I will."

Damon said goodbye. He tore the number off the paper, placed it in his pocket and pulled back onto the road.

Children's laughter greeted him as he walked into his mother's house. Pat and Cheryl and their kids were already there; they ran over to him, eager to see what was in the bags.

"Where are the twins?" he asked as he removed his hat and coat.

"Mona's not here yet, as usual," Pat said.

Damon was hanging up his coat in the hall closet when he noticed Sharon calling him into the kitchen with her finger.

"Where's Carmen?" she asked in a low voice so that the girls wouldn't hear.

"She left me." Damon spoke in a normal tone, contrasting her whisper.

"You're kidding." Sharon's face immediately twisted into a frown.

"Nope. She left. Took her things. I guess she's staying with Cathy or her mother."

"What happened?" Sharon's mouth was agape. She clutched her chest.

Damon shrugged. "She got tired, I guess."

"I knew things weren't right between the two of you. Are you going to try to get her back?" Sharon was still whispering.

"It's over. It's all for the best."

"You don't look like you're handling it so well.

"I'll be all right. Really...don't worry." Damon leaned in to kiss his mother. He hesitated. Is it okay to kiss her? Or was he the walking plague? He turned and walked out of the kitchen into the living room.

About ten minutes later Mona walked through the door with her arms full of gifts. Edward, Mona's husband escorted the bundled up twins, Noelle and Noah, into the house and sat the bags he was carrying down. He extended his hand to shake Damon's.

"Merry Christmas, man." He looked around. "Where's your wife?"

Damon looked at his mother. She looked away.

"We have been having some problems, lately." Damon said. "She decided not to come."

Pat stood up, "On Christmas, Damon? What could you have possibly done to piss that woman off on Christmas?" She walked toward the kitchen.

Damon shrugged his shoulders. "You know me." He tried to laugh it off. He knew he would have to explain everything to everyone later. It was a task he dreaded. He didn't even know how he would begin to tell them that Carmen was the least of his problems right now. He sat on his mother's sofa and watched the children on the floor playing with their toys. Would he live to see London grow up? Would Evan end up raising London? He decided that wouldn't be the worst thing in the world. He was miffed that Rachel had his son taking piano and drama lessons instead of playing sports, and was positive it was Evan's doing, but other than that, Evan was an all right guy. If he had to pick someone to raise him, he would want it to be someone like Evan. Secretly Damon admired him—his character, his accomplishments, and his wife were everything Damon wished he could have.

The time passed quickly. Damon handed out his gifts to his nieces and nephews and told everyone he was leaving. Sharon didn't protest. She seemed to understand he needed to be alone. He hugged everyone and said goodbye. As he walked out the door into the dark night he feared the next time he visited, the occasion would not be so joyous.

Chapter 37

Damon awoke on Monday morning and dressed for work. He put on his jacket, and on his way out the door, he stopped in the kitchen and picked up the phone. He pulled the number to the specialist Rachel had given him out of his pocket and dialed. The receptionist took his information, scheduled the appointment for Friday and he left for work.

Business was slow at the car dealership despite the many "end of the year" discounts they were offering. Damon spent most of his day talking with the other salesmen. It would be slow until the weather started to break. He wondered how he would manage to pay the bills without Carmen. As soon as the weather changed he would have to work extra hard to make up for the slow times. He loved the brownstone. He would get a second job if he had to.

On Friday, Rachel pulled up outside of Damon and Carmen's brownstone. She had been there many times before picking up, or dropping off London, but this visit was not a routine one; it was a follow up to the promise Rachel had made to accompany Damon to the doctor.

Damon got in the car. The luxurious buttery, black leather cradled his body. It was a stark comparison to the cloth seats he sat on every day. Evan treated Rachel well, and Damon could tell that giving her the finer things was one of his priorities. He was again resentful of Evan for being able to afford Rachel the lifestyle he wished he could have given her.

The new car smell filled his nostrils. "Thanks for coming Rachel." He closed the door. The sound was solid; like the car was cocooning him.

"Sure. Don't mention it." Rachel tried to reassure him as she drove down the block. "Damon, I'm sure you're okay. You look great. I'm sure you're as healthy as a horse."

Damon looked out the car window at the strangers walking down the street. His mind recalled each of the random illnesses that plagued him the past few months. Fevers, flu like symptoms, swollen glands. "I'm sure you're right, Rachel. Let's just get these results and sweep this whole thing under the mat." He tried to sound as confident as she did.

Rachel pulled around to the back of the South Side physician's office. The doctor was an infectious disease specialist she had found in the phone book. They entered the office through the back parking lot, checked in and sat down in the waiting area. Everyone looked so normal, not like anyone was HIV positive that was for sure.

Damon filled out his paperwork and was led over to the lab area where his blood was drawn. The technician explained the procedure to Damon and told him the doctor would give him his results shortly. He returned to the waiting area and sat next to Rachel. She was leafing through a *Good Housekeeping* magazine. She took a second, re-tied the lime green neck scarf that matched her pantsuit and continued leafing through the magazine. Damon could smell her sweet perfume.

After a brief period, the nurse came out and called Damon's name. She led him back to the doctor's office.

Damon sat down. He could feel himself starting to sweat a little.

"Mr. Harris, you have tested positive for Human Immunodeficiency Virus."

Damon groaned.

"I'm sorry. We'll follow up with a more extensive test, but preliminary results show antibodies in your blood. All indications are that you have been infected. There are several trials going on and you want to get started on the meds right away." Dr. Lipkin pulled out a packet of information. Damon jumped up, took the literature from the doctor and walked out of his office.

Rachel looked up from her magazine as he passed. She hurriedly put her purse over her shoulder and rushed out behind him, following him to the car. Damon got in on the passenger side. He tried to pull the seatbelt across him to buckle it, but he didn't have the strength. He released it. The tension in the belt caused it to clang against the window. Tears began streaming down his face.

"I'm sorry, Damon. Evan and I are here for you." Rachel put the key in the ignition and cranked up the smooth running engine. She drove him home and as he was getting out of the car, she touched his hand, "I'll call you soon."

Chapter 38

It was Saturday morning. A few weeks had gone by and Damon was still adjusting to the news. The doctor's office had called with confirmation of the final test results. It was time to tell everyone. He kept rehearsing what he would say. No matter how many times he said it, it still sounded bad. He feared he would be shunned by everyone. Everyone, except his mother. He called her first.

"Mom, I need to come by tonight. I have to talk to you."

"Great. Ronald will be here. You haven't seen him since Christmas."

"No, Mom, I need to talk to you alone."

"Sounds serious."

"It is."

Damon hung up the phone and dialed Carmen. When he couldn't reach her, he decided to drive to Cathy's condo. When he pulled up, he saw Carmen's car parked in front of the building. He walked up the stairs, took a deep breath and knocked. Cathy opened the door and slammed it shut immediately. Damon rang the doorbell again. He knocked several times. A few minutes later, Carmen appeared.

"What is it, Damon?" She was wearing cotton pajamas and holding a toothbrush.

"Can I come in?"

"I don't think so. I might fall for some of your sweet talk." She chuckled. "No hard feelings between us, we just weren't meant to be. As soon as I have the money, I'll file for divorce. We've paid off the majority of our bills, so it shouldn't be difficult for us to handle what's left. Perhaps we can split—"

"Carmen." Damon cut her off. "I need to tell you something."

Carmen frowned disapprovingly. "What is it?" She said tentatively.

"Last summer, you and I had a fight. I got real mad...I got drunk and I slept with someone...something terrible's happened."

Carmen's mouth fell open.

"I went to the doctor. I'm HIV positive. You need to get tested right away."

Carmen screamed, "Oh, God, no!" The sound pierced Damon's ears. She dropped the toothbrush and slid down the wall in the hallway. Damon tried to grab her hand, but she snatched it from his grasp.

Cathy came running out into the hallway. "What did you do to her?" Her voice blasted Damon. "Why don't you just go? Leave her alone!" She charged at him.

Carmen sat on the floor, sobbing.

Damon started backing away, watching as Cathy tried to pull Carmen up off the floor. "I'm sorry, Carmen. I never meant to hurt you. You have to believe me. I—I never meant for any of this to happen."

He turned and ran down the stairs. He rushed across the parking lot to his car and drove out of the lot. It was thirty degrees out and he was sweating. His hands trembled against the steering wheel as he drove back to the brownstone. He walked in the house and went straight to the kitchen. He opened the cupboard and pulled out a bottle of Carmen's wine. He grabbed a beer mug, filled it up and took a sip. It wasn't strong enough, but it was all he had. When his mind replayed the image of Carmen screaming and sliding down the wall, he took another swig.

That was followed by several gulps. He felt terrible knowing he had inflicted that type of pain on someone.

He sat on the sofa and placed the beer mug of wine on the table. He was getting used to the fact that he now *lived* alone. But *being* alone was a much more devastating feeling. Because of his condition, he was afraid it was a feeling he would have for the rest of his life.

He looked down on the coffee table and saw the *Next Steps* folder the physician had given him along with his diagnosis. He picked it up and started to read over some of the information. He needed to schedule a visit with the doctor, which would be one of many visits over the next several months according to the literature. There was also a section titled *Telling Others about Your Status*. It offered some suggestions such as planning ahead, picking the appropriate setting, and perhaps taking some pamphlets along. *Now you tell me*. He pulled a pamphlet out of the packet and set it on the edge of the coffee table. He would take it with him to his mother's house.

He lay back on the couch. In the past, he would be getting dressed to go to the pool hall. Craig would have been texting him for the last hour and Carmen would be preparing dinner, pissed. But today, he sat alone in his living room reviewing HIV information and preparing to deliver his mother this dreadful blow. He would trade anything to be fighting with Carmen now. He would trade anything to have her win the fight, forcing him to spend another boring night at home. He would trade anything not to be sitting alone on the sofa, drinking wine from a beer mug, and being HIV positive.

After a nap, Damon woke up and began getting ready to go to his mother's house. He seriously considered leaving town without a trace, but that wouldn't be fair to his family and most importantly, London. As he thought of him, tears welled up in his eyes. He and Rachel had spoken a few times since she went to the doctor's office with him. They decided they would wait until they had more information before they told London. How would they explain to him what this meant? *He* wasn't even sure what this meant? He pulled on his jacket and walked down the front steps into the cold Chicago night air, headed for his mother's house.

Damon walked up the front porch stairs to Sharon's house and knocked on the door. She greeted him with a smile and invited him in. She still had a few curlers in the front of her hair.

"What's going on with you?" she asked. "You miss Carmen, don't you?"

"I do, but that's not why I'm here. Sit down for a minute, Ma." Damon removed his coat and laid it across the arm of the sofa. As he did, he noticed the picture of his father that normally sat on the end table was gone. He took his mother by the hand. "Ma, I have something to tell you."

"What is it, boy?" she snapped. "I don't have time to play with you." She took the six curlers out of her hair and fingered the curls loose.

"Mom, I went to the doctor the other day."

Sharon placed her hand over her mouth.

"I'm HIV positive."

Sharon sat silently. Damon could hear the theme from Entertainment Tonight coming from Sharon's TV upstairs.

Her voice was solemn. "I know a good woman like Carmen didn't give it to you so that means you cheated. What have I always told you about keeping that thing in your pants?" Sharon shook her head. "I raised you boys better than that.

"I know, Ma"

"Is that why she left? Did you give it to her?"

"I didn't tell her until today. I didn't know I had been infected until after she was gone."

"Does she have it?"

"Like I said, I just told her today. I don't know if she has it. All I know is that she didn't take it well."

Sharon stood up. "I'm sure she didn't.

"I'm sorry, ma." Damon pulled the pamphlet out of his jacket pocket and laid it on the table.

"You're sorry? Why Damon? Why do you insist on messing up everything for yourself? Sometimes it seems as if you do stuff on purpose. As soon as you start behaving and acting responsibly, out of the blue you do something that doesn't make sense. Does this make sense to you?" Sharon glared at Damon. "If you were going to cheat, why didn't you use a condom?" Damon could see Sharon's eyes welling up with tears.

Damon stared at the floor. He still had to tell his sisters and Ike.

His mother interrupted his thoughts. "What did the doctor say?" A tear streamed down the right side of her face. "What now?"

"I haven't been back to the doctor yet."

"You need to get to the doctor right away. They have to start you on all those medications. I see people that have it at the food bank sometimes. When you all were small, HIV was rampant and then for several years you didn't hear that much about it. Now it appears it's on the rise again."

They heard a car pull into the driveway.

"That's Ronald. I'll tell him I can't see him tonight. He can come by tomorrow."

Damon stood up. "I'm fine. You enjoy your company."

Damon put on his coat and headed for the door. Sharon walked behind him. She hugged him and kissed him on the cheek. "Everything will be okay. This isn't the first time our family has gone through a tough time. God brought us through that and He'll get you through this. And we'll all be right there with you. Do you need me to come by tomorrow?

"No. I'll call you and let you know what the doctor says."

"I'll come with you."

Damon smiled, "I'm a grown man. What would I look like with my mother taking me to the doctor?

"Oh, now you're a grown man." She nodded her head, sarcastically.

Damon walked out the door. A full moon hung overhead.

"Bye, baby." Sharon said.

Damon greeted Ronald as he walked down the front steps. As he passed the house, he looked into the window and saw his mother collapse into Ronald's arms. His heart panged with regret. He had now told Carmen and his mother. Next in line was Craig.

Chapter 39

Damon stretched as the morning sun beamed through the window, slowly stirring him from sleep. Every morning, for the past few weeks, when he opened his eyes, he prayed that the nightmare was over. Today, he was having no such luck. It was Monday and he was still HIV positive. He looked around the room to orient himself. He had calls to make; the doctor's office, for one. He also wanted to call his job and notify his manager he would be out for the next few weeks. He needed time to absorb everything that was going on. Because it was a slow period, he knew his manager would not mind. He also needed to call Craig. They had traded a few texts and a few quick calls over the past few weeks, but Craig was unaware that Damon felt like his life was ending. Damon slowly got out of bed and adjusted his plaid pajama bottoms, scratched the baby fine hair on his stomach and walked to the kitchen. He poured himself a glass of milk, picked up the *Next Steps* packet off the kitchen table and reluctantly removed the cordless phone from its base. He called Dr. Lipkin's office and scheduled an appointment for Friday of the following week. After that, he called Carmen and left her another message. Finally, he called his manager at the car dealership and explained he had a personal emergency and needed to take a few weeks off. He had decided he would keep his status from his co-workers; the doctor explained it was in his rights to do so, as long as he didn't put anyone else's health in danger.

After the manager gave his blessing for the time off, Damon walked to the living room and sat on the sofa. He recalled how happy Carmen was when they bought it from a discount furniture store uptown shortly after he moved in. It barely fit through the front door, they had to remove the legs and reattach them once inside. He lifted his feet and placed them on the glass coffee table. He stared gravely at the phone he held in his hands. He slowly started pressing the buttons, dialing Craig's number. On the third ring, he answered.

"Where you been, man?" Craig's tone was upbeat.

"Where have you been?" Damon shot back. His voice contained a smile.

"Working…that's about it."

"How's Samantha? Has she forgiven you, yet?"

Craig laughed into the phone. "Not yet."

They laughed together and then Damon started with the nature of his call.

"Craig, I got some really bad news the other day." Damon said, knowing it had been almost a month ago.

"Yeah? What happened?" Craig was still laughing.

"This is serious, Craig."

Damon's tone turned Craig's mood somber. "What happened?"

"I'm HIV positive."

"Stop kidding around, man. That's not funny."

"I wish I was kidding. I went to the doctor and got the confirmation." His voice sank. "She got me."

"Carmen?"

"You know better than that. It wasn't her. Remember that fine chick at the pool hall last summer?"

Craig paused in order to recall the *fine chick*. "I think I remember."

"I was real drunk that night. You and Wendell stopped and talked to me while I was sitting at the bar with her.

After ya'll left, I went to her house. Biggest mistake of my life."

"How do you know it was her?"

"I bumped into her on Christmas Eve and she told me she had it. I went to the doctor and got tested. I've got it, too."

"I can't believe this?" Craig paused. "Did Carmen get it *from* you?"

"I don't know yet. I've been leaving messages for her and she won't return my calls. She moved out."

"Man…I had no idea. I'm sorry."

"It's all good." Damon tried to sound positive. "Now that Carmen's gone, I can hang out at the pool hall whenever and as long as I want. Maybe we can get together this week."

"Yeah…maybe. Damon, I gotta' run. I have another call coming in on the other line. I'll catch up with you later. Stay strong, man."

"Yeah…I will."

Damon hung up the phone secretly fearing that Craig wouldn't be able to handle his new HIV status. Perhaps the lifelong friendship he had with a man he was closer to than his own brother had just ended over three tiny little letters.

Chapter 40

Cathy sat with her foot on the bed, painting her toenails navy pearl blue. Carmen sat in a chair in the opposite corner of her bedroom.

"You're going to get that on the bed." Carmen cautioned.

Cathy continued to paint her toenails, albeit carefully, since her foot rested on her favorite blue comforter. "Did you talk to Damon yet?"

"Not yet. I'm going to have to return his calls, though. I'm sure he is worried sick over my test results."

"I wouldn't take it that far. If he had been that concerned about you, he wouldn't have slept with the slut in the first place."

"You're so cold, Cathy. Things happen in life."

"You're too forgiving. You and Momma, both. I'm a firm believer that life gives you exactly what you demand from it. I demand someone who will treat me the way that I deserve to be treated. No slip-ups, no mistakes. I won't settle for anything less."

"But look at us, Cathy. We're alone."

"Whoop–ti– do." Cathy said, still focusing on her foot. "I prefer it that way. Before I let a man treat me like a dog..." Cathy looked up from her toes and raised a sharp eyebrow, "I know you aren't thinking of taking Damon back."

"No, but I want to be married again. Don't you?"

"Of course, I do. But I have a low tolerance for clowns. That's why I kicked Stanley to the curb. He keeps begging me to take him back. He can dream on." She placed the applicator back in the bottle and shook it.

"Poor Stanley."

"Poor Stanley? Poor me. He's a liar."

Carmen stood up and arched her back in a stretch. "I need to get some sleep. I have to be to work early tomorrow for a meeting." She said goodnight and walked to Cathy's spare bedroom and crashed for the evening.

***

Cathy stood at her post sorting mail the next day. She hated sorting mail. Thankfully, that was only part of her duties. She had worked at the post office for nine years and fortunately, she made a decent living. Where would she go with no college education and earn the money she was earning? Besides, the benefits the government gave her were excellent. She wasn't going anywhere. She sorted away.

Sylvia walked up and tapped Cathy on the shoulder. Sylvia was Cathy's supervisor. She was plain and quiet—a little too quiet for Cathy's taste. She always looked like she was up to something and Cathy didn't know if she could trust her. When Cathy turned around to see who was interrupting her, she saw Sylvia holding a bouquet of two dozen red roses. Cathy knew immediately who they were from. She read the card anyway.

I'm sorry. If you would stop being so stubborn, I will explain. I love you...Stanley.

"You can keep them," Cathy told Sylvia, who looked at her with astonishment.

"He must have messed up really bad."

"He did."

Sylvia walked away admiring the flowers.

Cathy dropped the card in her pocket and returned to her duties.

At five o'clock she left work and headed home. She walked in the door, tossed her keys on the hallway console table, and began emptying her work apron pockets. She pulled out her ring, which she placed back on her thumb, two butterscotch candies, and Stanley's card. She sighed heavily as she threw it on the table, and then walked to the kitchen to make her and Carmen something to eat.

Cathy heard Carmen enter the house about thirty minutes later. Carmen came into the kitchen carrying the note Stanley had attached to the flowers. Cathy was standing at the stove.

"He obviously really cares about you." Carmen stood, waving the card.

"Yeah…lying to someone usually means they care."

"I wished Damon would have pursued me like that." Carmen sat down at the kitchen table. "I get it now. When a man really wants to be with you, he pursues you. It shouldn't be the other way around."

Cathy stirred the chili, turned off the burner and sat down at the other end of the table. "I wish he would leave me alone. He's been leaving messages every few days, and today he sent flowers to my job. That's where the card came from.

"Where are the flowers?"

"I let my supervisor have them."

"Cathy, you're a trip. What's giving the man's flowers away going to do?"

Cathy shrugged her shoulders.

"You should call him."

"For what?"

"I don't know...say thank you? Take it from me. A man that's making that much effort to get you back can't be all bad. Maybe he's telling the truth and there is a logical explanation."

Carmen walked to the stove and filled a bowl up with chili. They heard a knock at the door. Cathy turned and looked at Carmen.

"Cathy baby, open up. It's me...Stanley." He forced his voice through the door.

"I'm telling you, Cathy. That man really loves you."

Cathy sat at the table and continued to eat her chili.

"I'm letting him in." Carmen ran out of the kitchen toward the door.

"No, Carmen. Don't!" Cathy said in a loud whisper, trying to stop Carmen before she reached the door.

It was too late. Carmen ducked around the corner, opened the door and let Stanley in. She came back into the kitchen with Stanley following behind her. Cathy rolled her eyes as Carmen picked up her orange plastic bowl of chili and carried it off to Cathy's guest room.

Cathy frowned in amazement at Stanley who immediately dropped down on his knees in her kitchen. He lifted Cathy's hand and pulled a diamond engagement ring out of his pocket. The ring's size removed the look of anger from Cathy's face. She caught herself and put the scowl back on.

"What are you doing, Stanley? Get up off the dirty floor." She tried to pull him up by his arm. All she was getting was sleeve.

"Cathy, baby, I love you. I'm so sorry," he begged. "There's an explanation—a reason why I didn't tell you the truth about me leaving town. I can show you better than I can tell you."

"What kind of games are you up to, Stanley? It's over. Why are you making this so difficult? It really is simple...you need to move on." Cathy continued to yank his arm upwards, trying to get him off the floor. "C'mon, get up."

Stanley stood up. He grabbed Cathy's hand again, and tried to put the ring on. Cathy got another glimpse of the monstrous thing. Whatever the reason for lying, by the size of that ring, Cathy could tell he really was sorry. She snatched her hand back.

"Can we just go for a drive, Cathy? I'll explain everything." He placed the ring back in his pocket.

Cathy turned around to make sure Carmen was still in her room. She left her chili on the table, retrieved her coat out of the hall closet, and followed Stanley out into the night so he could *show her* the reason why he lied. This had to be good.

As they drove, Cathy continually asked Stanley to tell her what this was all about. She had the strongest suspicion that Stanley was married. Why wouldn't he just admit it? Perhaps he was a polygamist like the man in Utah she saw on *60 Minutes.*

Stanley pulled a white silk scarf out of the console between the seats. "Here put this on."

Cathy snapped her neck. "Okay...now you're crazy, or you think I am. No way, I'm wearing a blindfold...anywhere. You might try to dump my body somewhere. You can forget about that. If a blindfold is required, you can just turn around and take me back."

Stanley laughed. "I've missed you and that fiery temper of yours so much the past several weeks. Okay, that's fair. No blind fold. I only wanted to surprise you." He dropped the scarf on his lap and continued driving.

A few minutes later, Cathy and Stanley arrived at a quaint residential community. Stanley pulled up in front of a brick Tudor and parked the car. A white trellis arched over the sidewalk that led to the house. Stanley got out of the car and walked around to the passenger's side and opened the door for Cathy. She didn't budge.

"Whose house is this?"

"You'll see."

"Take me home, Stanley. I have had enough of this nonsense. I guess you want me to go in there and confront your wife so she can carve me up into little pieces and we'll all make the WGN news. Keep dreaming. Take me home, or do I need to hail a cab.

"This is my house. I just bought it. You always wanted to see my place. Well...this is my place. C'mon in and see the inside.

Cathy slowly got out of the car and cautiously approached the house. Stanley walked up to the door, unlocked it and escorted Cathy inside. He flipped the switch on the wall and the light came on. Cathy carefully looked around.

He led her into the kitchen and sat her down in front of some papers that lay on the table. Cathy looked down at the documents. She folded her arms across her chest. "What's this about, Stanley?"

"Read it."

Cathy looked over the documents. It was the deed to the house and it was in both their names.

"What is this?"

"I bought this house for us."

"Are you telling me this is why you lied?"

"No, this is why I lied." Stanley pulled another set of documents out of his inside coat pocket and slid them across the table. It was divorce papers.

Cathy stood up. She was disgusted. "I knew you were married."

"Wait a minute, Cathy... look at the date on the papers."

Cathy stopped and looked down. She scanned down the page looking for the filing date. It was June 24th, the day after they had met.

Stanley walked around the table and gently guided Cathy back down into her chair. He sat next to her. "I filed the papers the day after I met you. I was already unhappy, and had been for years. I had planned to file, but I got so busy with work, time dragged on. Then I met you and everything changed. It was like the heavens opened up. I got a lawyer and filed the next day. I knew if I told you I was married, you wouldn't understand. I was afraid you would stop seeing me if you knew I lived in the house with her, so I tried to keep it from you. I lied and told you I was out of town that day because her mother fell sick. She had family coming in from out of town, and I knew I wouldn't be able to get away. Even though things weren't right between her and me, I felt I still needed to be there for her and my son."

"Your son!"

"I also have a grown son I never told you about. He's 22. He moved to Texas right after he graduated. I've already told him about you.

"Wow, Stanley. This is a lot to absorb." Cathy flipped through the papers. She glanced over at the boxes in the corner of the kitchen.

"I know...I'm asking you to marry me. The divorce will be finalized this week. All I need is her signature. She's agreed to everything." Stanley grasped Cathy's hand. "Can I show you the place?"

Cathy tentatively got up from her chair. She followed Stanley as he began the tour in the kitchen. As she walked, she ran her hand along the white wood cabinets. She stopped and tried to get a view of what was outside the kitchen window, but it was too dark. She followed him upstairs to the master bedroom. She liked the house. It needed updating, but had more than enough room for her and Stanley.

"I like it," she smiled, inviting Stanley to smile in return.

Stanley sat her down on the bed. He pulled the ring out of his pocket and got down on one knee. He took her hand and placed it on her finger. This time she accepted it.

Stanley drove Cathy home. She couldn't stop looking at the ring. Once at the house, she woke Carmen up with the news. Carmen tried to wipe the sleep from her eyes as Cathy eagerly told her about Stanley's surprise. Cathy bequeathed her condo to Carmen and showed her the ring. Everything had happened so fast, but deep down, despite her outward toughness, she wanted to be with Stanley. She wanted him to be the good man she had been waiting for, and she just found out he was.

Chapter 41

Damon left the doctor's office on Friday with his head spinning. It was full of T–cells, CD counts and viral loads. Instructions on what to do, and what not to do. He had to protect himself from everything the doctor said or he could get very sick. He couldn't be around people with viruses or colds, he was to avoid pets and raw seafood—that wouldn't be a problem. He had to wash his hands frequently and carefully, as well as any fruits and vegetables he ate. He had to constantly check all expiration dates on the foods in the refrigerator; which would be a challenge now that Carmen was gone. He didn't know how many times he had poured clumpy milk into a glass and then noticed the date had expired. He had to keep the house clean. Keep the floors mopped. The doctor even told him to be careful with leftovers. They had to be reheated thoroughly, and if they were more than 48 hours old, he should steer clear. His mind was in a tailspin. On top of all that, he had six medications he had to take twice daily, which meant he would need to carry them with him at all times. He was overwhelmed. Most days it seemed fear and exhaustion would overtake him.

Damon entered his brownstone and went to his bedroom. His phone was vibrating in his pocket. He pulled it out and saw he had a text from Carmen,

Damon, my results were negative. Never in my life have I been so happy that a man didn't want to make love to me ;-) I will keep you in my prayers.
Carmen

A sense of relief washed over him. He flashed back to the months they were together. Their intimate moments had been sporadic—toward the end, hardly at all. Physically, he felt nothing for her. Maybe on some level he knew he was being dishonest. Perhaps it was guilt that kept him from desiring her the way that a man should. Every day he tried as best as he could to love her, but he couldn't. At least with Candy, everything was on the up and up. She knew he wouldn't be hers, but it was different with Carmen. All she wanted was for Damon to love her, and although he cared about her, it wasn't love. And he knew it never would be.

Damon pulled the blinds shut and crawled into bed. He slept off and on for the next two days. He woke up and watched TV and slept some more. Sharon came by and brought him some food. She had told his siblings the news and they had sent their love along with her, but no one had come to visit yet. Damon was afraid they had abandoned him. Sharon assured him they would come eventually and that he was making a mountain out of a molehill. She left behind a plate of greens, along with words of encouragement. He was terrified of how he would be treated by everyone—Ike, Craig, Pat, Mona, Cheryl. By the end of the week, he had reached the pit of despair. He stopped answering the phone and continued to sleep most of the day.

***

When Craig woke up, his mind was still reeling with the news Damon had given him. Every second of the day, he was consumed with the fact he had been playing Russian roulette by sleeping with random women for years. He usually carried protection, but the fact that he was more concerned about knocking someone up then contracting HIV chilled him every time he thought of it. What about those times—he could recall them vividly, he didn't have protection and refused to let the opportunity go by, so he tossed caution to the wind? Could he be sick, too? He had recently had a physical—what if the doctor missed something? Damon's news had shaken him. Not only had being a player cost him the woman he loved, he had been putting himself at a far greater risk than he had realized. He was done. He had to have Samantha, now. He wasn't taking no for an answer. As far as he was concerned, she didn't have a choice in the matter.

Craig got dressed and raced over to Samantha's restaurant. It was early and *Sam's Place* wouldn't open for a few hours. He parked his car and entered the kitchen through the back door. Samantha was slicing vegetables for the afternoon lunch rush. She looked up when she saw Craig walking through the door. She casually continued slicing.

"Samantha...the party's over. This is the end of this nonsense. You and I are going to get back together and move beyond this. I've told you I'm sorry, and that that girl meant nothing."

A wooden bowl was at the edge of the counter and Samantha slid it closer.

"Did you hear me Samantha? This is over." Craig raised his voice. "I'm telling you I'm ready to commit, one hundred percent. Do you hear me?"

Samantha looked up from the yellow squash she was slicing. She turned around and looked at her staff members who had taken notice. Jesse, who was much bigger than Craig, removed his chef's hat and stood in the kitchen doorway, wiping his hands on his apron, watching Craig carefully.

Craig's mood and tone were becoming agitated. He started to yell.

"Answer me, Samantha! I'm not going to keep wasting my time."

Samantha looked up from the squash again. Her face and words were stoic, "Once a cheater...always a cheater. Please leave my restaurant and take your lies with you."

Before Craig knew it, Damon's news, and the frustration of Samantha making him grovel had caught up with him. He grabbed Samantha's arm and pulled her away from the counter. In a matter of seconds Jesse, the waiter and the busboy were all over him. They pried his hand from Samantha's arm, pulled him out the backdoor, made a few threats and slammed the door shut. Craig regrouped and charged back in. Jesse stopped him in the doorway while Samantha picked up the phone to call the police. He violently shoved Craig to the floor. Craig stood up and was about to charge Jesse again when he heard Samantha on the phone talking to the 911 operator. Reason started to kick in. He stood at the back doorway, panting in frustration. He couldn't get around Jesse, and the cops were on the way. He wiped his brow and raised his arm to look underneath his armpit to make sure he hadn't ripped his navy Burberry blazer. He cut his eyes at Samantha and walked out the back door. His wheels tore through the gravel, tossing it everywhere as he left the parking lot.

He picked up the phone and called Damon to vent. His emotions had created a pressure cooker in his mind and it was about to blow. Samantha had his heart and mind twisted in knots.

He was frustrated when he got Damon's voicemail again. He had called Damon several times earlier during the week, but Damon wasn't returning his calls. Craig looked at his watch, it was still early—Damon didn't have to be at work until around ten o'clock normally. Concerned about him, Craig turned around and drove to his house.

Craig parked his Lexus on the street and ran up the stairs to Damon's brownstone. He felt guilty for not being there for Damon for the past several weeks. He had been so preoccupied with his strategy and quest for Samantha, he had neglected his best friend, whose wife had left, and who was now HIV positive. Craig's heart ached for Damon. He was still trying to process everything. HIV positive or not, Damon was like a brother and he knew he needed to be there for him.

He knocked on the door several times, but Damon didn't answer. How sick was he? He didn't say when he told him. Maybe he was in much worse shape than he had let on. Craig tried to lean over and look in the front window, but he couldn't see through the curtains Carmen had hung. He looked up and down the street for Damon's car and saw it a few doors down. He knocked again, but there was still no answer. He went to the backyard and rapped on the door loudly, kicking it twice. He had a feeling Damon was in the house and was clueless as to why he wouldn't answer his phone or the door. Concerned it might be the worst; he pulled out his wallet and withdrew a credit card. Time to rely on his old school, South Side skills. His knee creaked as he crouched down to examine the lock on the door, a leftover remnant of his high school track meets. As he went to place the credit card against the lock to pick it, he noticed he was holding his American Express Platinum card. That card was his lifeline. He pulled his wallet back out and placed the treasured card back in its rightful spot, taking out an old gas card. He went to work on the lock. It had been years since he had done it, but suddenly the lock popped and the door opened.

Craig slowly walked into the house. He stood in the kitchen still holding the back door open, and called out to Damon in a low voice. He walked into the living room and looked across the room. The door to the bedroom was closed. Craig walked over to the bedroom door and knocked. He turned the knob and slowly eased the tall wooden door open. Damon was in the bed. As he approached him, he was relieved to hear him snoring. He walked over to the window and began opening the blinds. Damon woke up.

"How long you been like this?" Craig asked.

Damon squinted at Craig and used his hand to shield his eyes from the sun.

Craig tapped his arm. "Have you eaten?"

Damon shook his head. He sat up in the bed. His voice was still sleepy. "How'd you get in?"

"Credit card. Just like back in the day." He fanned the air in front of his face. "You stink."

Craig walked to the kitchen and grabbed a beer mug from the cabinet. He was relieved to see him and glad he looked the same. He was probably just depressed...understandably so.

He poured Coke in the beer mug and found some ham and cheese in the refrigerator. He made Damon a sandwich and placed it on a plate. He carried the sandwich and the beer mug to the bedroom and placed it on the nightstand.

"You been to work?"

Damon shook his head.

"I'll camp out here for a while until you're feeling better."

Craig walked back to the kitchen and poured himself a glass of Coke. He went to the living room and sat on the sofa. He grabbed the remote and turned on the TV. He settled in to an episode of Jerry Springer and spent the remainder of the day on Damon's couch watching TV. When night came, he slept there.

The next morning, Craig awakened on the couch. He called his office to check in and told his assistant, Victoria, he would be in and out of the office over the next few days. He walked back to the bedroom. Damon was still sleeping.

He yelled out, "Damon, I'm going to go get us something to eat."

Damon turned over and placed his pillow over his head. Craig laughed and left. He went by his house for a quick shower and changed his clothes. On his way to McDonald's he called Samantha at the restaurant. She answered.

"Sam's Place."

"Samantha…don't hang up. I'm calling to apologize for treating you like that. I was wrong."

"You're right. You were wrong."

"You didn't have to sick Guido on me." Craig said with laughter.

"Next time I won't need Jesse. I've had a restraining order placed against you."

Craig thought about his business. "What?"

"You heard me. A restraining order."

"Samantha, really? It's come to this? All I want to do is love you and take care of you for the rest of my life and you file a restraining order? Good riddance."

Craig hung up the phone. He had done everything within his power to convince Samantha to take him back. He was finding out that mentally, she was his match. Always calm, always in control and always determined. With her by his side, he felt there was nothing in life that he couldn't accomplish. Now, all he had to do was get her to cooperate.

Craig went through the McDonald's drive through and ordered several items off the breakfast menu. He and Damon were close, but he had no idea what he ate for breakfast. He got two bags of food, paid the attendant and drove back to Damon's house. He entered the bedroom and placed the bags on the bed next to Damon. He pulled pancakes and sausages, and an orange juice out of the bag for himself, and sat the bags on the floor beside the bed. He returned to the living room sofa and picked up the remote. He would stay with Damon until the cloud lifted.

For the next forty-eight hours he hung out at his house. Finally, on Thursday afternoon he heard some movement in the bedroom. Craig turned the TV down with the remote. He smiled when he realized the whooshing sound he heard was water running. Damon was in the shower.

A few minutes later Damon emerged with jeans on and no shirt. He was brushing his hair. The scent of Irish Spring filled the air.

Damon sat down in the living room chair opposite him on the sofa.

"When do you go back to work?" Craig asked.

"Monday."

"You handling things okay? You've been dealt a tough blow."

Damon shifted in the chair. "Yeah, I'm alright, I guess. How's Samantha?"

"Still stubborn as ever. She filed a restraining order against me."

"What did you do?"

"I admit…I got a little pissed off. She's being ridiculous. All this over some stupid girl, whose name I can barely remember. I grabbed her—"

"You grabbed her?"

"Yeah. It was nothing. Seriously. She knows she's got the upper hand and she loves it." Craig slid his foot into one of his shoes and began to lace it up. "Have you heard from Carmen?"

"Yeah, she sent a text message. Her test results were negative."

Craig smiled. "That's good. Is she coming back?"

"I don't think so."

"Do you want her to come back?"

Damon shook his head. "It's better this way."

"I saw all those medications in the kitchen." He teased Damon, "Do any of them get you high?" He laughed at his own joke.

"Unfortunately, no." Damon smiled. Although, they both drank, getting high was never their thing. Still, he appreciated the levity from Craig.

"What did Ike and 'em say?"

"I haven't really talked to anybody yet. I think they're all in shock."

Craig stood up. "Might help if you answered your phone." He put on his jacket.

"I'm going to run to the office. I'll come by later and check on you. Don't make me jimmy the lock again."

"Carmen's key is in the kitchen window sill."

Craig walked over to Damon and they bumped fists. "Later." He walked to the kitchen, grabbed the key out of the window, left five crisp one hundred dollar bills on the table and exited through the back door.

Chapter 42

Carmen woke on Saturday morning and drove to her mother's house. She would soon be a divorcee, and with Cathy occupied getting her new house ready, she found herself with more time on her hands. Carmen told her mother that Damon confessed to an affair after she left him. Her mother insisted they could work things out, but Carmen knew better. She had remained silent about Damon's HIV status to keep Gert from worrying unnecessarily. Right now, as long as she was negative, there was no need to say anything about it. She was fearful that eventually Cathy would leak it, even though she begged her not to.

Carmen entered the house and found her mother in the kitchen making tea.

"Hey, Momma."

Gert looked over her shoulder. "Hey, baby girl. Have a seat." Gert walked to the refrigerator, took out a plate of sliced lemons and sat them on the table. Carmen could hear her father upstairs stirring around.

"Have you talked to Cathy?"

"She asked me to come by the house later and look at some drapes she picked out." Carmen took the cup of tea from Gert and sat it on the table. "I can't believe the wicked Witch of The West is getting married." She squeezed lemon in her tea and stirred vigorously, clanking the delicate porcelain with the spoon.

"How are you holding up?"

Carmen opened the sugar pot that matched her teacup, both bequeathed to Gert by her grandmother, and scooped out a small amount of sugar placing it in her cup. "I'm fine.

My marriage didn't work out, but I'm honestly happy for her. I think Stanley is a good guy."

"Are you upset about the way things ended between you and Damon?"

"Of course I am, but the reality is that things were never right between us. I had time to adjust and prepare myself. A few months into it, I became aware of the fact that he may never love me. As time went on, it became clear that he never would. I began to look back over things and could see how we ended up the way we did. I wanted to get married so badly. I pushed and pushed. He never showed any enthusiasm. I was so determined. I just didn't want to see it."

"What about your place?"

"I told him he could have it. It might be a little tight for him, but I think he'll be able to manage. Cathy told me I could take over the lease on her condo."

"When will the divorce be final?"

"I found a cheap attorney. He said the process will be simple since Damon isn't contesting, and there aren't any joint assets or children. Once we fill out the paperwork, we go to the hearing and that's it. I plan on having it finalized before the end of spring."

"Is this what you really want?"

"Yeah, I think so."

Gert breathed deeply and shrugged her shoulders. "Cathy dropped off some bridal magazines the other day. She wanted me to look at the dresses she's marked. You can help me. Although we both know that whichever ones we choose, she'll pick the opposite. I don't even know why she asked me. You get started while I fix your father something to eat." Gert removed a skillet from underneath the cabinet and lopped a huge hunk of butter in it.

"Have you eaten?"

Carmen's eyes bulged when she saw the amount of butter Gert had placed in the skillet. To think she grew up eating like that. "The tea is fine for now. I'll grab something later."

Carmen spread the magazines out on the table. She put the fact that her own wedding had been a huge waste of time and money out of her mind, and began leafing through the magazines looking for the perfect dress for Cathy.

Chapter 43

Damon purchased a whole chicken at the grocery store since it was cheaper, not realizing when he got home he would have to cut it up. He called Sharon and carefully followed her instructions on how to prepare it. He floured the chicken, found the largest skillet Carmen had, and filled it with Crisco. Sharon told him to make sure the grease was hot enough so he waited until the oil started to boil and dropped in the chicken. A searing sound rose from the skillet along with a puff of heat. It only took minutes for the kitchen to become a hot, smoky mess. He was standing in front of the T.V. trying to catch the last quarter of the Bulls game, and at the same time not burn up his chicken, when the phone rang. He wiped his flour covered hands on his jeans and answered it.

"Hello." He grabbed a fork and turned the chicken, tentatively, while dodging the scalding hot droplets of grease. His tank top left most of his upper body as well as his arms exposed.

"Damon, its Ike."

"What's up?" Damon was taken off guard. He walked to the living room, grabbed the remote and turned down the game.

"Momma told us what happened."

"Yeah."

"How are you?"

"I'm good, man. I have no choice but to be. How are Diane and the kids?"

"They're good. Dianne cried when I told her."

Damon winced. He had the utmost respect for Dianne. He was embarrassed that he had done something so irresponsible. His one little mishap was affecting everybody. "She cried? Why?"

"You know women, man. Who knows?" Ike said with a nervous laugh. "We're all here at momma's house. We were going to come over. We wanted to make sure you were home."

Damon paused. Here came the tough moment. He hadn't spoken to his siblings since the news hit. Now they were coming. He had to look them in the face."

"C'mon. I'm here."

Damon turned off the chicken and went to the bedroom and changed his shirt. He returned to the kitchen in a button-down and quickly washed and half dried the mountain of dishes in the sink. He rushed to the living room, picked up the old newspapers and fast food cartons and threw them in the trash. About a half hour later, the door bell rang. Damon opened it and saw Pat, Cheryl, Mona and Ike. He opened the door wide and they walked in. The five of them sat in the living room. Everyone was quiet for the first few seconds. Damon laughed to himself. It felt like an intervention.

Finally, Ike spoke. "We don't know what to say, Damon. Momma's going on like it's no big deal. We don't know what to think."

"Why think anything? The doctors say if I'm careful and do the right things; it doesn't have to be a death sentence. And no Mona…the kids can't catch it."

"Me?" Mona placed her bony hand to her chest. She was tall and lanky. "What makes you think I was thinking that the kids could catch it?"

"You didn't bring them here. You never go anywhere without the twins."

"That's not why. This is serious. My kids are small. They can't process something like this."

"They could have gone to the bedroom to watch T.V." Damon looked at the group. "The other kids could have, too."

Mona stood up, "Let's go, Ike."

"Wait a minute. Everybody's tense." Ike said. "Damon, we're scared. We're scared for you and we don't know what to expect." He looked up. "Mona, sit down."

Mona fell back onto the couch. "I don't understand how you could let something like this happen. You were a married man."

"I didn't do it on purpose."

"You cheated on purpose!" Mona stood up again.

"You don't know the whole story, Mona."

Ike grabbed Mona by the back of her sweater and pulled her down onto the sofa. "All this bickering can wait. Damon, tell us what the doctor said. The girls are just afraid. They don't want to admit it, but we are all afraid. I mean…HIV kills people."

"No, AIDS does. I don't have AIDS. If I do what I'm supposed to do, and take my medications I can expect to live for a while. They can't tell me exactly how long, but there is no need to believe that I won't be around for years to come." Damon walked to the kitchen and picked up the rest of the pamphlets. He came back to the living room and handed one to each of his siblings. "This will give you some more information."

They looked at the pamphlets until Pat said, "I'm starving and I smell chicken."

"There's some in there on the stove. I just cooked it." Damon nodded toward the kitchen.

Pat got up and went to the kitchen and Cheryl followed her. They opened the refrigerator, found a bag of frozen corn and put some in a pot on the stove.

"Momma said you got it from some girl you met in a bar." Mona said.

"Yep."

"You're so stupid, Damon. You could have given it to Carmen."

"Know that already." Damon was trying to be patient with his youngest sister.

Ike stood up. "I'm hungry, too." He turned to Mona, "You need to apologize." He joined his sisters in the kitchen.

Mona and Damon remained locked in a rigid glare. Damon already felt bad, but for some reason Mona seemed to want to punish him more for his mistake.

"Mona, I feel real bad for what I did. There was no excuse for it. I'm sorry, but I really don't understand why you're so upset. I'm the one that is facing an uncertain future."

"I never told anyone this, but about five years ago I looked on Ed's computer and saw he had been emailing some woman."

Damon sat up in his chair and looked directly at Mona.

Mona waived her hand. "No need to get all huffy. Besides, what could you possibly say to him? You're no better."

Damon relaxed back into his seat.

"The emails weren't real obvious, but I could tell from what I was reading they had become curious about each other."

"What happened?"

"I confronted Ed. He said they just emailed and that he hadn't crossed the line, nor did he intend to. Allegedly, she had a crush on him."

"Do you believe him?"

"Let's just say we moved beyond it. I'll never have the trust I once had for him and in a way…" Mona's gaze fell gently to the floor, "he doesn't know this, but I never saw him the same way after that."

Damon could feel Mona's anguish as she spoke. He realized that if Edward had done more than just emailed, there was a possibility he could have contracted HIV and given it to Mona. The thought of Edward being unfaithful to his sister blindsided him. There had been times, when he got real angry, that he wanted to blame his indiscretion on the fact that Carmen made him angry, or the fact that he never wanted to get married in the first place. Listening to Mona, he realized there could never be an excuse for betraying the trust of someone who loves you. Seeing his sister's pain made him consider deeply what that must feel like.

"I'm sorry that happened to you, Sis. I was wrong, and I'll be paying for that one mistake for the rest of my life. If I had the chance to do it all over again, I would become the poster child for monogamy."

Mona gave a solemn smile.

Pat, Ike and Cheryl came back into the living room and placed the plate of chicken and a bowl of corn on the cocktail table along with a loaf of bread, paper plates and cups, which Damon filled with wine from one of Carmen's leftover bottles. The five of them began to dig in. They laughed together about old times, their mother and Mr. Ronald, and toasted to new futures—assuring Damon that their bond was still as tight as ever.

Chapter 44

On Saturday, Damon pulled into the coffee shop where Carmen suggested they meet. She had contacted him earlier in the week regarding finalizing the divorce. As he walked through the doors, he was nervous about seeing her. The last time they met, he delivered such dreadful news and inflicted such pain. He was glad that this visit, although not exactly joyous, would be better than their last.

He spotted her sitting at a small square table in front of the window. She stood up and hugged him when he approached the table. "Hello, Damon." Her greeting soothed him. "How have you been?" Her eyes were filled with concern and it reminded Damon how thoughtful she was.

"I'm fine. And you?" Damon sat at the table opposite her. "You look great."

"Thanks." She smiled. "Things are going well for me. I can't complain."

"What's that crazy sister of yours up to?"

"She's busy planning her wedding."

"Cathy?" Damon couldn't believe she found someone that would marry her. Unlike Carmen, Damon felt she was just plain evil.

"Yep."

"Wow! Good for her." Damon reached his hand across the table and placed it on top of Carmen's. He leaned in and said, "I'm sorry Carmen...for everything."

"I know." Damon followed her gaze. It rested on a tall gentleman sitting in the back. He smiled at Carmen, she smiled back.

"Is he with you?" Damon asked in a low voice.

Carmen gently pulled her hand from underneath Damon's. "Yeah."

Damon smiled at Carmen and picked up the silver ball-point pen that Carmen had laid on the table. He eyed the manila envelope that was sitting next to it. "Well, let's get this over with."

Carmen opened the envelope and handed Damon papers to sign. He looked over the documents while she explained to him what would happen next in the divorce process.

After he had signed the papers, Carmen reached in her purse and handed him the business card of one of the nurses she worked with at the insurance company. She explained that she volunteered on the weekends with an HIV support program. She also gave him one of her Aunt's business cards.

"You still want me to go see that headshrinker?" He winked at Carmen.

She smiled, "If you ever need someone to talk to, she might be able to help."

He took the cards and thanked her before getting up to leave. He hugged her and told her goodbye. Damon watched her as she walked toward the back of the coffee shop. The gentleman pulled out a chair for her and she joined him at the table.

Damon walked through the doors to the parking lot. He could feel the warmth of the sun on his face. The moment was bittersweet. He was happy it was over, but hated the way everything had turned out. He still wished that he could have loved her.

He unzipped his jacket as he crossed the parking lot and removed it before getting in the car. He was now free. To do what, he didn't know.

Chapter 45

Damon sat in front of the T.V. The card in his jacket pocket called to him. He didn't want to admit he needed help, but he did. He was lost and alone. No one could understand what he was going through. No one could understand the fear. Only he could taste the regret.

He had to force himself to take the day off. The doctor told him not to push himself too hard and to avoid stress. He had been hustling, making up for the slow period at the dealership and trying to keep his mind off his troubles. Whenever he could, he worked extra hours and his sales were back up. It looked as though he would be able to keep the brownstone.

He went to the closet and pulled the tattered card Carmen had given him out of his jacket pocket. He returned to the living room and turned down the television. He dialed the number on the card. Carmen's co-worker answered.

"Jackie Thomas, R.N"

"Hello, Jackie." My name is Damon. "Carmen Harris gave me your card."

"She told me about you. I was hoping you would call."

After a few beats, Damon asked, "What is the name of the program and where's it located?" He fell backwards onto the sofa while staring at Jackie's card.

"The name of the program is *Red*. It's a full service program that offers assistance to people affected by HIV, either living with it themselves, or perhaps loving and caring for a family member with the diagnosis. There's a support group, food assistance, job search assistance, and some medical care. The services are free. Does this sound like something you might be interested in?"

"Yeah. Maybe I should check it out."

"The support group is probably the best place to start. The next meeting is Monday at seven o'clock. All you have to do is show up. They meet in the lower level of the Adam's building on Washington Boulevard."

"I know where that is. Thanks Jackie."

"Don't mention it."

Damon hung up the phone. His heart missed London. It had been a while since they spoke. He still couldn't face him. He dialed the number and after a brief conversation with Rachel, London was on the phone.

"Daddy!" he screamed.

"Hey lil' man. What have you been up to?"

"Nothing. Evan got me a turtle."

"He did? What's his name?"

"He doesn't have a name."

"What? Whoever heard of a turtle with no name?" Damon teased him. "How about George?"

"I like that."

"Daddy?" London said.

"Yeah buddy, what's up?"

"I miss you."

He spoke with such innocence. Damon could feel a huge knot forming in his throat. His eyes watered and he strained to keep the sadness out of his voice. "I'm coming to see you real soon. Daddy loves you."

"Bye Daddy."

Damon hung up the phone and the tears released. It became clear that it wasn't just him who was facing the unknown. He was dragging others along with him.

Damon left the dealership around six o'clock on Monday and headed over to Washington Boulevard. It was just blocks from where he grew up. He pulled in the lot around the back and walked through the heavy doors of the Adams building then down the stairs to the lower level. He could hear people talking toward the end of the hall. He slowly followed the worn linoleum until he reached a room where he was greeted by a pale, middle-aged, balding man. Thin brown wispy strands of hair circled his beaming crown.

"Are you here for the support group?" he said.

Damon nodded.

"I'm Gary, the group's facilitator. Thanks for coming. Make yourself at home. There are snacks and beverages available if you'd like some." The man pointed toward the wall.

"Thanks."

Damon walked to the side of the room. He placed a bag of green tea in a cup and filled it with hot water from the dispenser. He realized he hadn't had any herbal tea since Carmen had left. Someone walked up to the table and stood next to him.

"I'm Angel." The short, chocolate brown girl extended her hand, and Damon, who towered over her, shook it. She filled up her cup with water, carefully selected a tea bag out of the bowl and took a seat.

Damon sat down in one of the small schoolhouse chairs. He was nervous. He didn't know what to expect. He watched as the facilitator stood up and gave his name, Gary Woods, and a brief overview of the meeting. Then he asked any newcomers to introduce themselves if they wanted. One person stood up. She announced her son was just diagnosed with the disease. She cried as she spoke.

When she was finished. Damon reluctantly got up from his seat. Everyone turned to look at him. It felt like he was standing underneath a spotlight. "My name is Damon." He paused. "And I was recently diagnosed."

"Welcome, Damon," Gary said and the group joined him in his greeting. "First let me say to you both…you're among friends. Second…we're glad you're here." A wave of relief swept over him as he sat back down. He looked around the room as the facilitator spoke. He was glad he came. It felt good being around others he could relate to.

They started the meeting. Gary gave some information on new research being conducted in the area on treatment for the disease that was gaining a lot of attention. The program was looking for volunteers. He walked over and hung a flyer on the corkboard with a thumbtack on the left side of the room, and returned to his seated position on the desk. He opened the meeting and people began to share stories about life with the disease. Some were ill and it scared Damon. Other than flu-like symptoms in the beginning, he felt pretty much like he always did. He wondered what might be in store for him.

Lydia, the other newcomer to the group, began sharing her story. Her son, who was twenty-three and had experimented with drugs in high school, had contracted HIV. The woman stated she felt as though life was just beginning for her son. He had been drug free for several years, had enrolled in college and had met a wonderful girl. "And just like that…" she said, with a hard snap of her fingers, tears padded her words, "his life was changed just like that. It's not fair!" She screamed.

Angel walked over and sat next to Lydia. She handed her a tissue and took her hand and held it. Damon watched in amazement as others shared their stories. He felt comforted and terrified at the same time. Grief and pain swelled in the room. So much so, he could feel it. Why did he sleep with Candy, a stranger, without regard to his health and safety? How could he have been so careless? There was no way he was sharing his story. No way.

The meeting adjourned and Damon walked out of the building alongside the others. He made his way to the parking lot. As he drove off he waved at some of the people he had met as they got into their cars. As strangers, they shared a common bond. He could feel a kinship with them already.

A few blocks down Washington Boulevard, he saw Angel walking. He pulled up alongside her and reached over and rolled down the window. "Do you need a ride?"

"You're not a killer are you?" She responded. Her wide smile was accented by cocoa dimples.

"I don't think so." Damon returned the smile; Angel got in the car and closed the door.

"I live a little ways from here. I hope that's okay. I was walking to catch the train."

"Where?" For the first time Damon felt nervous talking to a woman. Something about her took him off guard. Maybe it was the way she seemed genuinely concerned about everyone in the group. Perhaps it was because she now knew his dreaded secret.

"I live over off Lairamie Ave."

"That's a long street."

"I know. I'll show you the way."

Damon drove along following the directions Angel gave him. When they neared her house, she asked Damon if he was hungry and extended an invitation to join her at a small sandwich shop. He accepted.

Damon parked his car, still at a loss for words. He wasn't sure what to say or why she had asked him to grab a bite to eat. All he knew was that her smile charmed him. And at barely over five feet, it seemed to have a spark that could propel her to the moon and back.

Angel and Damon took a seat at one of the tables in the restaurant. Angel recommended a salad and Damon followed her lead. He was new to HIV, but by the way she helped others at the support group, he could tell she was no newcomer to the disease. Perhaps eating salads was what he was supposed to do.

The waitress delivered their meals to the table. A few seconds into her meal Angel started the conversation.

"So how did you contract it?"

Damon didn't want to tell her, but at the same time, he wondered the same thing about her. Did she have it? Maybe she was just a caretaker? "I slept with someone who had it."

"Man or woman?"

She was direct and very casual as she spoke. Damon's eyes bucked at her question. "A woman." He said forcefully.

"Is that the truth?"

Damon's face immediately registered a frown.

"I'm sorry," Angel said. "There's such a stigma surrounding the disease that sometimes people feel as though they have to conceal that they're drug users, or gay."

"I'm none of the above." Damon stared at his salad. "How about you?"

Angel placed her fork on the table. She took her napkin off her lap and wiped her mouth. She looked Damon in the eyes before she started speaking. "I'm one of the unfortunate ones who thought they were in a committed relationship. I was married. He contracted the disease, and then gave it to me. He denied it was from a man, but I still have my suspicions."

"Where is he now?"

"We're divorced. He told me in a letter."

"I'm sorry." Damon said sincerely. He recognized he was one of the pack. So were Craig and a lot of other guys he knew. They had sex with other women behind their wife or significant other's back. He never thought of the risks. He silently thanked God, again, that Carmen was okay.

Angel shrugged her shoulders. "It is what it is. This is my life, now. And I'm determined to live it as fully and completely as I can, while encouraging others to do the same."

After a little while, the waitress came back to the table with their check. Damon handed her a twenty dollar bill and told her to keep the change. He and Angel left the restaurant and he dropped her off at her apartment. He wasn't sure what the evening had meant, but he was glad to finally have someone to talk to.

Chapter 46

Craig leaned back in the chair. Samantha sat across from him. They were seated in the back of Samantha's restaurant.

"Sam, you're being stupid. You've always said you wanted to expand your business, and I'm looking for a business venture to invest in. This just makes sense. You help me and I'll help you."

Samantha stared contemplatively at the lace tablecloth. "I don't know if I can trust you."

"We'll have attorneys draft up the whole deal. Mine as well as your own, if you can afford one."

Samantha looked up from the table sharply. "That's exactly what I'm talking about."

She stood up from the table.

Craig touched her on the apron she was wearing and coaxed her back down onto the chair. "What? I'm just saying...if you don't trust me, hire your own attorney."

"I ain't' got it like you, Craig. You're going to get some expensive 'snake-in-the-grass' attorney to come in here and both of you are going to swindle me out of my business."

Craig shook his head. "I promise you, I'm not trying to do that. Picture it Samantha. "He framed her face with his hands. "Sam's place...maybe right off Michigan Avenue. New venue. New decor. New ambiance. High-end clientele. More money. We could even hire a world renowned chef."

"I'm the chef." Samantha stood up again.

"Samantha, if we could hire some French dude or something like that, think of the money we could bring in."

"I am the chef!" Samantha pointed angrily at her chest.

Craig backed down. "Okay, you're the chef. You're a great cook. I'm sure it won't be a problem."

Samantha rolled her eyes. She folded her arms as she sat back down.

Craig could tell he had her thinking. "All you have to do is start dreaming up the new *Sam's Place,* and I have the resources to make it happen."

"What's your cut?" Samantha huffed.

"I've got a figure in mind, but we can let the attorney's come up with an arrangement we can agree on. Just tell me you'll think about it." Craig stood up and grabbed the keys to his Lexus. He walked over to Samantha and tried to kiss her on the cheek, but she leaned away.

"I'll think about it."

Craig left the restaurant with a huge surge of confidence. It had taken months, but he finally had Samantha exactly where he wanted her. He knew she wouldn't turn down an opportunity to make the dream she had dreamed ever since she was a little girl, come true. He smiled smugly. He had just added restaurateur to his resume.

That evening Craig went to the pool hall to meet the guys for a quick game of pool. Things seemed to be returning to normal. Samantha was at least talking to him now, and he was no longer scared *of* and *for* Damon. Damon had assured him that the meds he was taking lessened the likelihood of transmission, as well as helped to protect him against threats to his own immunity. He had insisted he was fine.

He parked around back and entered the building. He was glad to see Wendell and Damon racking up. Craig stopped by the bar and ordered a scotch before walking over to join them. Damon extended his hand to shake

Craig's, and Craig pulled him close for a brotherly hug as they gently bumped shoulders. Craig was so glad to see him. Glad he looked the same. Wendell took the break shot. After a few moments sitting on the stool watching them play, he couldn't keep his mouth shut any longer.

"Sam and I are opening a restaurant together."

"How'd that happen?" Damon seemed to know that somehow Craig had tricked her.

"This is me, man. When have I not gotten what I wanted?" He swirled the drink he was holding in his hand.

Wendell looked at Craig. He rolled his eyes and shook his head.

"Since Samantha busted you cheating." Damon laughed.

Craig laughed too. "All that's behind us now. In a short time, we'll be married."

"You? Married?" Damon said. "That's funny."

"It's time I settled down. Time for me to start a family."

"Since when does going into business together equal a marriage proposal?" Wendell said before taking his shot.

"Since its Craig Mincey—the smoothest brother in this town."

Damon cracked up.

Craig took a swig of his scotch. "You won't be laughing when you're being fitted for your best man tux."

"You're going to have to do a lot more than bankroll Samantha's business before you get her to say 'I do'. You might want to be careful. She's a smart chick. You might be the one who ends up getting tricked."

Craig ignored Damon. He stood up from the stool and placed his drink on a nearby table. "My game," he said and started racking balls.

Chapter 47

Damon eased the car up in front of Rachel and Evan's house, parking behind Evan's black Range Rover in the circular driveway. He had called her the night before and asked if he could pick London up to spend the night. She agreed. They discussed telling London about his condition, but they decided to wait until he was older.

Damon looked up toward the house to see Rachel standing on the porch. She waved at Damon as he got out of the car and walked up the driveway. "Where is he?"

"He's in there. Evan is putting his shoes on. He's excited about staying with you tonight."

"I know."

"How have you been feeling?"

"I'm okay."

Evan eased the door open and stepped outside. London was resting comfortably on his hip, his arms draped around his neck. Damon felt a twinge in his heart knowing they shared his son equally. Evan's hand clutched the small backpack bearing the Cookie Monster's face that Damon had given London last year for his birthday He wondered if he had packed it for him.

"Hey." Damon greeted. First he took the backpack from Evan. Then he picked up London.

"How are you doing?" Evan asked.

"Good."

Rachel hugged London and kissed him on the cheek and Evan rubbed his tiny head. Damon turned and walked down the walkway carrying London to the car. He placed him in the booster seat in the back, buckled him in, got in the car and made the drive over to his house.

London talked incessantly about his day, school, everything. He seemed to have lots he wanted to catch Damon up on. Damon smiled as he listened to him, occasionally stealing a glance of him in his rear view mirror. He had been away from him far too long.

At the house, Damon settled London into his room. He placed his back pack in a corner chair and hung his sweater in the closet. Afterwards, they went to the kitchen so that Damon could make something to eat. He sat London on the counter next to the stove and admonished him not to move. London's legs kicked back and forth in anticipation of one of his favorites—grilled cheese sandwiches, recommending Damon serve them with pickles like they did in school. Damon placed butter in the skillet and when it started to melt, he pulled out a butcher knife and began slicing the cheese. Suddenly, London must have kicked too hard. It appeared he was losing his balance. He was about to fall over onto the hot stove or hit the floor. Damon panicked. His heart pounded as he grabbed him quickly by the arm and eased him down off the counter slowly and safely.

London looked at the floor. "Daddy, you're bleeding!" He reached up and tried to grab Damon's hand.

Damon jerked it from his reach. "Never do that." His tone was strong, brimming on anger. Not at London, but at himself.

London's face was puzzled.

Damon turned off the stove. When he looked down, he saw bright red drops on the floor. "Don't touch it." He screamed as he reached and yanked a dish towel from the side of the sink and tightly wrapped it around his hand. "Come with me," He commanded.

London followed Damon to the bathroom where Damon forced him to stand in the doorway and directed him not to move. He threatened to spank him if he did.

Damon disinfected his hand thoroughly, covered it with a load of gauze then taped it up. He instructed London to follow him back to the kitchen and remain in the doorway, again. Damon reached underneath the cabinet and found some bleach. He poured it on the blood on the floor and wiped it up. He doused the towel he had used with the bleach, wrapped it in a plastic bag and tossed it in the trash can along with the entire stick of butter and block of cheese. When he was confident he had removed all traces of blood, he picked London up and carried him to the living room sitting him on the sofa.

"Listen to me."

London's doe eyes connected with Damon's.

"Daddy is sick. And if you touch his blood you could get sick too." London frowned.

"I need you to promise me you will never touch Daddy's blood. Ever. Do you understand me?"

"Yes, Daddy."

He went back to the kitchen and found chicken nuggets; he placed them on a baking sheet and shoved them in the oven along with a few frozen French fries. When they were done, he returned to the living room with the food and two paper plates. As London enjoyed the nuggets, he did that thing he always did when he was eating something that he liked. He made a sound, sort of a low humming growl, the sound of satisfaction. Rachel couldn't stand it, but it delighted Damon every time he heard it. He knew he had done well.

They were watching a *Cars* DVD for what felt like the hundredth time to Damon when London ran to his room to get his backpack. He walked back to the living room digging down into the bag. His tiny hands brought forth an IPad. "Look what Evan bought me!"

Damon eyed the IPad. He'd heard about them, but never seen one up close. "Nice."

"There are a lot of games on here. I think I'm going to go to my room and play for a while."

"Okay. In a little while, you need to brush your teeth and get ready for bed. I'll be in to tuck you in."

Damon went back to the kitchen and began cleaning up, careful not to get his bandaged hand too wet. His gaze rested on the spot on the floor where his blood had been. Could something still be there? What happens if London crawls on the floor and places his hand in his mouth? He disinfected the refrigerator door handle and the knobs on the stove realizing that he had become afraid of himself.

He eyed the clock. It was time for London to get ready for bed. After London brushed his teeth, Damon fluffed his pillow and tucked him in. He weaseled his way out of telling a bedtime story, too much on his mind, by agreeing to let London stay up thirty more minutes playing his favorite game. He kissed his head and headed for the door. He clicked off the light and stood, watching his son, the soft glow of the device illuminating his little face. He hung his head as he closed the door, horrified at how complicated his life had become.

The next morning he drove London home. When he pulled into the driveway to drop him off, London insisted he come in and meet his turtle. Damon complied and entered the house. He walked up the staircase to London's bedroom to meet George. Grey black, ugly looking thing. Damon smiled with forced excitement when he noticed London looking at him.

"Isn't he cool, Daddy?"

"Yeah, w-a-a-ay cool. What does he eat?"

"Mostly vegetables. Evan gets this stuff from the pet store for him." He took George out of the aquarium. "Wanna' hold him?"

He headed for the door. "No thanks, lil' man, I'll pass." He walked out of his room and hurried down the stairs, meeting Rachel at the doorway. He glanced around, making sure Evan wasn't nearby. "Can I talk to you for a second?"

"Sure."

He pulled her out the door onto the porch. "I told him."

She rolled her eyes and placed her hand on her hip. "I thought we agreed to wait." She whispered. "I wanted to be there."

"I had to tell him. I cut myself."

Damon could see Rachel cringe as she looked at the bandage on his hand.

"Did he understand?"

"I don't know. We'll see if he brings it up again."

Chapter 48

Damon had begun to look forward to his support group meetings. He still had trouble opening up, but he enjoyed hearing everyone else's story; reinforcing he was not alone. The best part of the meetings was seeing Angel. There was something intriguing about her. Maybe it was her confidence, maybe it was her dimples, and maybe it was her round behind. All he knew was he never minded seeing her again.

Damon drove Angel home after the meeting as he had done for the past several weeks. Angel moved around town by bus or train. She couldn't afford a car just yet, but she was saving money from her job at the library to do so. He pulled up in front of her apartment building.

"Why don't you park around back and come in." Angel extended an invitation to Damon in her blunt, matter-of-fact manner.

"Okay," was all Damon could think to say. For some reason Angel seemed to steal the words from his mouth.

Damon drove his car to the parking lot in the rear of her building. Her unit was small, Damon guessed no more than six families lived there, and all the spaces were full. "Will they tow me if I park next to the dumpster?"

"No, it happens all the time."

Damon carefully pulled up next to the dumpster on the side opposite the opening so people could still access it without damaging his car. He locked the doors and they walked to the front of her building. When they entered, Angel stopped at her box to get her mail. She frowned as she studied the envelopes, carefully flipping through each one. As she studied them, she lost her grip on her keys and they fell to the floor. Damon squatted down to grab them, but she beat him to it, his hand clasped hers instead. They looked up and their eyes met. Damon could feel his pulse. "Sorry."

She smiled and headed up the stairs. Damon followed her.

From the front door he could see the kitchen, living and dining room areas, and into the bedroom. She invited Damon to have a seat.

"Would you like something to drink?" She asked as Damon sat down. She flipped the switch on the wall and turned on the light.

He looked backward over his shoulder into the kitchen. "Water is fine."

Angel reached into a lower cabinet. "How about a little wine?"

"I thought we weren't supposed to drink."

She smiled, "All things in moderation. We still have to live. What's life without a little wine now and then?" She raised an empty wine glass, "Half a glass?" She beckoned.

Damon smiled. For the first time in a long time he felt joy. "Half a glass."

Angel walked over to him carrying two wine glasses filled half-full with red wine. She sat in a comfy chair opposite him and dangled her leg over the side. Damon started getting uncomfortable. She really rattled him. He never knew what might come out of her mouth.

"Tell me about yourself, Mr. Harris. What's your story?"

"Me? I'm pretty boring." Damon felt a grin sprawl across his face.

"There has to be more to you than going to an HIV support group and selling cars. Family?"

"Yes. I have three sisters, and my older brother that lives up north. I also have a son. He's six years old. His name is London."

"Nice." She looked him in the eye. "So what's your HIV story?"

"I told you. I got it from a woman. You didn't believe me, remember?" Damon could feel that stupid grin creep across his face again for no reason. He silently admonished himself.

"Right. Was it someone you were dating?"

"No. It was a careless mistake. I was actually married at the time."

Angel's demeanor changed. Her face showed obvious revulsion. "Same old song. You men out there throwing your penises around, leaving the rest of us unsuspecting faithful servants to pay the price."

Damon was speechless.

"Did you give it to her?"

"No, she doesn't have it." Damon sat up and raised his hands. "Can I explain?"

"Sure." Angel's tone mocked him.

"I met a woman. She was nice and a really good person. She wanted to get married. I didn't want to, but I wasn't man enough to tell her. I didn't want to let her down. People were telling me that a woman like that was hard to come by. Before I knew it, I gave in. I never loved her. I thought I was doing the right thing. I thought I could settle down and be her husband, but a few months in, I realized I couldn't. Things were never right between us, especially physically. It wasn't like I was sleeping with her, and then was out scoring chicks...it was nothing like that." Damon could feel his eyes well up. "I was alone, confused, and just plain miserable. There's no excuse for what I did. I wasn't thinking, that's all. There's no way I would have intentionally done anything to harm her."

"Yeah." Angel sighed. "I'm sure that's the case in most situations. They just don't think." Angel stood up from the chair. "You hungry?"

Damon nodded.

Angel finished off her wine before going into the kitchen. She returned seconds later with tuna salad in a bowl and a plate full of crackers. She set them on the cocktail table. "You should speak up more in group." She placed a dab of tuna on a cracker and put it in her mouth. "I think it will be good for you. Good for the others."

Damon took a cracker off the plate, "You think so?" he said. "Thanks for the tuna; it's one of my favorites."

"I do." Angel turned on the television. "Do you have to work tomorrow?"

"Nope."

"You should spend the night."

Damon continued munching on his tuna. This girl was like a ninja. She could take him off guard at any second. He decided he would take her up on her offer to stay, although he was slightly fearful of what she might say, or *do* to him before daybreak.

Chapter 49

Craig pulled up in front of Samantha's restaurant at nine o'clock. She walked around the car and got in.

"Good morning, baby."

"Good morning."

He pulled off in route to a place, a few blocks from Michigan Avenue. He was confident she would love it as the new spot for *Sam's Place*. Samantha had agreed to become his business partner. He had his attorney draft up an agreement. He would front the money as a loan to secure the new place, and complete the build-out, as well as take care of anything else that was needed. Samantha agreed to pay him back his front money, as well as give him ten percent of the profits. Unfortunately, she didn't seem as happy about it as he did. Craig continued to push her further into his corner.

"Have dinner with me, tonight."

"Why?"

"So we can talk some more about the plans. You're going to love the place. A colleague of mine owns the building. It's prime Chicago real estate."

"You can come by the restaurant and we can talk like we've been doing. That's been working just fine." Samantha's tone was cool.

Craig reached down and held her hand. "You act as if you've made a deal with the devil."

Samantha stared out the passenger side window of the car. "Maybe I have."

"C'mon Samantha. What do I have to do to make it up to you? I've apologized. I've begged. I've told you that that girl meant nothing to me. I deserve another shot."

"You sound like a fool. You don't deserve anything. Men like you can't be trusted, Craig. Plain and simple."

As Craig pulled around the back of the restaurant and parked the car she continued, "I don't even know why we're having this conversation. The only reason I'm in this car is because we have a business arrangement. That's the only reason." She got out of the car and slammed the door. "Which one of these doors is it?" She walked toward the building.

Craig closed his car door and pressed the remote to lock it. He pointed at a door. "That one."

Samantha barged over to the door and yanked on it before Craig had a chance to tell her it was locked. She huffed loudly. He walked up beside her with the key and let her in.

Samantha entered the spacious venue and studied the place. Her demeanor changed. Craig could tell she was turning things over in her mind so he tried to help her paint a picture. "Can you see it? Chicago A-listers seated everywhere. Wall street brokers, celebrities."

Samantha continued to walk the place. After a few moments had passed, she asked, "How much is it?"

"I've got you covered. He's a buddy of mine. He'll give me a good deal on the lease if I agree to sign something with a longer term."

"How long is longer? I plan to get this business up and running and pay you off immediately. I don't want you holding anything over my head any longer than is absolutely necessary." She spun around. "My primary goal will be to get rid of you."

Craig chuckled. So did Samantha.

"You'll warm up to me eventually. If I can get you to love me once, I can get you to do it again. I'm sure you've figured out that my extending this offer is only so I can be around you a lot more. I wanted the chance to show you what a great guy I am. The old Craig is no more. You'll see."

"Let's go." She headed for the door. "And as far as I'm concerned, there's nothing else for me to see. I've seen it already and it ain't pretty."

"Are you talking about me or the place?"

"I'm talking about you. The place is wonderful."

Samantha clicked her heels to the back of the room and out the door. Craig followed her, stopped to lock up, and then hurried to catch up. He opened her car door and she got in. He jumped in on the other side and drove her back to her restaurant.

When he returned to his office he called his colleague and told him to have his attorney draft up the lease papers. He then called an architect and asked him to meet him on Monday to discuss the new plans for *Sam's Place*.

Chapter 50

Damon and Angel parked in the parking lot outside the Adams building. He had started picking her up and taking her to the meetings since she still didn't have a car. Eventually, when she had the money, he would try to work out a deal for her on a used car at his dealership. As they descended the stairs he wanted to hold her hand, but he didn't. They took seats next to each other.

Angel's encouragement had caused Damon to open up and share more about his story with the group. A few women who had been infected by their spouses or significant others held such bitterness toward men. Damon sharing his story seemed to ease some of their anger. The women could tell he was genuinely sorry for what he had done, and his words seemed to comfort them. He felt a responsibility to speak in defense of men. He wanted to reassure them that not every man was a dog, and had he married for the right reasons—not fear or selfishness—but for love, he would have never cheated.

After the meeting, on the way to the car, Angel stunned him again.

"I spoke with my pastor on Sunday about you. He wants you to come speak to our congregation about your status."

"What?"

"I think it would be a good idea. People need to know about this disease. You don't hear or see as much about it because of the advancement in meds, and because the activists have fought for equal and fair treatment. But this disease is just as real, and just as rampant as it was years ago, if not more so, because of a lack of awareness."

Damon got in the car. He put the key in the ignition once Angel was inside. "I don't know if I can speak in front of a group."

"You need to do this, Damon. People need to see the faces of HIV. It's easy to think this is a gay man's disease. You and I are living proof of that lie. We can no longer look the other way. This is a pandemic. It's everybody's problem."

Damon's brakes squeaked as he coasted to a stop at the light. He didn't want to disappoint her, but he was terrified of speaking in public. He didn't speak well when he was talking to only one person. A whole church? "How many people?"

"My church is not that big. Trust me. You'll be fine."

Damon pulled in front of Angel's apartment building and dropped her off. He could add her to the list of everyone who seemed to think he was more capable than he thought he was. He wouldn't disappoint her though. He would spend the rest of the week thinking about what he was going to say and pray her church wasn't near the South Side where he grew up.

Angel gave Damon's number to her pastor and Reverend Michael called him on Thursday night. Damon explained his story and that he was genuinely sorry. The pastor told him to speak from his heart and let the Spirit do the rest. He seemed excited that Damon was coming to speak to his congregation. He was the only one.

Sunday rolled around. Damon put on one of the few suits he had and left to pick up Angel. They drove around the corner to her church. Damon's mouth felt like cotton. Every time he tried to swallow, his tongue would stick to some part of it.

Angel led him to the front of the church where Reverend Michael stood greeting his church members in order to make a formal introduction.

"Damon, meet Reverend Harvey Michael."

Damon extended his sweaty hand and shook the pastor's.

"You look nervous, son." The reverend said. His voice was commanding, but his smile warmed his tone and put Damon at ease a little. "Don't be." He reached into his robe, taking out a handkerchief and handed it to Damon.

Damon smiled as he accepted the handkerchief and wiped his brow.

"God has led you to this place, Damon. Relax and let him carry you the rest of the way."

He patted Damon on the shoulder as they walked inside. He motioned for Damon to have a seat in the pew. The reverend took a seat in front of the choir and the service began. When the choir finished singing, Damon was introduced by the reverend's assistant. He trudged up to the microphone and stood in the front of the church.

"Hello everyone. My name is Damon and I'm a friend of Angel's."

The church nodded and welcomed him.

"And I am HIV positive." Damon could hear a few groans.

Reverend Michael stood up. "Now...Now..." He motioned with his hands for everyone to calm down. "Let him speak. I invited him here. His story is not what you're thinking."

Damon understood where the resistance from the congregation was coming from and decided he would clear the air once the reverend sat down.

"I'm HIV positive and I'm not gay. I came here today to share my story. To talk about how you, or your sons or daughters might be at risk of contracting this disease."

Damon cleared his throat and continued, "I was married and I had a one night stand. Biggest mistake of my life. To all you brothers out there, it doesn't matter how good she looks; nothing is worth putting yourself, or someone you care about at risk. Once it's done, it's done. It's something you can't reverse. Condoms don't protect you. They can break, and once contact is made, transmission is possible. You never know who has it. Do I look like someone who carries the HIV virus?"

Damon looked at the face of a young black, corn rowed woman a few rows back. She licked her lips as she shook her head, no.

Damon continued telling his story. He felt compelled to tell people that although the medications helped, life with the disease was no walk in the park. As he spoke, he was surprised how easy the words kept coming. The congregation genuinely appeared interested in what he had to say. So much so, that after he finished speaking and the service was over, two young men came up to him and thanked him for sharing his story. Reverend Michael said he would make a few calls to some other churches in the area and see if they would allow him to come and speak about a topic that was largely affecting the community.

Chapter 51

Damon dropped Angel off after church on Sunday. He drove to his mother's house. Their visits had been infrequent the past several months. It wasn't because she found out he was HIV positive, it was because every spare moment she had outside of work she spent with Ronald.

He walked up to the front porch and rang the doorbell. Now that Ronald was always around he was afraid to just walk in the back door like he always did. No telling what they might be doing. He scanned the block and was relieved when he didn't see his car. A moment later Sharon answered the door.

"C'mon in baby," she patted him on the back before offering with a frown, "why do you keep ringing the doorbell?"

"I don't know." Damon walked into the living room.

Sharon sat opposite him on the sofa. "You look good."

"Thanks. I feel okay. How's Ronald?"

Sharon smiled. "He's fine. Great in fact. What brings you here?"

"Nothing. Just thought I'd stop by." Damon stretched out and placed his hands behind his head.

"There's chicken and dumplings in there on the stove."

"Is that what I smell?"

"You can have some if you want."

"I'm good," he smiled. "More for Ronald."

Sharon pulled a throw pillow from behind her back and playfully threw it at Damon. He leaned to the side and it landed on the back of the couch.

"You talk to Ike?" She asked.

"I did. He said everyone's coming up the fourth."

"Yep. Even Ronald and I are going." Sharon softly grunted as she got up off the couch and walked to the kitchen. She returned with a bowl of chicken and dumplings and a spoon. She handed it to Damon. "It's hot."

He plunged the spoon into the bowl. "I've been speaking at churches around town about HIV."

Sharon looked up with surprise. "You? Speaking in front of people?" She smiled broadly. "I don't believe it."

"Me either." He said, realizing that she said the dumplings were hot. He felt a sting in the tender spot behind his two front teeth.

"How'd that happen?"

"A girl from my support group." Damon choked back his grin. "She hooked everything up. Kinda' forced me into it. I like it, though. It feels as though I'm doing something good for the community."

"Oh, my word. I'm stunned. I'm happy, but I'm stunned. That must be some kind of girl."

Damon released his grin. "I'm thinking about asking her to come to Ike's with me."

"I think you should. I can't wait to meet her. A woman that can get you to speak in front of people must be something."

"She is."

Damon finished his meal and took his bowl to the kitchen. He rinsed it out and placed it in the sink. He returned to the living room and hugged his mother good bye. As he pulled away, he reflected on his visit with his mother. He noticed that his interaction with her had been different. Good, but different. He was starting to feel at ease with himself, surprisingly. And he was starting to appreciate every moment he had. He took nothing for granted. Not even a thirty minute visit, eating chicken and dumplings with his mother.

On Sunday, Damon stopped by the store and picked up six packages of hot dogs and buns. It was the Fourth of July. He and Angel were headed to Grand Rapids to see his brother Ike. He had invited the entire family for a cookout. Angel had volunteered her cooler to transport the hotdogs. Before taking those inside he scooped up all of his hip hop CD's and put them in the trunk.

He knocked on Angel's door and she opened it without greeting him. Literally, just turned the knob and headed back to the kitchen. She wasn't in a bad mood that was just Angel. She was dumping ice in the cooler when he approached her. He handed her the hotdogs and she covered them with ice. He picked up the cooler while she turned off the lights, and they were out the door, headed up the interstate to Grand Rapids.

Angel could be quiet. Damon wasn't exactly use to it, yet. He thought all women blabbed incessantly. When he was around Carmen and Cathy he couldn't get a word in edgewise. His sisters were the same way. It was if they were speaking some incomprehensible language of nothing. But Angel was different. When she spoke, she offered substance. You would pay attention to what she was saying. It appeared she didn't waste words.

Angel inquired about Damon's family on the drive up and Damon filled her in on the details. Each of their nuances, their childhood. He talked about Diane, probably more than he should. Angel seemed excited about meeting his family.

"Do they know about me?"

"Yeah. I told them about you." Damon smiled.

"Do they know I'm HIV positive?"

Damon paused. He had told them, but wasn't sure if she would want him to. He was afraid of responding with the wrong answer.

"It's okay that you told them." Her words brought forth relief. She seemed so open about everything he didn't think she would mind, but he knew that sometimes women didn't like men taking too much liberty. She was carving a niche in his heart—the last thing he wanted was to upset her.

A little while later they pulled up to Ike's house. Damon could see that the rest of his family had already arrived. They walked up to the door and rang the bell. A few seconds later, Diane appeared.

"Damon Harris." She hugged him and kissed him on the cheek. It was good to see Diane. When she smiled, she smiled with all of her heart.

"Hey, Diane." Damon could smell baked beans.

"And this must be Angel." She wrapped her arm around her. "C'mon in you guys. Everyone has been waiting for you."

Damon and Angel followed Diane past the living room and study to the family room and kitchen area. Pat, Mona, and Cheryl were already there. Ronald and his mother were sitting on barstools at the kitchen counter. Damon looked through the sliding glass doors to see the children playing in the backyard.

He introduced everyone to Angel. They looked around for a few uncomfortable seconds. Diane broke through the silence and approached Damon, telling him to take the hotdogs out to Ike in the backyard. She asked Angel to come help her in the kitchen. Everyone resumed talking at that point. Good old Diane, he thought. She always wanted everyone to feel her love.

Damon took the hotdogs out back. They were the last thing to be placed on the grill. He approached Ike, who was turning burgers with a long fork. He smiled when he saw Damon. "Open those for me and put them on that plate sitting over there."

Damon walked over to a table that was a few feet from the grill. He began tearing open the packages and placing them on the plate.

Ike was feverishly moving the burgers around on the grill. His body darted and swayed as he turned them. "This fire is getting too hot. Hand me that water bottle."

Damon handed him an unopened bottle of water and he splashed a little on the grill. Damon heard a sizzle and then saw the fire tamp down a bit.

When the threat was over, Ike turned to Damon. "I'm glad you came."

"Me too. I brought Angel with me."

"Good. I can't wait to meet her. Mom says you're henpecked."

"Is that what she said?"

"Those are my words, but she said this girl has you speaking all over town. Sounds like it to me."

"I've been speaking, but not because I'm henpecked. I actually like doing it."

Ike folded his arms. "It's not like you, not like you at all." His eyes were filled with suspicion as they traveled up and down Damon's body. After a few seconds he smiled and let his arms fall to his side." He glanced at the plate. "I'm ready for the dogs now."

After they had cooked, Ike piled them up on a plate and handed it to Damon. He grabbed the platter full of burgers and ribs and they went back inside the house.

Damon was glad to see his sisters and his mom chatting with Angel; being nosy he was certain, but at least they were talking.

Diane called the kids in and served them hot dogs and hamburgers along with baked beans, coleslaw and potato salad. After she cut up the ribs for the adults, everyone began serving themselves. Damon and Angel filled their plates, and headed for Diane and Ike's dining room. The two of them sat down at the table. Damon noticed she didn't have a napkin. He rushed to the kitchen to get her one.

"What do you think?" He handed her the paper napkin and sat down next to her.

"About your family?"

"Yeah."

"They're nice. That was an awkward moment after you introduced me." Angel put a forkful of coleslaw in her mouth.

"I'm not sure what that was about. I apologize."

"No need to apologize. It's probably because I'm positive, too. It's shocking to people. They don't know how to respond."

"Maybe it's because you're the first woman I've brought around them since my ex-wife."

"Could be. Whatever the reason was, they seemed to move beyond it."

Damon and Angel finished their meals and joined everyone in the family room. Angel sat on the sofa next to Ronald. Damon could hear him asking her questions about her family. He went outside to help Ike clean the grill.

"She's cute." Ike said as he saw Damon approaching. "Nice lil' honey you got there."

Damon smiled.

Ike handed him the wire brush and the top rack to the grill. "So how does that work between the two of you?"

"How does what work?" Damon took the rack and brush from him. Surely, he wasn't about to go there.

"With both of you having it, how do you...you know?"

"I don't get in the bed with you and Diane." Damon joked. Ike was moving into an area that was none of his business. He scrubbed the rack with the brush.

"C'mon man this is me. I know you. A fine little honey like that—something's got to be jumping off."

"Furthest thing from my mind right now."

"I see." Ike hosed down the rack he was holding and leaned it against the grill.

"Can you?"

"Can I what?" Damon grinned. He couldn't believe Ike wouldn't leave it alone. Only a short time ago, he would have reveled in having a conversation about sex with his older brother. It seemed so trivial now. Other things had definitely moved higher up on his list of important things in life—like staying healthy.

Damon decided to put this matter to rest. "If you are asking me if we've had sex, the answer is no. If you're asking if we can, the answer is yes. We just have to use protection."

"I bet you hate that don't you."

Damon handed the rack he was holding back to his brother. "Grow up, Ike." He returned to the house with Ike chuckling as he walked away.

Chapter 52

Craig and Samantha were busy putting the final touches on Sam's Place. The three month construction was complete. The grand opening was four weeks away. They had worked with the architect to give the restaurant an eclectic look to attract a wide array of customers. The menu also followed an eclectic style. Their specials would range from empanadas, to sushi, to rack of lamb. They hoped Samantha's desserts, which had been the backbone of her catering business, would be the crowd pleaser.

Samantha signed for the beverage delivery and directed the delivery man to the storage area in the back of the restaurant. Once he began unloading the truck, Samantha broke the seal on the box of white tablecloths the linen service had left her, placed them on a cart and rolled the cart to the dining area. She began shaking them out and draping them over the tables. Craig walked over to her.

"I never said thank you." Her red manicured nails smoothed the folds out of the fabric on the table she had covered.

"You're welcome. I told you it was a good idea. We make a good team." Craig picked up a tablecloth and began shaking it out.

"You were right. I can't believe we didn't fight throughout this entire process. I have to admit I find your ability to generate ideas, as well as your business knowledge, very impressive. I know I couldn't have gotten to this level this quickly without you."

Craig smiled. "Takes a big woman to admit that. That's what I love about you, Samantha. You have complete confidence in who you are. That quality is rarely found in people. Even I'm guilty of a little false bravado, more than I'd like to admit. But you seem comfortable in your own skin. I admire you so much for that."

A gentleman entered the restaurant. He approached them with a camera and tripod.

Samantha greeted him. "Can I help you?"

"I invited him here." Craig put the table cloth he was holding on the table and straightened it out. "He's from the PR firm I use for my other business. They're going to start generating buzz around the restaurant and get us the press we need."

"I'll need a few minutes to set up and then we'll get a few shots of you together," the photographer said. "You can email your bios and anything else you'd like to say, and we'll have our editor look it over and polish it up. Then we'll distribute to all local media outlets and wait for someone to pick up the story."

The gentleman began setting up his camera. Samantha and Craig continued to shake out tablecloths and drape them over the round tables that filled the dining area. Samantha went to the back and retrieved the bamboo centerpieces the decorator had left. She loaded those on the cart then brought them out, placing them on the tables in preparation for the pictures. When she was finished, the photographer was ready for them. He took pictures of her and Craig standing in various places in the restaurant. He took pictures of them standing alone. Then, together. Finally, he wanted to get a picture of them standing in front of the restaurant.

They walked outside. Samantha took advantage of the bright sun and stole a quick look in the reflection on the window. She fluffed her hair while the photographer adjusted his camera on the tripod. He instructed Samantha and Craig to stand below the restaurant's black velvet awning. *Sam's Place* sprawled across it in large cursive gold letters. The red light flashed on the camera and the photographer indicated he was ready. Samantha looked at the camera and prepared for her picture to be taken. Suddenly, Craig dropped down on one knee, grabbed her hand and jammed a ring on her finger. He smiled directly into the camera. While Samantha looked down in amazement, the photographer clicked away.

Samantha snatched her hand back. "Really, Craig? You can't be serious."

The photographer chimed in. "What a perfect photo op. We should be able to get this in newspapers and magazines all over town. Congratulations you two. A surprise engagement. This one will be easy." He began dismantling his camera and Sam stormed back into the restaurant. Craig dismissed the man and walked inside. Samantha was in the bar area pacing back and forth.

"I was just starting to feel good about this, Craig."

"So, what's changed?"

"You ambushed me."

"I'm still the same person I was thirty minutes ago when you were thanking me. Only now I gave you a ring."

Samantha pulled off the ring.

"Think about it Samantha. It could be the thing that gets us picked up by the papers. We might even get the news to come here and do a story. You heard him. We could have a full house the first night."

Samantha grumbled as she put the ring back on. She headed to the back storage room and pulled a stack of white cloth napkins out of a box that was sitting on a shelf, and began folding them.

Craig walked through the door and gingerly approached her. He picked up the large box of napkins and moved it onto the counter, closer to her reach. "You know what that ring means for me, but if you decide you don't want it after the restaurant opens I'll take it back." He left the restaurant and headed for his office.

Craig entered through the glass doors that read Mincey Technologies. Fourth quarter was a few weeks away and he had a ton of work to do. He had been so wrapped up with Samantha, he was getting behind on what should have been his number one priority—his own company. He was sacrificing a lot for her. Every time he thought about how happy she was, though, it made everything worth it. He took the messages Victoria handed to him as he walked past her and down the hall to his office. He closed his office door, tossed the messages, along with his keys and cell phone on his desk and sat down. He placed his face in his hands. Samantha *had* to say yes to him. She was irritated that he had surprised her, and he had stretched the truth trying to make Samantha think the ring was more of a publicity stunt. He had spent weeks looking for that ring. Knowing Samantha appreciated the finer things he had picked something exquisite. It was risky, but she fell for it. Now, the hard part would be to keep her from pulling it off her finger.

Craig's phone rang. He picked it up to see it was Damon. He needed to catch up on how he was doing and tell him about the grand opening. He answered the call.

"Hey, man."

"What's happening?"

"Busy, man. Crazy busy. The restaurant's almost done, and three new commercial contracts came in—both data and security. I'll be in a full court press through Christmas. But as long as my piggy banks' getting fatter—"

Damon broke through Craig's speech with laughter. He asked about Samantha.

"She's all I can think about. I'm getting to where I don't know if I can truly be happy without her being in my life. It's scaring me." His voice cracked.

"You really love her don't you?"

"Yeah, I do. I've been working real hard to prove it to her. I think she's about ready to give in. I can feel it." Craig shifted the conversation, almost as if it was too painful to discuss. "What's been up with you?"

"This girl has me speaking around the neighborhood about HIV. I've been educating people about the disease. I'm especially concerned about these young kids. They're one of the fastest growing groups, and when I talk to them about it, either they haven't heard of it, or if they have, they don't really know what it is. It's definitely nothing to play around with."

"Tell me about it. I've learned my lesson. My playing days are over. I never thought it could happen to me, or anybody I know. I could have gotten it just as easily as you did."

"Ain't that the truth?" Damon laughed. "You've been with way more women than I have. Your luck's always been better than mine."

Craig continued. "Tell me more about this girl. You don't speak in public so you've got to like her."

"I do."

Craig could hear the smile in Damon's voice. "Are you bringing her to the opening?"

"I'll ask her."

"Cool." Craig received another call while he was talking. He looked at the phone and saw it was Samantha. He told Damon he would call him back with the opening details and hung up. Damon didn't even get the chance to say goodbye.

Chapter 53

On his day off Damon took Angel by the car dealership after she got off work. He had several cars to show her in her price range. She was interested in a pre-owned Honda Civic. He committed to himself that he would do everything he could to get her the best price possible.

Damon and Angel walked the lot and he showed her the cars he had picked out, carefully discussing the features with her. As they were returning to his car he offered his unsolicited opinion.

"The gold one has the lowest mileage. It's also certified by the dealership which means the warranty is extended. The previous owners took excellent care—"

"I like the red one."

"That one's nice..." he coached her, "but it isn't as good of a car."

"It has a few more upgrades than the gold one. The Bose speakers are really nice." Damon opened the door for her and she got in. She pulled on her seatbelt. "Can we go get something to eat?" Damon took her to the sandwich shop where they first dined together. Angel was officially his woman. There was something about her that changed him. He would do anything within his power to see her happy. It scared him, but a part of him knew that was the way he was supposed to be—that this was what it felt like to love a woman.

They walked up to the counter and looked at the menu hanging overhead. Angel read the day's specials out loud.

"Meatloaf. Minestrone." She turned to Damon. "What are you thinking of having?"

Damon wasn't considering the menu at all. He was thinking about Angel's choice of car. He didn't want her to buy the red one and start having trouble with it, but her heart was set on it. He regretted showing it to her. "Just order me a sandwich. I'll go grab us a table."

Angel requested soup and salad, and ordered a bagel sandwich for Damon. They sat in a booth in the rear of the restaurant.

They discussed the cars she had seen, and Damon made sure he informed her of how to make the best choice. After that, the decision was hers. If he had his way he would make the choice for her, but he knew she wouldn't want him to. For her, his guidance was enough.

Damon listened to Angel talk as they ate. She encouraged him more and more each day. It was as if she could see what his mother had always seen. She dreamed a bigger dream than he ever thought was possible for himself. With her encouragement, he had gone to several churches and two high schools to speak about HIV. He was scheduled to speak at a community center the following week. She complimented him repeatedly on the work he was doing to help educate the community. She was proud of him, and he was drawn to that. He wanted to do more to please her.

"A friend of mine is opening a restaurant downtown," he told Angel. "It's this Saturday. I'd like you to come with me."

"Okay. Do I have to get dressed up?"

"We do. They have a minimum dress code." Damon giggled. "That's so like Samantha. If you don't have anything to wear we could go shopping and I could buy you something."

"I'll take a look in my closet when I get home." Angel wadded up her napkin and tossed it into her empty soup bowl. "If I can't find anything, I might take you up on that offer."

They left the restaurant and returned to Angel's house. As he pulled into the parking lot, Angel invited him in. "It's still early. Do you have plans?"

"No plan of mine could ever be better than spending time with you." Damon looked at her and got a glimpse of one of his favorite things, her cocoa dimples.

Once inside, he sat on her sofa and started looking for the remote. He found it between the sofa cushions and turned on the television. He changed the station from HGTV to ESPN.

Angel walked to her bedroom and came out in a purple fitted dress and silver high heels. Damon smiled when he saw her.

She twisted her hair up behind her head. "Will this work?"

Damon grinned even wider. "Turn around so I can see the back."

Angel turned around, giving him a view of her petite round backside.

"That will work just fine." He added enthusiastically, "More than fine…it's perfect."

"Good." Angel pulled off one of the high heeled shoes she was wearing, then the other. "Be right back."

A few moments later Angel returned to the living room wearing nothing but a baby blue towel. Damon's pulse quickened when he saw her. She approached him slowly. She pulled him up from the couch and guided his hands underneath the towel. She rested them on her hips. He began kissing her softly. She reached up and loosened her towel and it dropped to the floor. She grabbed him by the hand and led him to her bedroom.

It was Saturday. Damon was getting dressed for Craig and Samantha's grand opening. As he exited the shower he thought about the last time he was with Angel. The things she said. The things they did. His heart flooded with contentment when he retrieved the memory. He draped himself with a towel and began preparing his face to shave. His cell phone rang. He picked it up from the back of the toilet. It was a number he didn't recognize. He frowned as he turned off the water, wondering who it was.

"Hello."

"Damon this is Gary, *Red's* group leader."

"Hey, Gary." Damon was surprised but glad to hear from him. Any guy who would devote himself so tirelessly to people with HIV was an alright guy in Damon's book. And he didn't even have the disease.

"I would like to talk to you about something." Damon grew concerned. He had no idea where the conversation was headed.

"What's that?" Damon asked calmly but eagerly.

"Can you stop by Monday evening after you get off work? We'll talk about it then."

"It'll have to be late. I don't get off until eight o'clock."

"That's fine." Gary said, and gave Damon his address. "I'll see you Monday evening."

Damon ended the call and finished shaving. Afterwards, he pulled the tags off a suit Carmen had purchased for him months ago, put it on, and left to pick up Angel.

Chapter 54

Damon pulled up to the restaurant. He and Angel got out and Damon handed over the keys to the valet. He looked through the front glass to see *Sam's Place* was a packed house. He took Angel by the hand and walked through the doors into the restaurant's hostess area. After she greeted them he informed her that he was one of Craig's special guests, as Craig had instructed him to do when he arrived. The hostess—her tag read *Brittany*, picked up the walkie talkie and requested Craig come to the front of the restaurant. She took Angel's wrap and handed her a coat check ticket. Craig approached them with a huge braggart grin on his face. He greeted Damon with a hug and a pat on the back. He stepped back a ways to get a full view of Angel. Damon introduced him.

"Hello Angel." Craig greeted her. "It's nice to meet you." He turned to Brittany. "These are my special guests. Give them one of the best seats in the house, and tell their server the tab is on me." He winked at Damon.

Damon thanked him and they were lead to their table. Before he sat down he spotted Wendell and Sheila sitting at the next table. He walked over and Angel followed him.

Wendell stood up and hugged him, and introductions were made.

A few seconds later Craig bolted past the table. Samantha was on the other side of the room waving for him. He was in a hurry to get to her.

"Have you ever seen Craig like this?" Wendell asked Damon.

"No, I haven't, and it's definitely something to see. I think I like him like this. He seems..." Damon chuckled as he searched for the word.

"Like a human being..." Wendell interjected with laughter. "And not a barbarian?"

"Yeah." Damon joined in his laughter.

The server returned with the pasta and steak dishes that Wendell and Sheila had already ordered.

"How are the girls?" Damon inquired as the waiter sat down their plates.

Both Sheila and Wendell answered with laughter, "Bad!"

Damon laughed. "I'll let you guys get to your meals. Good to see you again, Sheila."

Damon and Angel returned to their seats and their waiter came by a few minutes later. Angel ordered the Atlantic salmon. Damon couldn't make up his mind, he hadn't heard of most of the dishes. Angel guided him through the menu as the waiter jittered with impatience. He settled on the Shrimp Etouffee.

"If you don't like it, we can switch," Angel told him.

"Thanks." Salmon was one of the few dishes on the menu he recognized.

While they waited for their meals to arrive, Damon explained that he and Craig had been friends since childhood, and that he owned the restaurant along with Samantha. He pointed her out to Angel as she stood in back of the restaurant outside the kitchen doors talking to one of their employees. Angel turned around to get a look at her. The employee was telling her something and in exasperation, Samantha smacked her forehead as if something had been forgotten.

"She's pretty," Angel said as she turned back around to face Damon. "Nice ring. When are they getting married?"

Damon craned his neck around a passing waitress and focused in on Samantha's hand. He saw she was wearing an engagement ring. The large stone sparkled from across the room. Confusion dawned on his face. Somewhere he had missed something. Craig had said nothing about a ring. Perhaps she was engaged to someone else. He waved at her. When she saw him she approached the table, she was wearing a fitted lavender cocktail dress along with a solitary string of white pearls, and that big fat diamond.

"Damon, I'm so sorry I haven't had a chance to come over and say hello," she said as he stood up to hug her. "Craig and I are running around like fools tonight. We had no idea the restaurant business would be this much work."

"This is Angel, my girlfriend." Damon proudly showed Angel off.

Angel smiled. "Nice to meet you, Samantha." She extended her hand to greet her.

"I love your dress. What a beautiful color." Samantha's wide eyes reflected her appreciation of all things purple.

Angel looked down at her dress. "Thank you." She gave a warm smile.

Damon conspicuously eyed the ring on Samantha's finger. She finally noticed him staring and spoke about it. "It's a stunt Craig's pulled for publicity. It doesn't mean we're getting married. I told him this morning I will at least wear it until I know for sure whether or not we have a chance. He wouldn't leave me alone about it. As if I need the extra stress right now." She smiled, and someone motioned for her from across the room. She nodded at their request, and then turned her attention back to Damon and Angel. "Are you guys being taken care of?"

"Yes." Damon said.

"Good. I'm off to put out some more fires. Craig's around here somewhere if you haven't seen him yet. Thank you so much for coming." She placed her perfectly manicured, bejeweled hand on Angel's shoulder. "Enjoy your meals." She walked away.

The waiter returned with their meals. Damon watched Craig as he greeted everyone. When he wasn't whizzing by, he was visiting tables and shaking hands like a politician. Damon couldn't wait to draw his attention. Finally, Craig looked in his direction. Damon held up his hand and wiggled his fingers indicating he had seen Samantha's ring. Craig's grin was huge. He tossed his head back jokingly and placed his hand to his heart as if he had received an arrow, indicating that cupid had shot him. He moved on to greet patrons at another table. There appeared to be no limit to what he would do to get her.

After they had finished eating, they walked to the front of the restaurant and Damon retrieved Angel's wrap from the coat check. He was helping her put it on when Craig walked past him headed for the bar. There was a look of intent on his face. He hadn't even noticed them.

"Yo...yo." Damon tapped him on the shoulder.

Craig stopped and spun around. He smiled when he saw Damon.

"You didn't tell me about the ring?"

"I know. Ain't got time right now. I'll tell you about it later." He shook Angel's hand. "Nice to meet you, Angel. Thanks for coming. How was everything?"

"The salmon was wonderful. Damon even loved the Etouffee. I was afraid it might be too fancy for him."

"I'm glad you enjoyed it. He turned toward Damon. "Call me tomorrow. I'll let you know what's up."

Damon nodded and Craig continued walking. Damon retrieved the car from the valet and he and Angel left the restaurant. He dropped her off at her place, drove home and laid his clothes out for church the following morning.

After church, Damon stopped by the pharmacy to fill his new prescription. He'd finally gotten over the embarrassment of getting his prescriptions filled. Everyone knew him there, and he was certain they knew what the prescriptions were for. Nobody cared. And finally, neither did he.

When he got home, he placed the prescription bag on the kitchen counter next to his other medications. Dr. Lipkin told him he might experience a little nausea with the change and he wasn't looking forward to that. But thus far, he had been pretty fortunate with the medications he was taking. The side effects had been limited.

As he undressed, he thought about Angel's church. He liked it and was starting to feel comfortable there. He enjoyed Reverend Michael's sermons, and they had talked intimately a few times, including a conversation about his relationship with Angel. He now looked forward to going to church. Didn't hurt that Angel was always sitting next to him either.

He went into the kitchen to make himself something to eat. Now that Angel had her own car, he found himself with a little more free time. If he had his way, he would still be chauffeuring her around. He didn't like being away from her. Today, after church, she told him she needed to drive to the beauty supply store to buy a deep conditioner for her hair, and she would spend the afternoon washing it. He told her he would see her later.

Damon made a sandwich and planted himself on the sofa. Before picking up the phone, he thought about Gary's call and wondered what he wanted to meet with him about tomorrow evening. He dialed Craig's number. He was laughing when Craig answered, eager to hear what he was up to.

"A publicity stunt?" Damon said as soon as heard Craig on the other end.

"That's the only way I could get her to wear it. I popped it on her finger during a photo shoot. The PR firm ran the story that we were opening the restaurant and getting married. It worked. Several papers and one of the news stations did a story on us."

"Bravo." Damon commended. "It might have worked on her, too. She told us that she agreed to keep the ring on until she made up her mind about you."

Craig smiled into the phone. "We'll be married by the end of next year."

"As crazy as it sounded at first, I'm starting to believe you."

"What about you and Angel?"

"Marriage?"

"Yeah. Why not? You're different with her. When you talk about her, your reaction's not the same as it was with Carmen. Something about her gets you to light up."

Damon smiled. "I could definitely see myself marrying Angel." His voice trailed off. "The future seems so far away, sometimes I really don't even think about it.

"Maybe you should."

"Yeah...maybe. "Well, congrats on everything. The restaurant. Samantha. It looks like you got what you wanted, as always."

"This time it wasn't just what I wanted. It's what I needed. She's the person I should have been with all along."

"Funny, I was just thinking the same thing."

Damon hung up the phone and went to the kitchen to take his afternoon medication. The pharmacist told him to go ahead and mix in the new one. He returned to the sofa where he fell asleep until he heard the shrill of the phone's ringer sitting next to him. He jolted awake as he reached for it and squinted at the clock.

"Hello."

"Hey. My hair's finished. Did I wake you?"

"I was just laying here. Are you coming?"

"Yeah, I'll stop and get a pizza."

"Pepperoni?"

"Cheese…I'll bring a bag of salad since I know you haven't had any vegetables today. And that's a clear 'no no.'"

Damon grumbled before laughing. "Alright, see you in a few."

Thirty minutes later, Angel walked through the door with a pizza and a bag of salad. Damon finished his meal and felt a little stomach upset. Probably the new medication. The doctor stated he would adjust. After she left, he climbed into bed. Sleep was slow in coming. Instead, he lay awake listening to his stomach gurgle as his mind kept thinking about Gary and what he wanted to meet with him about. He tossed and turned, got up and used the bathroom, read a little of the newspaper, and finally fell asleep.

Chapter 55

Damon finished up the last of his phone calls for the day. He always made his calls toward the end of the night when dealership traffic slowed. The calls he made could range from educating current or potential clients about the cars he sold, to general customer service on things like tags, repairs and license issues. He might also find himself tactfully explaining to someone why he was the best person in town to buy a car from. He liked the customer contact his job provided. He had also grown to like knowing that he was helping people.

He finished his last call to Mr. Campbell, a potential customer, about six minutes after the dealership had closed. He hung up the phone, turned off the light to his workspace and headed down the stairs to his car. He stopped at the door and pulled out the directions Gary had given him to his house. Out the corner of his eye he saw Cephus sitting in the waiting area in front of the T.V. As he approached him, he noticed he had nodded off.

"Hey, old man." He tapped him on the shoulder. "Time to go."

Cephus collected himself. He wiped his mouth and chuckled. "Man, I need to retire."

"See you tomorrow."

"Yeah, you too."

Gary lived about twenty minutes from the dealership. On his way over he tried to imagine what Gary wanted to see him about. Angel said she hadn't spoken to him about anything, but she knew he was aware that Damon had been speaking to various groups about HIV. Perhaps he wanted him to speak to another group, he thought. He hoped he wasn't about to tell him he was sick.

Damon followed the directions. Luckily for Damon they were exact since he wasn't familiar with that side of town. He found parking a few doors down from Gary's apartment building. He got out of the car. He could hear the bark of what sounded like a large dog. It grew more vicious when he opened the latch on the metal gate. He stood there momentarily to make sure wherever the dog was, it was contained and wouldn't maul him in Gary's front yard. The barking continued, but no dog appeared. He approached the building and pressed number four on the intercom. A voice answered.

"Is that you, Damon?"

"It is."

Damon heard a buzz and a click. He pushed the door open. He walked up the steps to find Gary waiting with his apartment door open.

"C'mon in."

Damon walked into the apartment. It had floral wallpaper, white crown molding and gleaming hardwoods. It looked as though you could eat a meal directly on the floor. Gary invited him into the living room and they sat down on the tailored sofa. A few seconds later a guy entered carrying a tray and offered Damon a glass of lemonade. He really didn't want it, but hated to be rude. He took the glass with a sugar encrusted rim and glass straw off the tray, and sat it down on a side table on a coaster the guy handed him.

"Damon, this is Aiden."

Aiden stretched out his hand.

Damon shook it. "Hello."

Aiden nodded and left the room.

By that time, the anticipation was at its height. Gary started talking about the group and its members. He commended Damon for his participation in the group meetings, and said that he seemed to have a way of being able to soothe the members that were hurting. He told him that his honesty was exactly what people needed to see and hear.

"You make my job a lot easier. The members seem to gravitate toward you even more than they do to me. And I'm the leader!"

Damon frowned. "You think so?"

"I know it."

Aiden entered the room. He handed Damon a piece of cake. "It's tiramisu."

Damon chuckled to himself. He admitted that having HIV had changed him. Here he was at the home of two white men having lemonade and Tiramisu. He smiled at what Craig would have to say about it.

Gary nodded a thank you to Aiden and he left the room again. Gary continued. "How would you feel about taking over the group?"

"Why would I take over the group?" Damon took a bite of cake. It tasted terrible; like tar with a hint of sweetness. He ignored the overwhelming desire to spit it out. He placed the tiny fork back on the plate and sat the plate down on the table. He grabbed the glass of lemonade that was sitting next to it and took a few gulps to wash down the nastiness. Surprisingly, bitter tasted better.

"Not just the group. The whole program."

Damon looked up at him.

"I've been promoted to Executive Director. It's an administrative role. I'll be working with securing funding, carrying out the directives of the board, branding, new partnerships, etcetera. Since the program director is a hands-on position, I want a replacement that I can trust to be just as committed to education, and the people that are afflicted with the disease as I am. You're the first person that came to mind."

Damon shook his head. "Man, I don't know anything about running any programs."

"The biggest job requirement is strong people skills. I've seen you interact with the group members, seen the way they respond to you. It seems as though people naturally gravitate to you. That's important in this position because it's a difficult subject to talk about. The second requirement is public speaking skills. I know you have those because more than one person has told me they've heard you speak at their church or school, and your story impacted them. Being a program director involves completing a lot of paperwork, and I'm sure you have to do that whenever you sell a car. The rest of the stuff, Devonna or I will help you with. She knows the organization inside and out." He handed Damon a job description. "Tell me you'll think about it."

Damon perked up when he saw the salary range displayed in the right hand corner of the first page. It was more than he currently made selling cars, and he was hustling big time. Plus, it would be a straight salary, not the ups and downs or slow periods of commission pay. And, he'd be doing something that mattered. He remained silent.

"Mull it over this week. If you decide you want to proceed we can set up a time for you to come by my office." Gary stood up. "If I wasn't confident that you're the man for this job I wouldn't have come to you."

Damon followed Gary to the door. "I don't know what to say." He responded with humility. "Thanks, Gary." He shook his hand.

Gary said goodbye and Damon walked down the stairs to the street. He got in his car, he was stunned by the conversation he just had. He thought a person would need a college degree for a job like that. Maybe Gary was pulling some strings. He drove off wondering how in the world he could have gotten the opportunity to become a program director. The only real job he had ever had was at the dealership.

He drove over to Angel's house to tell her about the meeting. It occurred to him that she probably wouldn't be surprised. She had been telling him that he should be doing more to further the cause. He parked the car and walked up the stairs to her door. She yawned as she opened the door with curlers in her hair, donning a pink bath robe that looked as though it had been washed too many times. Damon thought she looked cute. Unlike with Carmen, he didn't mind it when Angel wasn't looking her best. He could wake up to those curlers and that dingy robe every day of his life.

"What time do you have to be at work?" He spoke to her back, since; after she let him in she started toward her bedroom.

"Seven-thirty"

"Sorry." He said as he walked behind her.

"That's okay." She yawned again. I wasn't asleep yet. What did Gary want?" She lay across the foot of her bed and looked at the television. *Law and Order* was on.

"He offered me a job."

Angel sat up. "Doing what?"

"Program Director of *Red*. He got promoted." He leaned against her chest of drawers and rested his elbow on top of it.

"Really?"

"You sure you didn't have anything to do with this?" Damon smiled.

"Nope. But I'm not surprised. People have been talking about you. He's really connected in the community. Word's getting out about what you're doing."

"Must be."

Angel smiled broadly. "Congratulations. I'm excited for you and all you'll be able to do in that role." Angel looked at the clock. "You staying the night?"

Damon eyed her robe appetizingly. "As much as I'd like to...no. I want to go home and try to figure out if I'm going to take this job or not."

"Why wouldn't you?"

"I don't know if I can do something like that. All I've ever done was hustle the streets and sell cars, which are actually similar when you think about it."

"You don't give yourself enough credit. You're good at your job. You always make your sales goals and sometimes exceed them. You like working with the customers and you've seen the way the people respond to you in group."

"Women always respond to me like that."

Angel's eyebrow shot up. She rolled her eyes at his comment. "It's not only the women. It's the guys, too. Remember the guys that came up to you after you spoke in church?"

Damon walked over to her and kissed her on the head.

"Maybe." He turned toward the door. "Sleep tight. I'll call you tomorrow."

"Okay."

Damon walked out of Angel's apartment and headed home. His mind was filled with appreciation for all the things he had going for him. He thanked God as he drove along, not only for his current blessings, but also for the fact that he could feel the uneasiness and fear that had plagued him for so many months changing into something else. He was coming to know what desire and expectation felt like for the first time in his life.

Chapter 56

Damon spent the first part of the week contemplating whether or not he should take the job. He wanted to, but doubt was still plaguing him. He was excited about the opportunity to educate the public and help people who were living with HIV, but he couldn't help but wonder if he might fail at a job he knew nothing about. He decided to call his mother on Wednesday evening to talk to her about it. He had pretty much made up his mind by then. He felt he had more to gain than he had to lose. After all, he could always find another job selling cars.

He took the cordless phone off the wall and walked to the living room, sat down on the sofa and dialed his mother.

"I have some good news." He said when she answered.

"I can always use good news," Sharon encouraged. "What's going on?"

"Someone offered me a job."

"You didn't tell me you were looking for a job."

"I wasn't. My group leader got promoted. He's asked me to replace him. I'll be running the same program that has helped me adjust to living with HIV."

"That *is* good news!" Sharon exclaimed. "When do you start?"

"I don't have any of the details yet."

"It sounds like a great opportunity. I'm so proud of you."

"Thanks, Ma."

Sharon's voice bubbled with excitement. "I have to tell your brothers and sisters the good news. I know they'll be so excited for you. Congratulations, baby."

Sharon ended the call. She appeared more excited than he did. He thought about the times she told him he could do anything he put his mind to. He hoped she was right. He would call Gary in the morning and accept his offer.

Damon awoke the following morning with butterflies in his stomach. He was both excited and nervous at the same time. After he got dressed he walked to the kitchen to get something to eat. The impending phone call had taken his appetite. His heart fluttered every time he thought about it. He opened the refrigerator and perused the shelves waiting for something to peak his interest. Nothing did. He checked the expiration date on the milk. He would force down a bowl of cereal. When he finished eating, he rinsed his bowl and placed it in the sink. He took a few steps away and then recalled what Angel previously said about leaving unwashed dishes in the sink. That, since he lived so close to his neighbors, he could get roaches. They would be attracted to the food he always left out and the unwashed dishes. He'd never thought about it and was sure she was overreacting, but he went back to the sink and washed the dish and placed it in the rack anyway.

He put on his jacket, swiped his keys off the table and checked his pocket for the paper that had Gary's address and phone number on it, and then headed out the door to work. He started his car's engine and inhaled deeply. He forced the air out of his mouth and stared at Gary's number on the paper. He dialed the number as he pulled out of the space. Gary answered on the second ring. This was it, there was no turning back.

"Hey Gary, its Damon."

"Good news I hope."

"Yeah. Count me in. What happens next?"

"Can you come by the office this week during the day? I'll have you meet some of the people that help run the organization, and we'll have you fill out some paperwork. I start my new role November first. Do you think you can start around the second week of October?"

"That should be fine?" Damon said, although he wished he had more time to get his nerves together.

"Good. When can you come by the office?"

"I can come tomorrow on my lunch hour."

"See you then. Bring your birth certificate and Social Security card and we'll get the process started. I'm happy for you Damon. You've made the right decision."

"Thanks Gary."

Damon didn't know what to think. He had never had a job with any responsibility. Selling cars was easy; working with people who needed help was another thing. He had been a failure his whole life and couldn't fathom what was happening. It was a heavy responsibility. One he didn't know if he was up for.

He pulled into the dealership parking lot and parked the car. His phone was ringing when he walked into his cubicle and he immediately sat down and answered it. It was a woman who had been referred to him by a past client. He made an appointment with her and hung up. He stood up and pulled off his jacket. As soon as he did, he heard Cephus whistle, letting him know that an unaccompanied female had just hit the lot.

Chapter 57

Damon sold a mini-van to a single mother the previous day. He took the time to make sure she picked out the car that would best suit her needs and her budget. In the past he would have tried to coax her into the most expensive car on the lot. It didn't seem right to do that anymore.

Lunch time rolled around. Damon walked down to his manager's office and told him that he might be a few minutes late getting back. He asked Damon if everything was alright, prompting a twinge of guilt. His manager, Alan, hired him off the street without any solid work history. Because the position was commission only, Alan wasn't in a position to be choosy. He had to take whoever was willing to do the job without a guaranteed salary. To both of their surprise, they soon discovered that he had a knack for selling cars. After four years of working with these guys, he would soon be leaving.

He drove downtown to the Adams building and parked in the lot. He entered the building and went upstairs to the third floor. He pushed the door open and saw Gary standing in the hallway straight ahead. He was speaking to someone. As soon as he saw Damon he motioned for him to come over.

Damon walked up to him.

"Devonna, this is Damon." He turned to Damon. "Damon this is the genius I told you about. Without her, the activities around here would come to a screeching halt."

Devonna stuck out her hand and shook Damon's firmly. "Welcome to *Red*," she said in a fraction of the time it would normally take someone to speak three words. She launched right in, "Gary, I'm going to give him a tour.

After that I'll sit him down and orient him, and then I'll have him complete the new hire paperwork. I'll also introduce him to everyone in the office." She scratched her stringy blonde hair.

Diet pills, Damon thought. She was rail thin and high-octane. He could recall his sisters foraying into that world in the nineties, when they were popular.

Gary smiled at Damon. "You're in good hands. He pointed to a room occupying the back corner. "Stop by my office when you're done. I'll answer any questions you have. I will warn you, Devonna can be hard to keep up with. You'll come to appreciate it later."

"You eat yet?" Devonna interjected.

"No." Damon replied.

"Me either. There are snacks in the break room. Follow me."

Devonna tore down the hallway. Damon followed her. She stopped and introduced Damon to two employees that were walking past before continuing on to the break room. She pointed to the vending machine on the left side of the room and told Damon there were meal replacement shakes in the refrigerator. Before he could decline the shake because potato chips sounded tastier, she walked over to the refrigerator, snatched one off the door and tossed it to him. Then she withdrew a bottled water, walked over to the cabinet and retrieved a little packet. When she poured its contents into the water, it turned green.

Other than his response about not eating yet, he hadn't spoken a word to Devonna, but the green water begged him to speak.

"What's that?"

"It's wheat grass. It's good for you. Gives you lots of energy." She buzzed. "*You* especially have to be careful about what you put into your body. Only natural substances for me. This is my caffeine. Its plant based with no harmful ingredients. Want some?"

Damon stared at her. She was freaky. "Maybe later."

Damon and Devonna continued their tour and introductions. She sat down with Damon and began giving him an orientation of *Red*. He asked her for a pen and a piece of paper to take notes. She explained what the organization was about, the scope of their services, their funding and partnerships. Anything he might need to know. He completed his new hire paperwork and Devonna led him back to Gary's office.

Damon sat in a chair across from Gary's desk. His mind was reeling from the information dump he had received.

"That Devonna's something, ain't she?"

"Yeah. I can see she has tons of energy."

"That's what you want in an assistant. If you ever find yourself looking for an assistant in the future, make that your number one requirement—high energy. Whenever I'm not here I never have to worry. She can run this place without me." Gary chuckled. "Does this feel like something you want to be a part of?"

"Definitely."

"Good." Gary nodded. "Did you and Devonna come up with a start date?"

"Yeah. I'll let my manager know I'm giving my two weeks notice."

Gary stretched out his hand. "Welcome," he said. "You'll get to know more of the key players as time progresses." Gary patted Damon on the back as he stood up. "Everything will be okay. Trust me. Devonna and I will be right here to help."

"Thanks again, man."

Damon walked out of Gary's office and down the hallway to the elevator. He left the Adams building with excitement. He called Craig with the news and returned to the dealership feeling light as a feather.

Chapter 58

Damon gave his resignation letter to Alan, who was sad to see him go. He spent his last two weeks at the dealership entertaining questions from the other salesmen on how he convinced people, especially women, to buy cars. He tried to explain it to them as best he could, but realized that it was just something that he had a knack for—he couldn't put it into words. People seemed to trust him and would follow where he led them.

He left the dealership on Friday and started his new job on Monday. The first two weeks his fear had become exhaustion. Selling cars he knew. Budgets, boards, personnel, volunteers—he didn't. He came home in the evenings and studied the manuals Devonna gave him so he could learn how to run the program. He barely saw Angel for the next few months; work had kept him so busy. They made sure they talked on the phone every night.

The holidays had passed. Now, he was grateful for Devonna. Turns out she wasn't so freaky, after all. She made it her mission to help him succeed. She not only helped him professionally, but personally. She monitored what he ate and gave him tips on how to boost his immunity. She had even gotten him on her green drink. He drank one every day, and while he wasn't racing to the finish of every task like Devonna, he did notice he had more energy. He wasn't falling into bed at night exhausted, like he was a few months ago.

Devonna entered his office with pad and paper and sat down in his chair. "I've organized the event at the South Side community center. They were very appreciative that we've agreed to do this. Are you prepared?"

"Always. I just speak from my heart and share my story. Then I tell them about the program and how it helped me adjust. That always seems to work."

"Good. I won't be there. The board is meeting that night."

"I know. Thanks for covering for me."

Devonna winked. "You've got it."

****

Damon made his way over to the South Side community center to give his presentation. He parked his car in the parking lot. As he walked along he admired the life-size mural of Muhammad Ali that was painted on the building. Muhammad was his favorite athlete, but to Damon, he was more than that—a man of principle, and he admired the fact that he had the courage to stand up for what he believed in, in the face of opposition.

Damon greeted the staff at the center and they discussed last minute instructions as people starting milling into the gym and filling the seats. At seven-thirty Damon took the podium. The audience consisted of local residents, and Damon recognized the faces of a few well-known community leaders. His primary concern, though, were the neighborhood folks. He hoped that if there were people listening to him that either knew they were infected, or thought they could be, his message would inspire them to reach out for help. He wanted them to know that his agency could offer resources to ease the transition into living with the disease. He also wanted people to know that denial only made things worse, and that early treatment prolonged life. He had seen people come to *Red* when it was too late. The virus living undetected in their bodies until the damage had been done. Any attempts at treatment at that point were futile.

After his presentation was over he was putting on his coat when he was approached by a member of city council. "Councilman Jenkins," Damon shook his hand. "Thanks for coming."

"Great speech. Your honesty is admirable. I think we need to get this message to other community centers. Do you have a card? I'd love to chat with you to see how we can be a part of what you're doing."

Damon opened his binder and pulled out several. He handed them to the councilman.

"Me too." A woman approached, Damon didn't recognize her. I'm Sonya Rogers... school board." Damon handed her a few cards. "I'd love to invite you to one of our meetings. I think it's time we address this on a broader scale. Kids don't understand the risks." She handed Damon her card.

"Thank you."

"No...thank you," she said and walked away.

He placed the cards in his binder and buttoned his coat. He smiled as he walked to the parking lot knowing his message had just received the help it needed to reach a wider audience.

Chapter 59

Craig and Samantha had grown closer as the months passed. Every need she had he met with urgency. For a Christmas gift he had even sent her to Paris for six weeks to study under Chef Phillipe Jean Chien—a well known pastry chef. He ran the restaurant in her absence, as well as kept up with the responsibilities of his own business. As he had always suspected, their styles complimented each other. Now he was considering buying her a car.

He entered the restaurant and walked back to her office. She was preparing the previous nights receipts. He leaned against the wall next to her file cabinet. "I've been looking at the new Jaguar's."

"Good." She said, still looking at the receipts. "Those are really nice cars. I thought you were a Lexus man."

"I am."

Samantha looked up. A frown crossed her brow.

"I want to buy it for you." Craig smiled.

She shook her head. "You don't have to do that."

"Really." He insisted. He pushed away from the wall and stood tall. "I want to."

"Have a seat Craig. We need to talk."

Craig walked over to her desk and sat down. He prepared himself for bad news. Although she had on the ring, she seemed indifferent to him some days.

"Wait, Samantha. Before you say anything let me say something first."

"Okay."

"I love you."

"I know."

Craig looked at her in puzzlement.

"I know that you love me," she repeated. "You've finally convinced me. You don't have to keep spending your money on me to show me that. The tenderness in your voice, the care that's in every interaction, the joy or sadness on your face that corresponds to my every mood speaks to me much louder than your checkbook."

"But, I want to buy you the car."

"I know you do. But that's not what love is about. Love is about faith, trust, honesty, loyalty. It's the intertwining of two souls and the resulting connection that sustains two people. Do you understand that?"

"I do. But, it gives me great pleasure to do things for you. That's what men do when they care about someone."

"I understand that. But, what I feel for you has nothing to do with your money."

Craig leaned forward in the chair and scratched his head. "Are you saying that you do have feelings for me?"

Samantha hesitated. She leaned back. "I do. I've been waiting all this time to see something in your eyes. I needed to hear a message from your heart that you would never hurt me, again."

"Never, Samantha! You have my word. I would never do anything like that again."

"Now, I believe you. It's taken me a while to get here."

Craig walked over to Samantha, leaned down and kissed her deeply. He noticed she was kissing him back. "Does the ring now have some meaning?" He asked her.

Samantha sighed. "It does. I can finally admit it."

Chapter 60

Once Damon was acclimated to the job, he hit the South Side hard, marketing the agency's services and spreading the word about testing and early diagnosis being the key to sustaining health. He informed people about programs that would help them obtain medication if they couldn't afford it. Initially he was somewhat embarrassed about being on his home turf—seeing people that he grew up with, and they finding out he had the disease, but embarrassment was no deterrent to him accomplishing his mission. He wanted people to know that an insidious intruder lurked in the streets waiting for its next victim.

He had formed alliances with several churches and community organizations. He was most proud of the allegiance he formed with the school system to educate students about the consequences of risky behavior. This goal seemed to fuel him the most. He wanted to raise the awareness of a culture of youth that was largely affected by, not only HIV, but teenage pregnancy and other STD's as well. He wanted them to know that these things could have a negative impact on their lives, and all of them were one hundred percent preventable. He had started speaking about abstinence, which didn't always go over well with kids that had been raised in a sexually free society. For those that did receive the message, he started a support group. He realized that wouldn't be the choice for everyone, but if there were kids out there that wanted to protect themselves by means of abstinence; he wanted to make sure they received encouragement to do so.

He was speaking to a group of teens one night. He shared with them that although life with the disease is manageable; it still has a significant impact on your life. He shared with them that he was no longer the same person because of HIV, and that if he had it to do all over again; he would have never had the encounter with Candy through which he was infected. He told them it was an act he regretted.

He wrapped up the teen's group meeting and the kids filed out of the room. He was straightening up the chairs they had scattered everywhere, preparing the room for the next day's regular support group meeting when he noticed one of the group members, Lenore, was still there. She remained seated, her legs propped up on a chair in front of her. All the kids had a special place in his heart, but he had developed a fondness for Lenore. She was smart, and wasn't shy about letting you know what was on her mind. She had been quiet throughout the meeting. Damon could tell something was wrong.

"What's up, Lenore?" He approached her.

"I wanted to talk to you about something." She pulled her legs down from the chair and Damon sat down, facing her.

Damon cringed. *No...she didn't.* He waited for her to explain.

"Bryce asked me to, again."

Damon scratched the back of his head. And waited.

"I really don't want to...but there's pressure Mr. Harris. Pressure you don't understand."

Damon raised his eyebrows. "I understand. I used to apply that same pressure."

"I like him Mr. Harris...I mean, I like him a lot. If I don't, someone else will. He keeps telling me he has other girls that want to be with him—"

"And that's the point. He doesn't want you Lenore, he wants your body. Those are two totally different things. It might feel as though if you give him what he wants, he'll be with you, but there's a chance, a pretty likely one, that once he gets what he wants he'll move on."

Lenore picked at the chipped pink nail polish on her right hand.

He grabbed her hand, stopping her, and looked her in the eye. "You think that if you give him sex, in exchange, he'll give you his heart, but a man who's found the woman he wants, will willingly surrender his heart. She doesn't have to *do* anything to get it."

Lenore spoke in a shallow voice, contemplation on her face. "In the past the guy never stuck around afterwards."

"What makes you think this guy is any different?"

"He's real cute, though," Lenore said with an acquiescing chuckle.

"Love yourself, Lenore. Love yourself." Damon stood up. "I've got protection if you need it, but I think you're strong enough."

Lenore stood up, "Me, too." She picked up her plaid umbrella from underneath the chair. She reached out and hugged Damon, surprising him. "Thanks Mr. Harris."

"You're welcome, Lenore. See you at the next meeting?"

She headed for the door. "Of course."

Damon dragged the last few errant chairs into place and threw away the soda cans. He looked around at the meeting room. He couldn't believe how far he had come. He couldn't believe that, the once hustler from the South Side, was now doing something that mattered. He walked over to the door and paused before he turned off the light. He thought about what he had told the group about HIV changing him. Perhaps he hadn't been totally honest with them. He regretted contracting HIV, but he knew he wouldn't be the person he was without it. It matured him in a way that wouldn't have been possible had he not been diagnosed. He wouldn't have met Angel. He wouldn't have had the opportunity to make a difference in people's lives. He wouldn't have learned to believe in himself. He turned off the light, locked the door and left the building for the night.

Chapter 61

Fall came quickly. Damon had spent the summer in the parks, at fairs, and other venues getting to know people. Getting people to trust him and listen to his story. Getting them connected to *Red*. Angel even chipped in sometimes by helping him hand out flyers, or delivering a meal to someone who was sick. She supported him by volunteering with the teen group in the evenings. He was glad that she could be there on the nights he couldn't make it.

Damon loved his work and had finally made peace with his life. He forgave himself for all the mistakes he made in the past. He tried to make amends for the selfish person he used to be by never missing an opportunity to show someone kindness. He worked hard to strengthen his relationships. He visited his mother more often and he called his brother and sisters regularly. And he cherished every moment he had with his son.

Damon sat in his office looking over the previous year's budget. He wanted to get started early and he knew he would need help. He was scratching his head with a pencil when Devonna came into his office and sat down. He chuckled when he looked up at her.

"I'm cat woman."

"Is that who you're supposed to be?" This time he laughed out loud. "You look more like a mouse than a cat. If it wasn't for the tail...I mean...really."

"At least I dressed up." There was admonishment in Devonna's tone. "Where's your costume? We always dress up for Halloween."

"I didn't have time to pull anything together. I'm with you in spirit though." He pumped his fist in the air as a symbol of solidarity.

"I have something for you." Devonna pulled a white envelope from the stack of papers she was holding and handed it to him.

"What is it?" He asked with curiosity.

"Open it."

Damon opened the envelope. He wondered why Devonna wouldn't tell him what it was since she opened all his mail and screened it for him. He slowly read down the card. He sat back in his chair, shocked to discover he had been nominated for the South Side Man of the Year Award. Being from the South Side he had heard about the award, but he had no idea what the criteria was or that he could even be considered. He smiled at Devonna and placed his hand to his heart. "Wow." A gentle breath escaped his mouth. He couldn't believe what he was reading.

"It's exciting isn't it?"

"It is."

Devonna stood up. "I'll have to tell the staff."

"Thanks Devonna. It's because of everyone's efforts, but I want to personally thank you for all you do for me."

"That's my job." She smiled. "Speaking of which, when we do the budget we will need to build in money for hiring. Because of your hard work, activity has doubled. The number of people we test each day has gone way up. We'll have to see if we can get approved for an additional staff member for the testing center. " She stroked the sickly looking tail of her costume. "I'll talk to Gary about it."

"Thanks Devonna."

Devonna left the office. Damon picked up the phone and called Angel at work with the good news.

"Congratulations! That's awesome!" she said when he told her. "You deserve it. I've seen a change in the community. I've seen a change in you too. I've watched you become a man. One who stands for something and is not just interested in himself. Damon felt his eyes mist. He was glad no one was in his office to see it. He had spent a lifetime being interested in himself. Now, he cared more about people.

"Thanks."

"How about dinner tonight to celebrate?"

Chapter 62

Damon and Angel left her mother's house and drove over to Sharon's. When they got out of the car, he wrapped his arm around her to protect her from the bitter cold air and the ominous South Side streets. They hurried up the front walkway to the house. A delicious aroma floated from underneath the door. As he knocked, he could hear the muted sounds of people talking inside the house. A few seconds later Ronald answered, dressed in grey dress slacks, a white shirt and a grey pullover sweater. Damon flashed back to when he was a boy. He remembered his father answering the door wearing similar clothes on Thanksgiving. He also remembered him putting on his fedora and heading for the pool hall as soon as the guests left. "Hey, Ronald," Damon smiled as he let Angel walk through the door first.

"Hello, you two." Ronald warmly greeted them like he was very much at home. "Everyone's in the kitchen."

Damon helped Angel with her coat and she headed in the direction of the voices coming from the back of the house.

Sharon walked up and stood beside Ronald before Damon could completely get his coat off. Her face brightened. "Congratulations, baby."

Damon returned the smile. "Thanks, ma, but you've told me that already."

"She's just proud." Ronald patted him on the back. "And she should be."

They started toward the kitchen while Damon finished taking off his coat. He grabbed a hanger out of the hall closet. He was hanging up Angel's coat when Ike approached him.

Ike extended his strong, dark, senior in stature hand and shook Damon's. "Congrats, man," he said and gave him a firm shake.

In a way it was confirmation for Damon. He had always looked up to Ike. Ike had made good choices. Had a great job, a beautiful wife, and amazing kids. His presence always reminded Damon of how much he had screwed up his life, as well as the lives of others. To hear the genuine pride in his brother's tone was something that he always longed for. It felt good to be affirmed by him.

"Thanks, man." Damon hugged him. No longer feeling like his little brother, but his equal.

"Where are Diane and the kids?" He grabbed another hanger.

"She's in the back. The kids are downstairs playing."

Damon could hear everyone greeting Angel from the kitchen. He was pleased they were accepting her as a significant part of his life.

They walked to the kitchen in the rear of the house and Damon greeted his sisters. Mona was standing at the stove. She took a fork out of Sharon's drawer and scooped up a forkful of turnip greens. She shook off the juice and twirled them around the fork. She looked at Damon. "You? Man of the year?" She gently blew on the bite of greens that rested on the fork before placing it in her mouth. "I can't believe it."

Damon shrugged his shoulders. "Me, either."

Sharon slapped Mona across the back and snatched the fork out of her hands tossing it in the sink. The prongs bounced against the porcelain with a clatter. "Dinner's ready." She rolled her eyes at Mona. "Everyone wash up and get to the table."

The family filed into the dining room and sat at the table. Sharon and Ronald began serving dinner. Ronald placed the turkey on the table while Sharon gathered the fixings. Damon watched him interacting with his mother—doting over the meal they'd made together. Admittedly, he wasn't so bad. Initially, Damon gave him a hard time, but he seemed to be making his mother happy. What more could he ask for?

After dinner was finished, Ike leaned back in his chair and unbuttoned his pants.

"You're such a thug," Diane teased. "Have you no manners?"

"No. And no more room in my stomach either." Ike said, and a few others at the table could identify with him. They laughed.

Sharon stood up." Why would you stuff yourself? You know I made you all a German Chocolate cake."

"Who are you kidding?" Ike ribbed Sharon. "We all know that cake is for Damon. Your favorite, and now, Man of the Year nominee."

Sharon laughed as she continued on into the kitchen. She returned with the cake and sat it in front of Damon. "Here you go, baby." She winked at Ike.

Damon thanked her. When he looked down at the cake the word *Congratulations* was written across the icing in chocolate ganache.

Sharon began slicing the cake. They passed the small plates around the table.

"The ceremony is in two weeks. I have tickets for all of you to attend."

"We'll be there." Sharon said.

"Yeah." Mona placed a bite of cake in her son's mouth. "We all will."

Chapter 63

Damon was awakened by the alarm on his phone. After he had eaten a sandwich and taken his medication, he laid down on the sofa to watch the football game. He was afraid he would doze off during the second half so he set the alarm for six o'clock, just in case he overslept.

After he showered and brushed his hair, he walked to the closet and pulled out the tuxedo he'd been married in. When he eyed it on the hanger, he thought of Carmen and hoped she was well. He thought about the days, weeks, and months of drama that had transpired since he first donned it. The last time he wore it, he felt a feeling of dread, as if he were attending his own funeral. Today, as he put it on, the feeling was entirely different. He felt as though it was a symbol of a new beginning. He walked to the dresser and opened the box that held his cuff links and put them on. Cuff links reminded a man of the importance of an occasion. He never remembered his dad wearing them. He headed to the bathroom and opened the cabinet. He dabbed a small amount of Ralph Lauren aftershave on his hands, rubbed his hands together and patted his face. The familiar sting was gone. He welcomed the protection his newly grown beard offered, plus he liked how he looked. He turned off the light, walked to the closet, put on his overcoat and headed out the door for Angel's house.

After he let the car warm up for a few minutes, he pulled off and drove down the block. He was excited that all of his family would be at the ceremony. He couldn't remember a time in his life when they had come to something he was involved in. Probably because he had never been involved in anything. It was a proud moment for him. His family and closest friends would be there showing him their support. Ronald was the only one who would be missing. The weather forecast projected a heavy snow for the evening. The city had called in as many workers as they could to treat the roads. Ronald would be working most of the night and wouldn't be able to attend. They would pick up Sharon on the way.

The three of them entered the Regency hotel lobby. They were greeted by a group of women seated at a banquet table. One of the ladies took their coats. After Damon gave his name, they were presented with name tags and one of the ladies escorted them to where they would be sitting. As they entered the expansive room filled with round tables draped in linen table cloths and linen covered chairs, Damon began to feel the weight of the honor he was receiving. He wasn't used to formal table settings, big and little forks, fine china or fancy stemware. As he looked around the room at the hoity decor he realized it was a very big deal. He questioned whether he deserved to be nominated along with the others.

Their escort seated them at a table in front of the podium.

The room began to fill quickly. Damon waved at people he recognized, and spotted people he wanted to meet. Eventually, Devonna joined them at the table wearing a gold sequined gown.

At eight o'clock the emcee began the ceremony. The key note speaker—Mayor Thomas Benson took the stage. He welcomed everyone and gave the names of the seven nominees. He thanked them for the work they were all doing in order to improve the South Side communities. "In my eyes," Mayor Benson said, "you are all winners."

Next they played video clips detailing the work of each of the seven nominees. They interviewed people that worked with them, or had been impacted by their work. Damon was shocked when he saw Devonna on the clip. He had no idea that they had come to the office and filmed her. They also had a clip of him speaking to a group, as well as interviews with Reggie and Pamela—two people who stated that Damon had a positive impact on their lives. Reggie teared up as he shared that, before he met Damon, he considered suicide. Damon wondered how they obtained the footage. Devonna again, no doubt.

He continued watching. The gentleman working in genetic research, or the special education teacher who developed programs for children with physical and mental disabilities would probably win. How did he even get in the same category?

When the film stopped, the mayor took the stage again. This time he was holding an envelope. Damon leaned over and tried to kiss Angel on her neck. She nodded at the mayor on the stage admonishing him to pay attention.

The mayor cleared his throat. "Again, all of you are winners. The work you're doing is invaluable to all the residents who live and work in the South Side. We are forever indebted to your service." He opened the envelope. "But there's one whose work has stood out in the eyes of our panel, which consists of people who live and breathe, and work extremely hard, to see the improvement of the South Side communities. It is a decision they deliberated over for weeks. They conducted interviews and extensive research to qualify this candidate for this award." He glanced down at Damon and spoke directly into the microphone. "I'm pleased to announce the South Side Man of the Year is Damon Harris."

Everyone stood up. The mayor invited him to the stage. Damon could hear applause, but the rest was a blur as he made his way up to him.

The mayor shook his hand and handed him the large clear, Lucite plaque.

"Thank you," Damon took it, surprised by its weight.

"You deserve it." He motioned for Damon to step up to the podium as he backed away.

Damon swallowed hard. He paused for a few moments to gather his thoughts. He reminded himself to speak from his heart like he had always done. He breathed in deeply, adjusted the mic and began his acceptance speech. From the elevation of the podium he could clearly see all in attendance. Happiness swelled his heart as he looked out into the large audience of people, dressed to the nines in his honor. He saw Craig and Samantha sitting at a table to his right. He saw his brother and sisters to the left. Sheila and Wendell were sitting in the back. People that he worked with in one capacity or another over the past year filled the room. He even saw Cephus scamper in, in a nick of time, to hear his speech. He was still in awe over how far he had come as he spoke. He never imagined that he would one day be celebrated by the community. Never imagined he would love again. Never believed that one day his life would matter, and he would have something of value to give. It was as if his smile couldn't contain what he felt in his heart. He continued his speech and in his closing remarks, he gave thanks and acknowledgements.

"I never dreamed I'd be here. I thank you for this award, and I accept it with great humility. I dedicate this to the people who believed in me when I didn't believe in myself." Damon glanced down at the table in front of the podium and smiled at Angel and his mother. He searched the room for Gary and found him sitting in the back. When he saw him, he smiled and nodded his head graciously expressing thanks. He continued. "And I will continue to work tirelessly to educate, and eradicate this disease from our community, and beyond."

Damon finished his speech and was met with roaring applause. He stepped down off the podium and returned to his seat. The mayor took the stage and closed out the ceremony.

As the evening was winding down, Damon stood shaking hands and saying thanks to a group of people who were congratulating him. Rachel and Evan walked over with London. Damon was amazed at how much he had grown. For the first time Rachel wasn't holding his hand or Evan carrying him on his hip.

"I'm proud of you." Rachel said.

"We both are." Evan echoed.

"Thanks. That means a lot." Damon replied with genuineness. "I want you to meet someone." He told them. He turned toward the table where he had previously sat and motioned for Angel to come over to where they were standing. When she approached he turned to Rachel first. "Rachel this is Angel," he said with pride. It felt good to finally be free from loving her. Then he introduced Angel to Evan. The envy he once felt for him was now gone. Damon squatted down and kissed London on the cheek and made the last and most important introduction.

Angel smiled when she greeted London. "Nice to meet you, young man."

London held out his small hand and politely shook hers. "Nice to meet you, Angel." He said in a tiny voice.

Damon thanked them for coming and promised London he would pick him up the following weekend.

When they walked away, Damon returned his attention to the people in attendance. He spent time shaking hands, hoping to form future alliances with some of them as they meandered out of the room. He was always working to further the cause.

When the room was almost empty, he walked over to his mother who was still sitting at the table. "Where's Angel?"

"Ladies' room. She'll be back in a few minutes." Sharon stood up holding her purse in preparation to leave.

Damon kissed his mother on the cheek. "Thanks for coming, Mom."

"I wouldn't have missed this for the world. This is what I was trying to get you to see all those years." She straightened Damon's bow tie. "You had it in you all along."

Damon smiled at his mother. He heard Angel's heels striking the floor behind him and seconds later smelled her perfume. He turned around. "You ready?" Damon asked her and she nodded.

They stopped by the coat check and picked up their coats. Damon helped the two most important women in his life with theirs before he bundled up. He wrapped his scarf around his neck and they walked through the hotel lobby and out the front door. Large snowflakes gently floated down from the sky, blanketing them in stillness. He closed his eyes and savored the feel as they gently caressed his face. He stuck out his tongue and allowed one to land, tasting the purity of the snow.

"Couldn't have happened to a better man," Angel said.

He put his arm around both Angel and his mother to protect them from the winter's chill. He could feel great things in store for him. He thought of all the things he wanted to do. In a short while, he would ask Angel to marry him. He walked down the snow-covered street with the confidence that his once unknown and depressed future was now as bright as a star.

About the Author:

Tonya Lampley's first novel was titled *A Taste of Love* and was a National Indie Excellence Book Awards finalist. She lives in Ohio with her husband and is currently working on her next book. For more information about Tonya, please visit her on the web at www.TonyaLampley.com.

CPSIA information can be obtained at www.ICGtesting.com
Printed in the USA
LVOW08s2123260715

447743LV00001B/20/P